THE
MUMMY
RETURNS

UNIVERSAL PICTURES PRESENTS AN ALPHAVILLE PRODUCTION

A STEPHEN SOMMERS FILM BRENDAN FRASER "THE MUMMY RETURNS"

RACHEL WEISZ JOHN HANNAH ARNOLD VOSLOO ODED FEHR

PATRICIA VELASQUEZ AND THE ROCK AS THE SCORPION KING

MUSIC BY ALAN SILVESTRI FILM EDITOR BOB DUCSAY

SPECIAL VISUAL EFFECTS & ANIMATION BY INDUSTRIAL LIGHT & MAGIC PRODUCTION DESIGNER ALLAN CAMERON

DIRECTOR OF PHOTOGRAPHY ADRIAN BIDDLE B.S.C. EXECUTIVE PRODUCERS BOB DUCSAY DON ZEPFEL

PRODUCED BY JAMES JACKS SEAN DANIEL WRITTEN AND DIRECTED BY STEPHEN SOMMERS

THIS FILM IS NOT YET RATED

www.themummy.com A UNIVERSAL RELEASE

© 2001 UNIVERSAL STUDIOS

UNIVERSAL

THE
MUMMY
RETURNS

A novel by
Max Allan Collins

Based on a motion picture screenplay written by
Stephen Sommers

BERKLEY BOULEVARD BOOKS, NEW YORK

THE MUMMY RETURNS

A Berkley Boulevard Book / published by arrangement with Universal Studios Publishing Rights, a division of Universal Studios Licensing, Inc.

PRINTING HISTORY
Berkley Boulevard edition / April 2001

The Penguin Putnam Inc. World Wide Web site address is
http://www.penguinputnam.com

ISBN: 0-425-17926-5

BERKLEY BOULEVARD
Berkley Boulevard Books are published by The Berkley Publishing Group,
a division of Penguin Putnam Inc., 375 Hudson Street,
New York, New York 10014.
BERKLEY BOULEVARD and its logo
are trademarks belonging to Penguin Putnam Inc.

PRINTED IN THE UNITED STATES OF AMERICA

10 9 8 7 6 5 4 3 2

For Chris Christensen—
monster musician

"Death is just the beginning."
                                    —Imhotep

·◖ PROLOGUE ◗·

The Scorpion's Curse

EDITOR'S NOTE: *The following is an excerpt from chapter 6 of* Curse of the Pharaohs: Myth and Mystery *(Bembridge Press, London, 1930) by Dr. Evelyn O'Connell. Though holding a doctorate in library sciences, Dr. O'Connell was known as a leading expert of her day in the fields of archaeology and Egyptology. The daughter of noted Egyptologist Howard Carnahan—who with Sir Gaston Maspero discovered Tutankhamen's tomb in 1922—Dr. O'Connell was curator of the Cairo Museum from 1925 until 1927, when she retired to raise a family with her husband, noted explorer Richard O'Connell; in later years, Dr. O'Connell was curator of the British Museum.*

Although no artifacts exist to confirm his existence, and the hieroglyphs that tell his story date centuries later, the Scorpion King is very much a reality to the children of modern Egypt. Just as the Western world has its Boogeyman, the land of the pharaohs has its Scorpion King, a personification of evil invoked—often at bedtime—as a threat by parents to misbehaving offspring.

Yet hieroglyphs of the Scorpion King portray not a monster, but a figure both fearsome and majestic—a muscular, decidedly brutal-looking, strangely handsome warrior, who towered over the thousands of Akkadian soldiers under his command.

The image of his namesake—that desert arachnid of the nipping claws, jointed tail and deadly stinger—appeared in bas-relief on his shield, and on the golden breastplate bedecking a brawny frame otherwise clad in loincloth, animal skins and various mementos of war. The soldiers who followed the Scorpion King served under that same sinister symbol, fighting beneath banners topped with gold discs embossed with gold scorpions carried into battle on poles.

Most significantly, the scorpion imagery carried over to a certain massive golden bracelet that never left the Scorpion King's right wrist. This, the so-called Bracelet of Anubis, was said to provide passage (in some mysterious fashion lost to antiquity) to the fabled Lost Oasis of Ahm Shere.

Scholars date the Scorpion King's grand campaign to unite the known world to a five-year period ending in 3112 B.C. The warrior king is said to have marched at the head of five thousand soldiers whose attack on the fantastic walled city of Thebes was met by fifteen thousand Sumerian defenders.

Bellowing commands, thrusting his scimitar high, the Scorpion King was no general directing his men from a far-off encampment. This was a fierce warrior at the forefront of his troops, charging on foot across the desert to meet the foe, his eyes blazing, almost crazed, braids of hair swinging in tandem with his flashing blade. Fighting like a man possessed, the Scorpion King and his stinging scimitar cut down the enemy like so many weeds, inspiring his soldiers to new heights of bravery—and butchery.

But still the Sumerians came, until the army of the Scorpion King was overrun by the defenders of Thebes, swallowed up in the desert dust they themselves had so unwisely stirred.

Defeated, driven by the Sumerians into the sacred desert of Ahm Shere, the Scorpion King and his army fought another battle, an even more hopeless one, their foes this time the sun, the sand, and an absence of water. The decimated remains of an army that had thought itself invincible staggered into the vast wasteland, slogging up and down dunes on an expedition to nowhere; and, as hours turned into days, the warriors died off, one by one, their scattered corpses feeding the birds, leaving bones for bleaching, a terrible trail no one would ever dare follow.

And then the Scorpion King was an army of one. At the foot of an enormous pyramidlike dune, he gazed up where the sun painted the dune's crest golden, winking at him, as if promising treasure. Convinced that an oasis awaited over this rise, he stumbled, staggered, swayed, but never crawled, climbing, climbing, until he reached the pinnacle . . .

. . . from which he could see more endless sand, more rolling dunes.

Now, at last, the Scorpion King fell to his knees. Sturdy though he was, the days of baking on these desert sands with no water, no food, had taken a toll—within him, the spark of life was flickering. He looked to the burning sky and shook his fist, the scorpion bracelet reflecting the sun; and he bellowed a curse that echoed across the sandy canyons.

"Anubis!" he cried, the rasp of his voice like the scampering of his namesake over the sand. "Spare me, give me back my life, and let me conquer my enemies— and I will give you what the gods have denied me: a pyramid of gold. I will build you this great temple!"

The sky did not reply; but a skittering drew his attention to the sand into which his knees were sunk: a scorpion . . . a real, live one, not a golden symbol . . . was crawling toward him, as if in mockery of the grandiose imagery of the warrior's battle regalia.

The Scorpion King cast a defiant sneer toward the sky and grabbed the wriggling thing, allowing it to sting him. He winced in pain, then shoved the scorpion into his mouth, and chewed, chewed, chewed some more . . . and swallowed.

"A pyramid of gold, and my soul!" he yelled, challenging the sky. "This is my offer! I await your answer."

And in the sands around him, in a bewildering

4

flash of green, lush vegetation sprang suddenly up, almost exploding out of the desert, plants and trees reaching heights and achieving luxurious splendor that should have required months and years but took seconds . . . and the sound of water, gently lapping, drew the Scorpion King to his feet, and he walked down the dune through exotic foliage to the sparkling waters of life, where he bathed his cracked lips and washed away the bitter taste of his namesake.

And so, legend has it, was the oasis of Ahm Shere born out of the Scorpion King's pact with the great god Anubis.

A golden temple was built, with the bounty and slaves acquired by a pillaging army led by the Scorpion King . . . but not an army of men, like those whose bones were scattered across the desert, markers of the failure of the prior campaign. These soldiers were fiends, monsters; Anubis-bred warriors whose tall canine exoskeletons were covered in striated muscle; whose eyes glowed like fiery coals in the hairy, horrific, doglike heads that barked and growled and shrieked with sadistic glee as scimitars slashed, heads rolled, limbs scattered, blood sprayed everywhere.

The last city to fall in this hellish campaign was, fittingly, Thebes.

Thousands of these hideous Anubis warriors swarmed through the once-grand city, laying waste. The Scorpion King no longer sought to conquer, but to destroy; buildings were torched, battering rams collapsed buildings, men and women screamed in terror as the sadistic dog-soldiers pursued their every evil whim.

In the midst of the carnage, in a swirl of smoke as black as his soul, the Scorpion King—caked with blood and mud, streaked with soot and sweat—basked in his triumph, savoring the completeness of his revenge. His massively muscular chest heaving under the golden arachnid breastplate, he swiveled to watch his grotesque warriors—these creatures who, like a great flood, had washed away all that lay before them— wander the ruins they had created. These dog-soldiers seemed lost, suddenly, with no one left to kill, nothing left to burn, no city to sack, their task done.

A spasm—as unexpected and electric as lightning— shook the Scorpion King's body. Pain sent him to his knees, just as he had been atop that sand dune, and he howled in impotent rage as his very spirit was sucked from him, withering him, the golden bracelet dropping from his wrist to the ground.

Around him were the yowling shrieks of the canine creatures who had been his army, disintegrating, dissolving into black sand.

According to myth, Anubis then returned his army to the desert sands from whence they had come, where still they wait, silently, until the day when some other fool might strike a bargain with the gods and waken them once more.

The next time they awake, however (it is said), so will their commander, and the next great campaign of the Scorpion King will be to lay waste not just to a city, like Thebes, but the very world itself.

PART ONE

The Mummy's Shroud

·❨ 1 ❩·

Temple of Doom

Upon the left bank of the blue, shimmering Nile—the longest single stream on earth—not far above Luxor, site of ancient Thebes, lay the stone ruins of a magnificent temple. There three camels waited patiently for their masters, who were exploring the sun-baked remainder of pillared galleries, halls and chambers, designed to celebrate Ammon, the God of the Dead, and Ammon-Ra, the God of the Living and the Dead.

The temple had been completed around 1280 B.C., its design—and construction supervised—by Imhotep himself, Grand Vizier of Zozer, High Priest of Osiris, a man of great learning and power, said to have devised the means of transporting and lifting the massive stones of which the great pyramids were constructed.

Imhotep, however, had betrayed Pharaoh Seti, and

suffered the singular fate of the curse of the *hom-dai,* his very memory banished from the kingdom; and so it was that Imhotep's glorious temple had fallen into ruin and decay long before the birth of Christ. Today, in modern times—the summer of 1933—its majesty could only be imagined, much like examining a withered mummy and trying to picture the great warrior king it had once been.

Within the temple—its darkness sliced by sun seeping through the cracked ceiling—enormous pillars rose from the rock-strewn floor of a dead chamber alive with history, memories and, perhaps, ghosts . . . such as the small figure, casting a large shadow, that crept through the darkness to a far wall adorned with hieroglyphs, only to slip inside a fissure.

In the catacombs below, Richard O'Connell looked sharply up from his work—his eyes at once alert and wary—reacting to the sound of movement above and to his left. Stepping into a shaft of light, he pursued the source of that movement, that sound. . . .

O'Connell was not an Egyptologist—the newspapers, periodicals and newsreels had dubbed him with such fanciful terms as "explorer," "soldier of fortune," and "adventurer," frequently citing his status as a former colonel in the French Foreign Legion . . . though the latter distinction occurred only when Corporal O'Connell had received a battlefield commission of sorts when the real colonel had deserted.

That had been almost ten years ago—the beginning of the adventure that had changed his life, although of late that life had been considerably less eventful. Nonetheless—even if he did not realize it, and found these romantic press characterizations of himself faintly ridiculous—Rick O'Connell retained the dashing demeanor of a modern man of action, his strong-jawed, steely-eyed, collegiate good looks aging well. Bronzed by the sun, shock of unruly brown hair touched ever so lightly with gray at the temples, O'Connell had the same trimly muscular frame of his Foreign Legion days. With his collar open, shirtsleeves rolled up, chinos tucked into his boots, and a sidearm in its snap holster at his hip, O'Connell could have given Douglas Fairbanks a fair run for it in the hero department.

And right now a hero might be called for: footsteps were echoing through the coolness of the catacombs, intermingled with unidentifiable sounds, those spooky noises any dark unsettling place seems able to manage to generate.

O'Connell, moving stealthily along the rough rock walls of the tunnel, unsnapped the holster strap and withdrew his revolver, sliding it silently from its sheath.

Noises, footsteps, echoed—*something was coming.*

What a wonderful idea, O'Connell thought, jaw taut, *exploring a damn temple built by our old buddy Imhotep. . . .*

Pausing at a dark intersection, every muscle in his

11

body tensed, O'Connell waited in what had become dead silence.

Then he bolted around the corner, revolver poised to shoot . . .

. . . scaring the ever-living hell out of his eight-year-old son, Alex.

"Whoa!" the boy said. The angelic lad, with his shock of blond hair—at least as unruly as his father's—clutched his heart half-comically, half for real. "My heart almost stopped!"

"Mine did," his father said, swallowing, spinning the weapon and holstering it, then snapping it in. "I told you to wait up in the temple!"

Alexander O'Connell, who wore a shortsleeve white shirt and navy-blue short pants, replied in a manner standard of boys his age. "But, Dad—"

"No 'buts,' son. It's dangerous down here—uncharted territory."

Alex moved closer to his father. "But I saw something! Something I had to tell you about, right away!"

"What did you see?"

"Your tattoo!"

O'Connell didn't know what the hell his boy was talking about—Alex had long been fascinated by the small tattoo on the side of his father's hand, so of course the boy had seen it!

"I mean, I saw the same drawing on the wall," Alex explained quickly, words tumbling. "Up by the entrance, there's a cartouche marked just like your tattoo! I'm telling the truth."

"I don't doubt you, son—"

"It looks just like this," the boy said, latching onto his father's hand, turning it so his father could view the tattoo—as if O'Connell hadn't spent his own sweet time, over the years, wondering who had put it there, in O'Connell's youth, before his own memory: a mariner's compass pointing down, with falcon's wings pointing up, forming a pyramid . . . and in the center, the eye of Horus.

Alex was saying, "It's got a pyramid with the eye and everything!"

"Swell, son, good work . . . I'll be up a little later to have a look, okay?"

The angelic countenance winced in disappointment. "Can't I stay down here, exploring with you, till then?"

"No."

"But—"

"No 'buts.'" O'Connell placed his hands on the boy's shoulders and turned him around. "Back up to the temple and wait, Gunga Din. Scoot!"

"And do what?"

A rat scuttled past them, down the tunnel, and the boy whitened, grabbing his father's arm.

"Surprise me," he told the boy, ruffling his hair. "Build a better mousetrap."

The rat's appearance had apparently made Alex less enthusiastic about staying down in the catacombs.

"See what I can do," the boy said, and scurried back toward the temple—in the opposite direction of the rodent's path.

13

Which was exactly the direction O'Connell took, although he was not looking for the rat, nor was he looking for a snake, though the latter was what he got.

Stepping into the cartouche chamber where he and his wife Evelyn had been working prior to hearing strange sounds, O'Connell saw Alex's mother standing at a sealed rock door, using a brush to better reveal an ancient engraving—the hieroglyph story of two lovely Egyptian princesses locked in hand-to-hand combat.

Evelyn Carnahan O'Connell was as beautiful as any Egyptian princess, including Nefertiti herself. Tall, dark-maned, slender, shapely, richly tanned—a fetchingly "gone native" effect underscored by beaded necklaces and her flowing black-brown-and-white Egyptian print dress—she was, typically, lost in her work.

She did not seem to notice the big black snake, uncoiling itself next to her right boot.

As O'Connell's hand dropped to his holster, the snake hissed, and Evy—not flinching—said, "Go away . . . don't bother me," and hooked the creature over the toe of her boot and tossed it across the room.

O'Connell ducked as the thing flew over his head.

Glancing into the tunnel, where the snake was fleeing for dear life, O'Connell said, "You're getting pretty good at that."

Without looking back, staying at her work, Evelyn asked, "Did I hear you and Alex talking?"

"Yeah."

14

"What did he want?"

Then O'Connell was next to her at the sealed rock door, admiring her handiwork—the carved hieroglyphs stood out boldly now. Perfect for photography.

"Just to spout off about something he found," O'Connell said. "Ready to have me pry this baby off?"

She glanced sharply at him, almond-shaped blue eyes flashing in the lovely heart-shaped face. "No. We'll do it the right way."

"By the right way," he said, "I presume you mean *your* way."

She nodded.

He sighed, bending to the rucksack beside her, finding the brown leather pouch of archaeologist's tools and handing them to her. "Where were we? Oh, yeah . . . pick."

Evy selected a geologist's rock pick from the pouch and passed it to him like a nurse attending a surgeon, saying, "Pick."

O'Connell chipped carefully, delicately at the seam of the sealed door. Minute fragments of stone fell, like dandruff.

"File," he said, intent upon his work.

She selected a small metal file from the pouch, passed it to him, saying, "File."

Like a seasoned archaeologist, O'Connell used the file to smooth out his work. *This shouldn't take too long,* he thought. *No more than a century . . .*

"Chisel," he said.

15

Evelyn withdrew a chisel from the rucksack, saying, "Chisel," placing it in her husband's outstretched palm.

Delicately, O'Connell eased the tip of the chisel into the gap he'd created.

Sighing heavily, Evy said, "Oh, to hell with it—let's do it your way."

He grinned at her, dropping the chisel. "Pry bar!"

From the rucksack she withdrew the heavy pry bar and handed it to him, saying, "Pry—"

But O'Connell had already slammed the thing into the door's seam, and popped it loose. With an appreciative squeal, Evy jumped back and the huge stone slab hit the floor between them with an echoing *whump,* raising ancient dust.

"This moment," Evy said, rather grandly, eyes glittering, "is all I've been thinking of . . . ever since I began having the dreams."

Recurring dreams of Egypt—of this temple, Imhotep's temple—had led the couple and their young son to these ruins. O'Connell had long since accepted that, because of his wife's work, Egypt—the ancient land of the pharaohs—would always be a major part of their lives.

But this was more than work, much more than research—vivid dreams of ancient days had possessed the normally cool, even reserved former librarian. Such an obsession was simply not like her—but O'Connell loved his wife more than life, and far more than reason; and could not deny her this trip, this most bizarre of research expeditions: to discover not the history of the pharaohs, but the meaning of her own dreams.

And now the first door had been opened.

"My dreams are nothing like this," O'Connell said, illuminating the moldy chamber with a torch.

Rotted mummies leaned against walls, while scorpions skittered and snakes slithered about the stone floor in a tuneless, malevolent dance.

The creatures moved away as Evelyn fearlessly stepped into the vile chamber.

"I've been here before," she said, words resonating in various ways.

"Impossible."

"Rick, I *know* I have been here before!"

"Baby, nobody's been here but these snakes and scorpions, not in three thousand years."

Like a woman sleepwalking, and yet with calculated determination, Evy reached out and latched onto what seemed to be a torch holder, and pulled.

A doorway, concealed in the rock, yawned open and revealed a dark passageway.

"If I haven't been here," she asked her husband coolly, "how is it I seem to know exactly what to do, and where to go?"

Grabbing his rucksack and slipping it around his shoulders, O'Connell handed Evy the torch and stepped into the adjacent dark chamber, with her just behind him. As she fanned the torch around the small, empty room, its walls decorated with faded painted hieroglyphs, something strange happened to his wife, although O'Connell himself was incognizant of it. . . .

. . . Evelyn's view of the room, in a flicker of torchlight, changed, fantastically, as if she had been catapulted thousands of years into the past, the small alcove suddenly, gloriously new, the hieroglyphs vivid, golden glittering furnishings adorning what was clearly an elaborate antechamber. A beautiful woman—a shapely young Egyptian princess in head-dress and golden jeweled jewelry and clinging gown—moved through a doorway into the antechamber. The woman's head was lowered; Evelyn could not see her face, but did glimpse the larger, even more opulent chamber beyond, where two massive, fearsome warriors with swords and shields stood at either side of a small, ornate, gold-encrusted chest. Closing the door behind her, the princess locked it by twisting a sundial mechanism—twice to the right, once to the left. Strangely, Rick was in this vision of the chamber room as well, a jarring modern-day presence, but apparently oblivious to this manifestation of opulence . . . a fact which he confirmed by walking straight through the princess, as if she were a ghost!

. . . and then Evelyn was again standing in the dark, ancient antechamber, its hieroglyphs faded, the precious golden furnishings gone.

O'Connell had neither seen nor sensed any of it. He was approaching a stone door, which oddly enough bore what seemed to be a sundial, and—not anxious to go through the pick and file and chisel routine again—withdrew the pry bar from his rucksack and jammed it into the door seam.

As he strained his muscles prying at the thing, Evy was rather deliberately fanning her torch around the room, wearing a peculiarly awestruck expression.

Breathing hard, O'Connell glanced over his shoulder at this odd activity and said, "What're you trying to do? Write your name in the air?"

"I'm trying to make it happen again."

Leaning on the pry bar, catching his breath, he asked, "Make what happen again?"

"This room—I saw it differently."

"Differently . . ."

She described to him what she'd seen—what she'd experienced.

"It was the same as in my dream," she concluded, "but even more real, more vivid . . . as if I were actually standing here in ancient times."

"But this wasn't a dream—it was a vision."

Her lovely eyes flashed, nostrils flared. "Yes. Yes! A vision . . . that's the only word for it."

O'Connell stared at his wife, her beauty bathed in the orange glow of the torch, shadows playing on the perfect planes of her face, the supple curves of her body. He was sincerely hoping she wasn't insane, because he really, really loved this woman.

"Dreams I don't mind," he said softly. "Visions make me nervous. . . . Are you all right?"

"I'm . . . fine. Yes, I'm fine." She drew in several deep breaths, then her eyes locked with his, and—seeing his concern—she said, "Really, darling . . . perfectly fine."

O'Connell sighed, wiped the sweat from his brow

with the back of a hand, then returned to the hard work of prying at the stone door. "Well, baby," he said, grunting, "if you were really here a few thousand years ago, maybe you can think back and show me how to open this damn thing."

Then she was at his side, casually reaching forward to twist the sundial—turning it twice to the right, once to the left. The sound of the lock giving way was followed by the door cracking open with a hiss, as if air were escaping a punctured tire.

O'Connell met his wife's gaze—she was as surprised as he was.

"Okay," he said. "Now it's official: you got me worried."

She swallowed. "Now I'm starting to worry myself."

O'Connell, pry bar in one hand, with the other took the torch from his wife. "I'm right behind you."

She gave him a look. "That's not very heroic."

"Hey, you're the one who knows the way around the joint."

Evy stepped into the cool dark chamber as her husband, just behind her, raised the torch to light the way. Turning to her left, she found herself facing a hideous visage and screamed.

O'Connell saw it, too, and—as Evy's shriek rang in his ears—swung the pry bar like a saber, decapitating the menacing figure, sending its skull ricocheting off the stone walls.

"What the hell . . ." O'Connell said, stepping forward, lowering the torch.

20

The head, it seemed, had belonged to a mummy—not a reanimated one, of the sort O'Connell had dealt with when Imhotep had made his twentieth-century return, around a decade ago—just a good old-fashioned bandaged-wrapped dead one who'd been propped up here as if standing watch. But the shield and sword indicated this long deceased warrior had been a solider, like the ones guarding the chest in the vision Evy had told him about.

Taking the torch from her husband, Evy lighted the other side of the chamber, showing him that there were indeed two soldier mummies, positioned on either side of an ornate chest.

"This is what you saw in your vision?" O'Connell asked her, kneeling to have a look at the lid of the chest, on which rested a golden disc with the grotesque bas-relief image of a scorpion.

But Evy did not answer him; instead, she said, "The Scorpion King!"

O'Connell looked up at her. "Oh, I don't even begin to like the sound of that. . . ."

"That disc is the masthead of a battle banner . . . of the army of the Scorpion King."

"Oh-kay. . . ."

"The Scorpion King was supposed to be a myth—no contemporary trace of him has ever been found, and the writings date centuries after his supposed death. . . ."

"Go on."

Quickly, she told him of the myth, and as she

21

wrapped it up, O'Connell said, "Well, unless they cremated him, he's not in that chest."

Eyes wide, she said, "Darling, you don't understand—this is a major discovery. . . . That disc is the first historical evidence that the Scorpion King actually existed. What was myth before we entered this chamber is now fact."

He stood, brushed off his knees. "Great. That's something else you can ram up the collective wazoo of the Bembridge scholars."

Nodding gleefully, she clasped her hands and said, "Rick . . . Rick, let's open it."

"What, the chest?"

"Of course the chest. Who knows what precious—"

"Baby, I don't think that's such a swell idea."

"Don't be a ninny. It's just a chest—no harm ever came from a chest."

He held up a palm. "That has kind of a familiar ring to it. Wasn't there this book, once? And didn't you say no harm ever came from a book, right before we unleashed plagues and—"

Her eyes were bright, the reflection of the torch-light dancing in them. "Oh, Richard, we can't stop now! Where's your sense of adventure?"

He sighed, hefted the pry bar. No use arguing with her when she called him "Richard." "Okay, baby— but remember . . . Rick O'Connell was the voice of reason, this time around."

"For once," she said, her smile impish. "Now . . . give me that pry bar."

As she huffed and puffed, working the pry bar, doing her tomboy best to open the chest, O'Connell tilted the torch toward the fallen headless mummy who had stood guard here for a few thousand years. Around what was left of the figure's neck was a gold chain and what might have been a key. O'Connell helped himself.

"Oh, to hell with it," O'Connell said, mocking her sweetly. "Let's do it your way."

And he knelt and slipped the key into the lock and turned it, ancient tumblers clicking.

"Where on earth did you find that?" Evelyn asked, her eyes saucers.

"Came to me in a vision. Listen, stand back . . . we've run into booby traps before, remember?"

Nodding, she stepped well back, saying, "You be careful, too, Rick."

He removed the golden disc from its resting place, setting it on the stone floor, then flipped the lid back, ducking, as air hissed softly from the chest. No acid bath, no poison gas, no spring-loaded spear or other deadly surprise emanated from the object.

O'Connell peeked in.

Cradled lovingly in a cushion of ancient velvetlike material lay a thick gold bracelet with that same bas-relief scorpion design as the golden disc that had been atop the chest.

Evy approached, and uttered, her voice tinged with surprise, reverence and fear, "The Bracelet of Anubis!"

And she slammed the lid shut on the chest.

O'Connell blinked and got back to his feet. "Little late for that, isn't it, Pandora?"

She was trembling. But she swallowed and said, "Put those things in your rucksack."

The disc and the chest, she meant.

"Hey, I got an even better idea—let's leave the sons of bitches behind."

She arched an eyebrow at him. "Little late for that, isn't it?"

As if in reply—negative reply at that—a terrible sound, a sort of rumble-edged groaning, made its way into their chamber from the outer catacombs.

He looked sharply at her. "What the hell is that?"

She frowned. "Nothing human . . ."

The grating sound increased, echoing down the tunnels.

O'Connell said, "That's stone grinding against stone! An earthquake?"

"If so, these ruins will collapse! And Alex is up there!"

He loaded the golden disc into the rucksack, then forced in the chest—which fit snugly—and slipped the backpack on, saying, "Let's get out of here—to Alex."

Nodding, she held out her hand and he grasped it, and they ran like hell, just as the wall behind them exploded, stones tumbling under a geyser of water!

They sprinted through the antechamber, and into a room beyond that, and out into the catacombs, with the rush of water screaming in their ears, the sound

24

of it gaining on them, propelling them ever faster down the tunnel.

"That's the antechamber," he yelled, pointing ahead to a doorway as they ran, "with the stairway, right?"

A wall of water was splashing behind them, chasing them, racing them through the catacombs.

"I don't know!" she yelled over the water's roar. "Maybe!"

He yanked her through the doorway and his torch illuminated a small room with no exit—a dead end.

They turned to go back, but the water was on them, erupting through the doorway in a tidal wave, putting out the torch, beginning to fill the room with gushing, dizzying speed.

"This is a goddamn desert!" O'Connell yelled over the waterfall-like sound. "Where did all this bloody water come from?"

Her expression was more tortured than afraid. "Oh, Rick—what have I done?"

"Evy, don't—there's a way out! There's always a way out!"

Trying to wade through the cold, now waist-high water to get back out in the tunnel, where perhaps they could swim under the surface, to somewhere, the rushing force of the flood drove them back; within a minute it was up to their necks and they were still in the same chamber, breathing in stale, thinning air.

"Evy—"

"Rick!"

Then they were under the surging, swirling water, arms wrapped around each other, hugging tight, their fear and desperation outweighed only by their love.

·❦ 2 ❧·

Rat Trap

Beneath the relentless desert sun, three white men on horseback paused atop a dune just beyond the ruins of the temple of Thebes, their leader—"Red" Willits—using binoculars to scan for activity. He saw only the three waiting camels, and said, "They must be below—in the catacombs."

Astride horses as they were, all three wearing wide-brimmed hats, bandannas knotted at the neck, and sidearms holstered at the hip, the trio had an air of the American Wild West, though the scimitars they carried said they were not new to this part of the world. Their clothes were dingy with dust and sand, their faces unshaven, their eyes as cold as the desert was hot.

Red, six foot one and a brute, was an American. At a burly six three, Jacques Clemons, the Frenchman of the group, made Red look delicate. By comparison, the Brit, Jake Spivey, six foot and as lean and mean as a snake, seemed undernourished—but nothing that a little blood money wouldn't cure.

These three personified the difference between a soldier of fortune like Rick O'Connell, and mercenaries like themselves.

With a nod to his partners, who followed him, Red rode easily down the slope of sand, unaware that his binoculars had missed the presence of one of the O'Connells—young Alex—who was busying himself within the temple's great hall.

At first, Alex didn't hear the men coming, distracted as he was by the task at hand. Over the last several days, his parents had gathered numerous artifacts from the dig below, and they were assembled, sorted, into little groupings, set out on the temple floor not far from where Alex worked. The towheaded boy in short pants had collected bamboo shoots, stray mummy wrappings and rotted bones, and was well along in the process of building a cagelike contraption, into which he had already inserted a generous chunk of cheese from their provisions basket.

Build a better mousetrap, his father had said. Now and then, Alex would cast a wary eye on the scuttling rats in the corners of the temple. Big mice!

That was when he heard the bigger rats—their voices anyway, as Red, Jacques and Spivey tied up their horses and began approaching on foot.

The boy had inherited his mother's intellect and his father's courage; but he was eight years old and he was frightened, particularly when he made out a voice (belonging to Red) whispering, "We won't need to bury 'em. . . . What do you think the damn sun and the birds are for?"

Other deep, harsh voices laughed at that, but Alex was already on his feet, looking frantically about, eyes fixing upon the forty-foot wood-plank-and-steel-pipe scaffolding left over from a stalled restoration project of the Egyptian government.

Grabbing his rucksack and slinging it on, Alex scurried over to the scaffolding and began to climb; he did so quickly, nimbly, as if scaling a jungle gym on a park playground—though, disturbingly, even under his scant weight, the flimsy structure swayed some.

Nonetheless, he was soon safe at the top, belly-crawling across the planks to look down into the temple, where he saw three dirty-looking, scruffy-looking, *evil*-looking men enter—slowly, cautiously. Each man had a gun in one hand and a scimitar in the other and both weapons were poised to do harm.

The son of Rick O'Connell knew at once that this was a vicious crew, and a professional one; this rabble was here to kill his parents—and him. Eyes wide with fear, heart pounding like a trip-hammer, Alex peered over the edge of the scaffolding and watched as the redheaded one who seemed to be the leader knelt to examine the various piles of artifacts.

"Spivey, Jacques," he said, pointing, "pick through that junk and see if you can find that damn bracelet."

Spivey blinked at his boss. "What are you gonna do, Red?"

Red nodded toward a wall with a prominent fissure, which Alex knew to be the "doorway" down to the catacombs. "I'm gonna drop in on the O'Connells. . . . You sort out that crap, and I'll sort them out."

His partners laughed and Red headed toward the fissure, pistol in hand. Jacques knelt at the piled artifacts and began fingering through them, saying, "What are you doing, you idiot?"

"Just seeing what this thing is," Spivey said, his rodentlike features twitching with curiosity as he crouched before Alex's contraption. "Hey! Cheese . . ."

Alex could not restrain his smile as the skinny mercenary stuck in his hand, seeking the hunk of cheese that sat on a plate in the bamboo and human-bone cage.

But Alex winced and looked away, avoiding the sight of what happened next: the spikey bamboo shoot spearing down hard into Spivey's hand with a *thwack!*

Spivey's scream echoed across the desert, and Jacques's reaction was merely to laugh. Red had disappeared through that fissure, and Alex wondered if the man—and Alex's parents, deep in the catacombs below—would have heard the cry of pain.

Spivey was muttering obscenities, bandaging his hand with his bandanna, while atop the scaffolding, Alex was quietly digging in his rucksack. Then the

30

boy—with a smile that turned his angelic countenance devilish—withdrew one of his prized possessions: a wrist-rocket slingshot. Digging again in the rucksack, Alex came up with a small handful of pebbles he had collected as ammunition, never dreaming such a good purpose would avail itself.

Spivey, hand bandaged, still muttering, had joined the burly Frenchman and both were carelessly, even savagely ransacking the precious historical artifacts his parents had worked so hard to find and preserve.

Alex took aim, and sent a pebble zipping through the air, bonking Spivey in the back of the head, a perfect hit!

"Blimey!" Spivey spun around, getting to his feet, clutching the back of his skull. "Something hit me!"

Jacques looked up suspiciously, pausing in his rifling of the artifacts. "What hit you, nitwit?"

"I don't know! A rock, maybe! Damn . . . I'm bleeding!"

Jacques shrugged, returned to his work. "It's nothing. Come on, you fool—help me find that damn bracelet."

Spivey sighed, muttered more obscenities, but did again crouch and begin roughly sorting through the antiquities.

Up on the scaffolding, Alex had reloaded and was once more taking aim—this time at the skinny guy's bony butt, which was sticking up in the air, begging the boy to hit him.

Which, with another zinging shot, he did.

"Yow!" Spivey said, and got to his feet and did a

little dance, clutching his behind. "Damn! Goddamn! That *hurt*!"

Alex was laughing, silently, and down below Jacques barked a laugh as well ... but then the Frenchman's eyes turned cold and began slowly scanning the temple around them.

"Get back to work," Jacques said, and, reluctantly, casting a suspicious glance over his shoulder occasionally, Spivey did.

Alex waited perhaps two minutes before letting fly again, but this time Jacques—who had seemed intent upon his work—spun around and caught the rock in midair, inches from striking Spivey's skull, a motion so blindingly fast Alex could almost neither believe nor perceive it. . . . How could such a big man be so fast?

Alex ducked back, but suspected the brute below had spotted him. Trembling, cowering, the boy waited, hoping he was wrong, hoping the man's eyes hadn't met his, and almost sure they had.

The boy did not see Jacques slowly stand, with Spivey looking up at him in confusion. Jacques opened his fist and displayed the jagged pebble in his palm.

"What the hell . . . ?" Spivey said.

"A little mouse," Jacques said, and closed his fist again, and squeezed.

When the big Frenchman opened his palm again, all that remained was dust. He brushed the powdered rock off on his filthy shirt and rose.

Now Alex braved a peek over the edge.

"I'll take care of him," Jacques said, and he withdrew from his side the scimitar, with an ominous *shing!*

Eyes widening, Alex scurried back, a mouse with no hole to hide in.

Unaware of any of this, the brutal Red was below, exploring the catacombs, scimitar in one hand, pistol in the other, an explorer seeking not artifacts but victims, specifically the parents of the boy above. As he peeked in doorways, he had no sense of history, and when he stepped inside one area, he had no idea he was in the cartouche chamber of a princess, nor that that fallen oval object he stepped on was the priceless and holy cartouche itself.

Nor, not at first anyway, did he realize he had somehow triggered one of those fabled Egyptian booby traps that had been the demise of so many, much more knowledgeable explorers than himself. He merely heard a soft if terrible groan that at first seemed human, then—as it built—revealed itself to his ears as the nails-on-blackboard whine of stone shifting against stone.

Massive stone against massive stone . . .

Then the chamber around him began to shudder, as if repelled, sickened, by his foul presence.

And as the entire tunnel system, the very catacombs themselves, began to growl like an enraged beast, Red got the point: eyes huge with terror, he performed his first intelligent act of the day . . . he turned and ran like hell.

33

Red, sprinting back through the chamber, stomped across the cartouche of the princess as he went, intending no disrespect, as if the gods would make such a distinction; the catacombs seemed to bellow in anger.

He fled out into the tunnel in time not to see (though indeed he heard) a wall bursting open, raging water blasting through a narrow but ever widening crevice.

In the temple above, none of this had yet become apparent to Spivey and Jacques, the latter in the process of scaling that scaffolding, scimitar in his teeth, like a pirate climbing a mast.

Alex could see him coming, and fired down several pebbles at the brute, trying to take out an eye; but the monstrous Frenchman ducked or batted the tiny stones away, and only laughed.

"More, my little mouse," he called up to Alex. "Fire more stones! It stokes my anger!"

Not liking the sound of that, Alex backpedaled to the edge of the scaffolding, and suddenly there was nowhere else to go and that ogre was almost to the top.

"Such a nice fillet you'll make, my son," the Frenchman was saying.

But before Jacques had reached the top, a rumbling below asserted itself, and the Frenchman glanced down just as his leader, Red, came scrambling out of the "doorway" fissure and ran pell-mell across the temple floor.

"Get the hell outa here!" the redhead yelled. "Now!"

"What are you talkin' about?" Spivey demanded, gesturing to the piles of artifacts at his feet. "We ain't even found the thing yet!"

"Keep looking, then, and die!"

Red was sprinting out of the temple, toward the horses. That was enough to convince Spivey, who fell in behind him, hotfooting it out of there.

Having heard this exchange, Jacques—who was at the edge of the scaffolding—glanced down at his partners sprinting out of the temple; then he looked at the terrified little boy, who was poised to shoot another pebble at him, said, "Damn—you are the lucky little mouse," and slid all the way down the scaffolding, like a fireman down a firehouse pole answering a call.

But at the bottom, the brute took the time—before fleeing the temple—to kick a balance board out from under the scaffolding.

As the Frenchman scurried out of the temple, Alex—still atop the scaffolding—felt the structure rock, and sway. As if standing on a teeter-totter, Alex struggled to keep his balance, as the world under him lost its.

The structure—none too steady to begin with—began to pendulate wildly, creaking, groaning, as if striving not to topple, a drunk trying to maintain his equilibrium. Terrible sounds were emanating from the catacombs below, and Alex's fear for himself was matched by dire concern for his poor parents. Still,

35

he rode that swaying scaffolding like a surfboard, and kept steady . . . at least until the scaffolding collapsed, pitching sideways, slamming into one of the massive temple pillars.

The impact hurled the boy from the collapsing-house-of-cards scaffolding, and he landed on the pillar, hugging it, riding it, bucking bronco-style, then—realizing he had a decent grip—he began to slide down the pillar, and it was almost fun, like sliding down a huge banister, and then he was on the floor, breathing hard, but relieved, despite the grotesque groaning sounds from beneath that floor.

The boy, catching his breath, watched helplessly as the falling pillar knocked into the next pillar, which toppled into the next pillar, one pillar after another slamming into its neighbor, *whunk, whunk, whunk,* echoing across the great hall, a terrible game of dominoes that raised clouds of ancient and modern dust alike and soon left the boy standing in the ruined ruins of a once majestic temple that, now and forever, had been destroyed.

A single pillar remained standing, none too steadily.

The boy—who had a touch of one of his mother's few faults, which is to say occasional clumsiness—said, "Oops," which seemed at once insufficient and yet did cover the situation.

The noise below, the rumbling, grew to earthquake proportions, and the floor seemed to shudder, to shake. That last remaining pillar—caught on a beam—was slowly slipping. It seemed to Alex the least he could do was try to prevent its destruction; so he raced over and, like a tiny Samson who had changed his mind, did his best to keep that pillar from tumbling and taking down what little remained of the temple, pushing against the massive pillar with all his meager might.

Not surprisingly, the lad lost the fight, and the pillar went tumbling toward the wall that bore the hieroglyph mirroring his father's tattoo—mariner's compass and falcon wings forming a pyramid with an eye in the middle—and the pillar collided with that wall, crashing right through it, removing the image Alex had hoped to point out to his father, caving a huge hole in the wall, but . . .

. . . at the same time creating an escape valve through which an enormous wall of water exploded!

A huge gush erupted through the hole Alex and his pillar had made, a wave on which his parents rode, spilling out onto the floor of the temple, drenched, exhausted, gasping for air, flopping like fishes, finally looking around them at the ruined temple with wide, bewildered eyes.

"Mum . . . Dad," Alex said, holding up both palms, as, panting, dripping, they sat up, taking in the enormous mess around them that had not long ago been a beautiful remnant of antiquity. "Count to ten. . . . I can explain everything."

·❨ 3 ❩·

Fly in Amber

As if searching for escaped prisoners, floodlights
swept across a desert dig at Hamanaptra, aiding a
starry night whose full moon had already painted the
ruins of the City of the Dead with a patina of ivory.
Native workers, like parasites picking at bones, in-
fested the skeleton of this once great city, with its
crumbled pylons, wind-worn columns, partial walls
and statues topped with lions' and rams' heads. Such
remnants of a great, vanished society were over-
whelmed by the realities of the modern, mechanical
age, the dead temple alive with the sound of grinding
gears, the ruins towered over by bulldozers and
cranes.

Along the periphery of various smaller sites within
this larger site, groups of armed men—Arab warriors
in red turbans, loose white garments and dark flowing
robes—supervised the efforts of perhaps a hundred

natives. Some of the red-turbaned, rifle-bearing guards had been charged to guard the boundaries of the camp from invaders who might materialize from the darkness of the desert at night.

The guards and the diggers alike answered to a small dark man in a red fez and off-white suit; his sharp features and sharper dark eyes gave an edge to what might have been dismissed as a mild demeanor. Hands folded patiently and resting on a modest rise of belly, Faud Fachry stood poised at the edge of a deep pit in the sand, where dozens of natives were digging in the floodlight sweep under Fachry's supervision—and the watchful eye of guards with red turbans and raised rifles.

Fachry was curator of the Egyptian wing of the British Museum—and indeed, "the Curator" was the only designation by which he was known at this site.

The Curator's attention was drawn from the pit by the sound of an approaching vehicle. He turned to see a Marmon Herrington all-terrain truck pulling up to a stop, the mercenary Red Willits at the wheel, the other two—Jacques and Spivey—riding. The men climbed from the open vehicle and met the Curator halfway as he approached them.

An urgency in the Curator's voice was at odds with his placid bearing. "Did you succeed?"

"Well," the redheaded mercenary said, scratching his stubbly cheek, "that depends. . . ."

"Did you acquire it? Have you the bracelet?"

"Well . . ."

A rumbling interrupted the conversation, the

ground trembling, shaking . . . then it stopped.

The three mercenaries exchanged wary glances. The Curator did not know that the trio had experienced a similar sensation at the Imhotep temple at Thebes.

Before the conversation could resume, the rumbling beat them to it, the sandy earth beneath them shaking, vibrating, more violently now, as if an earthquake were imminent, as if . . . some great beast were moving closer to them, traveling under the ground.

And, again, the rumbling stopped.

The Curator turned his head toward the pit—the sound had seemed to emanate from there. He resumed his position at the pit's edge, the mercenaries trailing after, curiously.

Down in the pit, eyes were huge, jaws open in fear, as the native workers paused, looking at each other, at the sandy walls around them, at the gun barrels pointing down, encouraging them to stay put.

"Get back to work!" the Curator snapped at them, in their tongue.

But before they could, the natives found themselves confronted by a mound of sand in their midst that began to swell, as if the hole were trying to refill itself, a hill that seemed to be forming of its own volition, growing, rising from the bottom of the pit like a cake in its pan. The diggers moved back, looking at each other with wide-eyed perplexity, just standing there, shovels in hand, giving it room, staring at this magical phenomenon, transfixed.

Then all hell broke loose.

The mound burst like a boil and thousands of beetles—those rancid dung beetles known as scarabs—came spilling out, and rose in a chittering, wriggling wave to flood the sandy pit, turning it black, and red, as the hard-shelled, flesh-eating insects swarmed over the workers and fed an insatiable appetite.

Screams of terror, shrieks of agony, rose from this pit of hell as the diggers tried frantically to scramble up the sandy walls, helplessly grasping for purchase, legs and hands churning in the sand, and those walls weren't all that steep, actually, but progress was slow and the scarabs were quick. The black shells of the insects glittered under the sweep of the floodlights, as did the glisten of blood and the sheen of freshly exposed bone.

"Holy Christ," the hard-boiled redheaded mercenary said.

The Curator, who had been observing the scene with scientific detachment (having anticipated this particular scenario), noted with some small amusement that the three tough cutthroats had turned pale and stood trembling like frightened schoolchildren. Hadn't they ever seen men eaten alive by scarabs before?

The trio ran to their truck and climbed up into its relative safety, Red ready to drive off at any moment.

One digger, miraculously, clambered up and out of the pit; shreds of his flesh were gone, however, and under what remained were moving bumps, like huge rolling sores: creatures were crawling under his flesh.

41

The three mercenaries screamed.

So did the digger, or at least he tried to: the result was that a small army of black beetles swarmed out of his gullet, as he seemed to vomit up the insects.

As if to make up for the digger's inability to actually cry out, the three hard-bitten men screamed louder, clutching each other like scared children at a horror-movie matinee.

Chuckling at this, the Curator straight-armed the digger, pushing the unfortunate fellow back down into the pit, then stepped quickly away, seeking higher ground—since a few of the scarabs were at large—and, nodding to his red-turbaned guards, said, "Now."

Robes flowing, guards moved in and sprayed the escaping scarabs with flame-throwers, herding them back into the pit, and as the insects scurried and scrambled to their hole, from which only a few human screams now emerged, the guards chased them to the pit's edge and blasted fire down in on them. The wind caught the stench of burning human flesh and the Curator, delicately, covered his nose with a handkerchief.

As this vile activity continued, voices shouting excitement, not fear, announced a discovery at one of the nearby sites. Red-turbaned figures began to point, and the Curator's eyes followed to the man-made monster that was a crane swiveling over nearby ruins, with a prize catch in its claw: a huge rock that, he could see even from this distance, held within it— like a fly in amber—what had once been a man.

Forgetting the scarabs (he had long since forgotten the diggers), the Curator—clapping his hands, as elated as a child presented a longed-for new toy, ran to the site, heading for that crane and its prize.

"You found him!" the Curator burbled. "You have found our lord! *We have found him!*"

Minutes earlier, within a tent at that same site, two other discoveries dug from the ruins of the City of the Dead had been examined by the Curator's collaborator, one Meela Pasha, and her trusted bodyguard, known only as Lock-nah.

Despite her interest in the distant past, Meela was a modern woman, as intelligent as she was alluring, as formidable as she was sultry. Tall, with long black hair, bangs cut bluntly in the traditional Egyptian style, her slenderly shapely figure well-served by tight-fitting khakis, Meela possessed a bearing at once regal and businesslike.

Lock-nah wore the same red turban, flowing dark robe and loose white garments as the various guards serving both the Curator and his mistress, Meela. But Lock-nah stood taller than the rest, a muscular figure with chiseled features and hard dark eyes.

He had just slammed down an object upon a table in the tent, raising a small duststorm: a book.

Not just any book—an oversize, improbably heavy, brass-hinged volume, its obsidian covers carved with ornate, vaguely ominous hieroglyphs.

"The Book of the Dead," Lock-nah announced in his resonant baritone.

"It gives our lord life," Meela said matter-of-factly, in her melodic alto.

"And *The Book of Amun Ra—The Book of the Living*—takes it away."

Now Lock-nah slammed another book on the table, next to the black one, raising more dust, the table legs shuddering under the weight. This book was the black one's golden twin, similarly hinged, similarly decorated with hieroglyphs, though nothing was ominous about this precious-metal artifact, whose value was unimaginable.

Meela bent over the golden volume and pursed her lips as if to bestow a kiss and, like a child blowing out the candles on a birthday cake, blew dust from its cover.

Straightening, she granted her bodyguard a smile. "We're getting closer."

At this point the screams of the diggers being eaten alive by scarabs easily found their way into the tent, and Meela arched an eyebrow at Lock-nah, saying, "We're getting *very* close. . . ."

The beauty and the handsome beast who guarded her rushed into the night, across the grounds of the ruins and their encampment; Lock-nah carried *The Book of the Dead,* and Meela—despite its weight—lugged *The Book of the Living.*

A turbaned chauffeur, standing at attention next to a cream-colored Rolls-Royce, bowed for his mistress and opened its door as Meela and her bodyguard approached; the chauffeur seemed not to hear the screams of terror and pain that echoed across the City of the Dead.

"Not now," she said dismissively, moving past the driver and the vehicle, heading for the pit where the Curator had been supervising the dig. She could see the little man in the red fez at the next site over, as a crane lowered a large object, a chunk of rock.

As they walked, Meela asked her bodyguard, "This golden book, this is what they used to defeat Imhotep? To condemn him, correct?"

"That is so, my lady."

"And it is the only thing on this earth that can harm our lord, yes?"

"Yes, my lady."

At the pit—from which the stench of human flesh and charred beetle wafted like foul incense—Meela paused and, as if discarding a used tissue, flung the priceless object down into the foul, smoky darkness of the hole. Not missing a beat, the woman and her bodyguard moved on, ignoring the chitter of scarabs below.

Meela also did not notice the three mercenaries, sitting in the truck nearby, who had seen this action of hers. Nor did she hear their comments.

"Did you see what I just saw?" Jacques asked.

Spivey said, "That bloody thing was made of gold! That book was pure gold!"

Red, their leader, behind the wheel of the motionless vehicle, was still shaking; he backhanded the sweat from his brow and nodded toward the pit.

"Well, why don't you girls scramble down there and fetch it, then?"

Neither Jacques nor Spivey accepted this offer, and they sat, mute observers, as a bulldozer approached and began shoving sand down into the pit. Trapped scarabs chittered, and the disgusted trio shivered.

In the gentle sweep of floodlights, Meela and Lock-nah strode through the night over to the euphoric Curator just as the claws of the crane lowered the slab of rock to the sand. Molded within the rock was a petrified corpse, deformed in anguish and death, frozen in a silent scream—whether of agony or defiance, that was hard to determine.

Meela's emotions were mixed—to see Lord Imhotep caught in this nightmare in stone broke her heart, even as that heart swelled with love. She stepped up to the corpse-in-stone and touched its cold cheek, smiling—a smile at once affectionate and devious.

The muscular, cruelly handsome bodyguard—*The Book of the Dead* still tucked under one arm—stepped next to his mistress and said, "We must now raise those who served our lord."

She nodded.

"The urn," Lock-nah said, turning to a servant, who scurried into the night just as the three mercenaries were approaching on foot.

"That's quite a nugget you dug out there," Red said, too casually, pitching a spent cigar into the night, sputtering sparks.

46

He and the other two mercenaries had just been confronted with the grotesque, unsettling sight of the man mummified within stone.

The Curator frowned, their presence reminding him of the conversation interrupted by scarabs. He thrust out his open palm to the scruffy redheaded American. "The bracelet! Where is it? Give it here at once!"

"I don't exactly have it."

"What does that mean?" the Curator asked, struggling to maintain his dignity.

The mercenary shrugged. "It was sort of a . . . missed opportunity."

Lock-nah—whose fury was anything but contained—dropped *The Book of the Dead* to the sand, and lurched forward and grabbed the American by the shirtfront. "We must have that bracelet!"

The other two mercenaries, scowling, moved forward, hands on their sidearms.

Lock-nah released the American, who huffed a face-saving laugh at the Arab, and his two companions grinned, feeling superior.

That was when Lock-nah whipped his scimitar from his side and its *shing!* sliced the air—though not, thankfully, anyone present.

The Curator stepped forward, hands outstretched like a referee. "Gentlemen! Please! Let us be civilized."

Meela—who had been standing with arms folded, watching these foolish men—merely raised a gentle hand, and Lock-nah nodded respectfully and took a step back.

Then Meela approached the Curator and touched his arm, saying, "I advised you to allow Lock-nah and myself to handle this . . . acquisition."

"Yes, I know, my lady," the Curator said, sheepish, "but I did not want your . . . shall we say, past history? . . . to cloud the issue."

The redheaded mercenary stepped forward, holding his palms out in a peace-making gesture. "No need for excitement—nobody needs to blame nobody. We got this situation in hand, if you'll just let me explain."

Her voice as cold as her eyes, Meela said, "Explain."

Shrugging, Red said, "We know where the thing is. We know where to find it, anyway. We're professionals—we'll take care of it."

Meela approached the mercenary. "Where is the bracelet?"

"On its way to merry old England. London, to be exact." The redhead filled them in on what had happened at the site. "Once the O'Connells were on to us, we kept our distance . . . but when all that water got soaked back into the desert, they packed up their trinkets and took the boat home. To London."

Meela arched an eyebrow. "And you presume the bracelet is among those 'trinkets.' "

"Yeah."

"So you did not *see* the bracelet."

"Not exactly . . ."

The Curator frowned.

Red smiled at Meela, his tone almost sweet, even flirtatious. "Look, we can handle this. We'll take care of it for you."

The Curator stepped up to them, saying to Red, sharply, "No! No. . . . We will handle this ourselves."

Red scowled at the Egyptian. "But what about our money?"

Chin raised, the Curator said, "You'll be amply rewarded for your efforts."

"You got something else in mind for me and my boys?"

The Curator's smile was ambiguous if creepy. "Indeed I have." He turned to Meela. "It would seem London is where we need to go."

The servant Lock-nah had sent to fetch a certain object now scurried back with it—a large black urn covered in hieratic.

Meela took the urn from the servant and held it caressingly.

Then she turned to the dead man frozen in rock and whispered tenderly, "Soon, my lord . . . my love. Soon."

Nearby a digger had heard much of this, just another of the anonymous *fellahin*, ignored by all, an invisible man. Not the Curator or Meela or Lock-nah or any of them suspected that among them, all this time, spying, had been Ardeth Bay himself. . . .

. . . Ardeth Bay, chieftain of the Med-jai warriors, a sect whose mission for centuries had been to guard the City of the Dead, to prevent the return of the

49

Bringer of Death, He Who Shall Not Be Named, the creature who would not stop until the earth had been consumed in pestilence and flame.

The creature in that shroud of stone.

·《 4 》·

The Bracelet of Anubis

Dusk can be a magical time in any city, and for a great city like London, sheer enchantment, the perfect time for a tourist to board an omnibus near the Strand and ride to the Bank, and from the Bank cross London Bridge to be whisked by tram for a view of the Surrey side of the Thames. Or, what better time of day or night to board an excursion steamer for an exquisite view of the Thames and its bridges, to enjoy the shimmering twinkle of lights on the river crossing under Tower Bridge, to see to best advantage the Parliament Houses and the dome of St. Paul's. Or even just to take a walk along St. James's Park, by the Mall, that stately avenue connecting Buckingham Palace and the Admiralty Buildings.

But this twilight, the double-decker omnibuses were in little use, the excursion steamers waiting at the dock, and few hardy souls were out taking constitutionals on this brisk evening. The magic of dusk had been overruled by the electrical wizardry of an impending thunderstorm, the sky gray and blackening as thunderheads rolled in and lightning flashed, diminishing Big Ben to a pocket watch on its vast charcoal vest.

A few miles west, in the lushest countryside to be found so near the city, a taxi pulled quickly out of a long, graveled drive, hoping to beat the storm back to London, having delivered passengers from Croydon aerodrome to this stately Tudor-style manor house. The luxuriantly green, well-tended grounds might appreciate the coming storm; but the O'Connells—whose residence this was—would soon find it bothersome.

Looking less than fresh in his tan jacket, white shirt and lighter tan trousers, Rick O'Connell—having deposited several bags as well as Evelyn's trunk in the entryway—was lugging two suitcases brimming with artifacts into the library. Improbably lovely in another flowing, Egyptian-print dress, his wife—carrying nothing at all, except a giddy enthusiasm that belied the long ocean and air voyages they had just weathered—was just behind him, having instructed her husband to take their discoveries directly into what was more a private museum than a library.

Two echoing stories high—with a magnificent stained glass skylight, and the wide central stairway of the manor off to one side, tucked under an archway—its shelves contained not only enough books to stock any two university libraries, but a dizzying array of priceless Egyptian artifacts representing both Evy's father's findings and their own. The white walls and black-and-white diamond pattern of the marble floor gave the vast chamber an oddly modern ring, though the richness of the walnut paneling and shelving harked to an earlier, more elegant time, more befitting the precious contents of this gallery.

"According to my research," Evy was saying, voice resonating in the room, "that bracelet provides a veritable guide to the Lost Oasis of Ahm Shere."

He set the bags down, heavily.

"Careful!" she said.

"That's good advice," he said, turning to her, wanting nothing more right now than a good night's sleep. "Evy, love of my life, light of my soul . . . I know how you think, and the answer is 'no.'"

She placed her hands on her hips and looked at him with friendly defiance. "That doesn't sound intriguing to you? Finding the lost oasis of the Scorpion King—a 'mythical' figure who, incidentally, we have proven actually existed!"

He sighed. Put his hands on her shoulders, gently. "Baby . . . we just got home!"

Her eyes danced; her smile was vivaciousness itself. "That's the beauty of it! Why do you think I went to the trouble, back in Cairo, of having all of our things laundered?"

"You're an efficient housewife and a loving mom?"

"That goes without saying. The point is—we're already packed!"

Groaning, he sat down in the nearest chair, shaking his head. "Give me one good reason. . . ."

She sat his lap. That was a start, anyway.

"We're not talking about finding a mere book, much less some rotting mummy—this is an *oasis,* darling." She put her arms around his neck, snuggled close. "Think of it . . . the moon glistening on the water, the sand gleaming like endless diamonds . . . picture it, beautiful, exciting, romantic. . . ."

He put his arms around her, and gave her a lascivious look. "Palm trees swaying? A white, secluded beach? Cool water to swim in—with no bathing suits?"

She cuddled. "Now you're getting the idea."

He dropped the act, held her out at arm's length, arching an eyebrow as he said, "What's the catch?"

"The catch?"

"The catch. The hidden agenda. The part that's going to cost me."

She shrugged, lifted herself off his lap and headed across the library, all business, half-heels echoing off the marble floor; she paused to gesture to the bags. "We can sort through these things tomorrow. . . . Supposedly, the oasis is the resting place of Anubis's army, is all."

He was up and after her. "See, I knew there'd be a catch. This wouldn't happen to be an army of the dead, waiting to be led by this Scorpion character?"

She glanced over her shoulder. "I wouldn't worry about that. He only reawakens every five or six thousand years."

"Yeah, but something tells me he's about due for his wake-up call!"

"Don't be silly."

He stopped her with a hand on one shoulder—a firm one. "If he does rouse, what then?"

She didn't look back at him; she said nothing.

O'Connell said, "If someone doesn't put him back to sleep again, then he wipes out the entire world?"

Now she looked at him, brow furrowed. "I'm impressed, Rick. You've become quite the scholar."

"No, baby, I've just been down this road before."

He fell in at her side as they went up the wide staircase. "Must that always be the story? . . . So what are the details—give."

"In eleven fifty B.C.," she said, crisply, teacherly, "Rameses the Fourth sent the last known expedition to actually *reach* the oasis. An expedition one thousand men strong."

"Don't tell me—none of 'em were ever seen again."

Pretty eyelashes fluttered at him, innocently. "You're sure you haven't been doing research on this?"

Sighing, shaking his head, he said, "Just taking a wild guess. Keep going."

"Did I mention there was a golden pyramid?"

"Oh, good, fine. Treasure involved, now—greed always helps spice things up a little."

They had arrived at a landing, and Evy stopped, her smile impish—she was playful, goading him now. "Alexander the Great sent troops in search of it."

"No kiddin'."

"And Julius Caesar."

"Really."

"Not to mention Napoleon."

"Not to mention Nappy. Of course, they didn't go personally. They were smart enough to send somebody else who could never return."

"True."

"I mean, we wouldn't do that, right? Go ourselves? 'Cause we know better."

"You're right . . ."

"Good. Finally you see the light."

". . . none of them ever returned."

Then Evy trotted up the stairs and wandered onto the balcony of the library and began pulling books from the shelves, and withdrawing maps from document drawers. O'Connell followed, exhausted, and—though he would never have admitted it—afraid . . . afraid of where his wife's latest obsession might lead them. His mind raced, seeking some way to get through to her, to weaken her resolve.

He was unaware of a fact that might have helped his case: two limousines—red curtains concealing the side and rear windows, headlights doused—were at this very moment creeping up the driveway, heading for the O'Connell manor. One of the vehicles vanished around the side, while the other drew up in front, a curtain pulling back as a dark, chiseled-featured passenger peered out: Meela's majordomo, Lock-nah.

And, as luck would have it—bad luck—Lock-nah could see, through an open window onto the library, the O'Connell boy, Alex, toting a small but heavy object, a most precious object: the ornate chest that held the bracelet of the Scorpion King.

In the library, the boy was staggering under the chest's surprising weight. He had been allowed by his parents to bring the artifact—which, though not terribly large, was too big to fit in a suitcase—in from outside, into the house.

"Ugh!" the boy said, pausing, out of breath. He was in short blue trousers and a matching jacket. "This God-darn thing weighs a bloody ton!"

From the balcony, his mother scolded, "Alex! Language!"

"Rather weighty, this," the boy said, mock-poshly.

Then Alex set the heavy chest down, harder than he meant to, and—possibly as a result, perhaps triggering a mechanism—heard a sharp click from within.

He looked up at the balcony, where his mother and father were busy talking, and dug into his pocket for a certain key. Checking again, making sure Mom and Dad were distracted, the boy knelt; then he worked the key in the lock.

Up on the balcony, O'Connell—standing close to his lovely wife, brushing a stray lock of auburn hair from her heart-shaped face—was saying, "Evy, the first of these strange dreams . . . you had it exactly six weeks ago . . . right?"

Puzzled, she replied, "Well . . . yes. I guess that's so. . . . Here." She thrust a stack of books into his arms and headed down to another section of shelving.

O'Connell stepped into her path. "Six weeks—which just happens to coincide with the Egyptian new year."

Impressed, she said, "I *knew* you'd been researching. . . ."

"Egyptian new year, baby—a.k.a., the Year of the Scorpion."

Now her expression turned thoughtful—even, perhaps, a trifle troubled. "Yes . . . the Year of the Scorpion. That's right."

He put a finger, gently, under her chin, locked eyes with hers. "All I'm saying, Ev—let's just be a little cautious for a change."

She mustered a tiny smile. "We've never been cautious before."

Below them, out of their sight, Alex had opened the chest and discovered what that clicking sound had been: cushioned in velvet within, the golden bracelet with the decorative scorpion had sprung open. He stared at the object, which caught the light, winking at him, daring him. . . . Then he looked up at his parents, who were paying no attention to him whatsoever. . . .

"So we haven't always been cautious," O'Connell was saying to his wife, "that I'll grant you—but you've never conjured up ancient princesses before. These, these hallucinations—"

"I prefer to think of them as 'visions,' thank you."

"Whatever you call them, back at that temple we were that close"—he showed her an inch between thumb and forefinger—"to buyin' the farm."

She frowned in confusion. "Whyever would we buy a farm when we have this place? Not that there's anything left of my parents' estate to do otherwise. . . ."

"Ev, it's a figure of speech," he said, mildly exasperated. "Buy the farm—die?"

"Well," she huffed, "I should think I would rather die than buy a farm."

As oblivious to his parents' conversation as they were to his activities below, Alex—eyes glittering with fun in a manner available only to children—pulled back his jacket sleeve and, rather gingerly, placed his wrist in the open bracelet . . .

. . . which snapped shut, like a crocodile taking a bite!

Alex managed to stifle a *yipe!* and, with appropriately wide eyes, jumped back, staring at the heavy gold bracelet that had virtually fastened itself to his wrist.

Above, O'Connell sat a stack of books Evy had handed him onto a chair, and took his wife into his arms, savoring the supple feel of her.

"You surely know," he said softly, sincerely, "I would rather die than allow anything bad to happen to you . . . again."

She brushed a lock of stray hair from his eyes and beamed at him. "Oh, darling, you know I feel the same way."

"You and Alex are the only things on this earth of any real importance to me."

She hugged him tight; he hugged back.

Below them, the son they both held so precious was experiencing something not unlike what had occurred to his mother, back at that temple, which is to say a vision . . .

. . . *a floating three-dimensional diorama of the Giza Plateau—three pyramids, one Sphinx . . . all as newly minted as a fresh coin. When he reached out to touch the geometric shapes, the diorama floated off—or did Alex float away?—as he experienced the sensation of racing down the Nile, as if in an autogyro, sweeping over the desert, stopping at the temple of Karnac, circa 2000 B.C. (Alex knew this was the date, though how he knew, he could not say) . . .*

. . . and then the vision seemed to dissolve into nothing at all, leaving the boy slightly dazed, and staring at the heavy gold bracelet locked to his wrist.

Alex shook his head—as if to rattle his brains loose—and frantically began fumbling with the bracelet, trying to get the God-darn thing off. But there was no clasp or hasp or anything—it was if the bracelet had fused itself to his wrist!

Above him, his parents were kissing, a long, tender kiss, and when she finally broke away, Evy—holding onto her man, tight—said, "I hate it when you do that."

60

O'Connell frowned at the woman in his arms. "Oh?"

"When you do that, it makes me feel like agreeing to anything."

O'Connell grinned at her. "Including doing nothing? Putting this exploring and digging behind us for a while?"

"Well . . . the Bembridge scholars *have* been after me to take over the Egyptian wing of the British Museum. That would keep us close to home, and allow me to be a good mother *and* a modern woman."

"I like the sound of that. . . . Now what was that about agreeing to anything . . . ?"

She laughed, hugged him tighter, and that's when O'Connell noticed the frilly pink brassiere hanging from a nearby chandelier.

"I don't imagine that's yours, is it?" he asked her.

"No."

With a sigh, O'Connell released his wife from his loving grasp, saying, "I believe we've forgotten about our housesitter."

"Ah," she said, glancing at the dangling brassiere. "Brother Jonathan . . . That would seem his style . . . so to speak."

"I'd better let him know we're home," O'Connell growled, "and suggest he send home any . . . houseguests sharing his quarters."

Evy laughed, and said, "At least it's lingerie hanging from the chandelier, and not Jonathan himself."

O'Connell leaned over the balcony railing, looking down at Alex, who was sitting by that small gold chest from the temple, the one bearing the bracelet Evy was so fired up about. "Son! See if you can behave yourself down there for a few minutes, will you?"

"You bet!" the boy said, yanking down his sleeve over the bracelet, praying his father hadn't noticed—which he hadn't.

O'Connell headed off down a hallway, and Evelyn started down the stairs, thinking it was time to check up on her precocious son.

Hearing the footsteps, Alex closed the lid of the chest and picked it up, only to discover that, without the bracelet, the thing was feather light! Quickly he took a heavy vase from a nearby table, thrust it in the cushioned chest and slammed it shut . . . just as his mother was rounding the bookcase.

Ruffling his hair, she asked, "Nice to be home, isn't it?"

"It's heaven," the boy said, wearing his biggest, most innocent smile.

"Open that for me, would you?" she asked him, nodding to the chest.

"Open what?"

"The chest."

"Why?"

His mother sighed—her patience clearly running out with this line of discussion. "Because I'd like to put its contents—that golden bracelet?—in our wall safe. It's quite priceless, you know."

"Well, I would . . . if I could find the key."

"You've lost the key? Alex, if you have lost that

key, you can kiss your allowance good—"

"I haven't lost it! I . . . I just can't find it." He tried to summon his cutest grin. "There's a difference, you know."

His mother was smiling in spite of herself. "Well, I suppose I've mislaid my share of things. All right, then . . . start looking."

"I will, Mum—there's nothing to worry about . . . but, really, I'm . . ." And he stretched out his arms in a facsimile yawn, pulling them back when he realized his jacket sleeve nearly betrayed the golden object on his wrist. ". . . I'm simply exhausted. Couldn't I just go up to bed?"

"Alex O'Connell, asking to go to bed early? That's a first . . . but, well, all right. I suppose this can wait until tomorrow."

As if in contradiction, a deep voice came from the doorway to the library: "I will have that chest, now!"

Mother and son swept their gaze to the tall red-turbaned figure striding toward them; a cruelly handsome Arab, he wore a dark glowing robe and the white loose-fitting sort of desert apparel that always reminded Alex of pajamas.

"Stop where you are!" Alex's mother demanded.

The Arab strode forward. His hand flashed out from under the robe and a scimitar's blade caught the light in menacing reflection. "The chest—give it to me!"

"Who are you?" Alex's mother stepped forward, blocking her son from the approaching intruder. Alex could hear no fear in his mother's voice, and her chin was high, defiant. "I demand to know what you are doing in my house!"

The Arab was almost upon them. "Give me the chest!"

On the wall just behind them hung a large Roman sword—Alex's mother plucked it off, deftly, swinging the heavy weapon around, assuming a combative posture.

"Whoa!" Alex said.

"Get the hell out of my house," his mother said coldly to the Arab, who had—wisely—stopped in his tracks.

"Mum . . ." Alex touched her sleeve. "This may not be your best idea. . . ."

"Shush," she said to him, then to the Arab, she said, "Leave now—before my husband sees you . . . and kills you."

Three more red-turbaned desert warriors poured into the library, each wielding a scimitar.

Swallowing hard, Alex tugged at his mother's dress, saying, "I think it's time to yell for Dad now. . . ."

"Stand aside," the Arab said, "and I will take the chest, and spare you and your son."

"No," she said.

The Arab shrugged. "Then I will kill both of you now and take it anyway."

Another voice—a deep, sand-papery voice— boomed through the chamber: "I think not!"

Alex looked past his mother, who also glanced toward the source of the words, and saw a solemn, dark-robed, dark-garbed, angular-faced, trimly bearded desert warrior—his cheekbones touched with strange puzzle-like tattoos. He had come from somewhere, from anywhere, as if he'd materialized.

"Med-jai!" one of the turbaned warriors shouted . . . though not the one nearest them, the leader, who stood frozen.

"Well," Evelyn said to this new player, almost casually, holding the sword up as indifferently as if it were a flashlight, "as Rick might say, long time no see. And what brings you here?"

Bowing to her, but keeping his fiery-eyed gaze on the turbaned intruders, the dark-garbed warrior said, "Perhaps explanations are best saved for later."

The red-turbaned leader took a slow step forward— the man seemed, to Alex, to be glaring at the dark-clad warrior with both hatred and respect. With a nod of a bow, he said, "Ardeth Bay."

Ardeth Bay nodded back, smiling pleasantly, saying, "Lock-nah," and swiftly withdrew a sword from under his cloak.

The response was immediate, as Lock-nah and his three warriors charged forward, swinging their scimitars, the blades viciously slicing the air.

Ardeth Bay leapt forward, parrying Lock-nah's blows, and those of a second warrior. As the blades clanged and whanged and echoed in the great gallery, Alex clutched the small precious chest to him and retreated to a corner, from which he watched, with startled pride, as his mother—Roman sword in hand— stepped forward with no fear and great confidence and parried the blows of the other two scimitar-wielding Arabs, lunging, thrusting, feinting and parrying like a lady Zorro!

"Mum! Where did you learn to fight like that?"

"I . . ." She parried a blow, grunting as she expended great effort, maneuvering with the heavy sword. ". . . I haven't the foggiest!"

Her next blow knocked the scimitar from the grasp of one of the warriors, but the other came pressing in, hammering with his blade, his superior strength finally forcing her back. Then, with a savage forearm, he slammed her into a wall of books, and she cried out in alarm, and pain.

"Mum!"

Rather than finish her off, the warrior decided to gloat, and perhaps to enjoy her beauty, and he leaned forward, laughing in her face, through yellow rotted teeth.

Alex saw his mother cringe, which was hardly surprising, but then he also saw her knee the warrior between the legs, in his naughty bits, which was surprising, both to Alex and the warrior, who screamed in agony, folding in half. Alex's mother used her knee again, this time in the fellow's face, and he yelped, but popped back up, like an ugly jack-in-the-box, only to have Mum smash him in the teeth with a right hook, decking him, sending him down and out.

"That," she said, breathing hard, "I learned from your father!"

The other warrior had recovered his scimitar and

was soon back on top of her; she parried and feinted with daring and skill. Alex had always known he had a remarkable mother—but *this* remarkable?

Alex, glued into his corner, clung to the chest and watched as the battle raged, the library getting up-ended, with many an irreplaceable artifact biting the dust. When one of the warriors came charging toward him, Alex darted out of the way, in so doing slamming against a freestanding bookcase, which toppled over and pinned one of the turbaned warriors, crushing him.

With all this brouhaha, the boy wondered, why hadn't his father heard, and come running? The manor was sprawling, yes, but surely all this racket would carry. . . .

Then that other warrior was looming over Alex, grabbing a handle on the chest with one hand, raising a scimitar high. Perhaps because Alex was just a boy, the warrior could not bring himself to bring that blade down, and the man and the boy stood there for some time, having a tug-of-war over the chest.

But finally the adult's greater strength took precedence, and the chest was yanked from the boy's grasp. The warrior grinned in triumph, just before Ardeth Bay thrust forward with his sword and skewered him.

And the dying warrior dropped the chest, and himself, to the floor.

Alex wanted to pick that chest back up, but the fighting was between him and it, and he was afraid—he was eight; being afraid was allowed.

In the midst of trading blows with Lock-nah, Ardeth Bay yelled, "Mrs. O'Connell! What is in this chest?"

Alex saw his mother blithely dump a big glass case filled with priceless artifacts down on top of one of the turbaned warriors, felling him, smashing the glass and much of the case's contents to smithereens.

His mother was out of breath. "The . . . the . . . Bracelet . . . of Anubis!"

The dark-garbed warrior's shock was apparent. "You *have* this?"

Catching her breath in a momentary lull, she nodded.

"Get it!" Ardeth Bay yelled. "Get it now and get out of here!"

"But . . ."

"*Now!* They must not get the bracelet!"

Alex watched as his mother dropped her sword and picked up the chest.

That was when a mountain of flesh in a red turban and dark robe emerged from the shadows to scoop up Alex's mother and carry her off, her protestations—both physical and aural—yielding no result.

"They got Mum!"

Ardeth Bay turned at this distraction, and Lock-nah swung his scimitar and gashed the dark-garbed warrior across his left arm, sending the man tumbling backward, into a display case.

Spinning around, Lock-nah spotted Alex cowering against the wall, and hurled the scimitar—it whipped end-over-end across the room, Alex dodging to the left just a fraction of a moment before the blade slammed into the wall, quivering there, just two inches from the boy's head.

Alex closed his eyes, breathing hard, and when he opened them, the red-turbaned warriors—like his mother—were gone.

·❆ 5 ❆·

Party in Jonathan's Room

The slender, fortyish, boyishly handsome man in the slightly disheveled tuxedo lay back atop the covers of the canopy bed in an elegantly appointed guest room of the O'Connell manor, one arm around a lovely young woman. A blonde, she wore the sort of silver-glittery, snugly-fitting, low-cut dress best served by the voluptuous figure of a showgirl, which she had, and was.

With his free hand, Jonathan Carnahan (who greatly resented being described as Evelyn O'Connell's ne'er-do-well, freely imbibing brother, however accurate that designation might be) was battling an invisible enemy, using a priceless Egyptian relic—a certain golden scepter—to sword-fight in the air.

"And that," Jonathan was saying, with just the faintest bourbon-induced slur, "was how I killed the mummy and all his minions . . . and wound up possessing this, his golden scepter!"

The blonde snuggled next to him, cooing, "Oh, Jonathan . . . you're wonderful!"

Which was about the extent of her conversational abilities, and that was just fine with Jonathan, who preferred Anita Loos to Noël Coward.

Inspired, Jonathan leapt from the bed and continued fighting invisible foes, saying, "You should have seen them, my dear—mummified soldiers! An army of the undead! A lesser man might have fainted, not feinted . . . get it? Fainted, not . . ."

She looked at him blankly.

He resumed battle. "At any rate, these creatures were not of this earth. They could literally march up and across and down a ceiling."

Her eyes widened, her mouth dropping in fright. Jonathan smiled, pleased that his storytelling skills were inspiring a condition in the showgirl that could be cured by holding her in his arms.

But then she was pointing, to something behind him.

He glanced around and there, having let themselves in . . . rude bounders . . . stood a trio of desert warriors in red turbans, dark robes and flowing garments, all but one bearded, every man of them tall, formidable-looking and, well, decidedly unpleasant.

Entering behind them was a small, dark, sharp-featured man in a red fez and an off-white suit; his eyes were so dark as to appear black, and they glit-

71

tered in the bedroom's muted lighting like polished obsidian.

Jonathan turned to them and displayed a charming smile, saying, "Gentlemen, I must apologize. My lady friend and I have had a long, hard evening of over-indulgence, and we have clearly stumbled into the wrong house . . . these manors are so dashedly inter-changeable. . . ."

The blonde was sitting on the edge of the bed now. "This isn't your house? You said this was your house!"

Jonathan glanced to her and whispered crossly, "I was mistaken."

"Take him," the small dark man said.

"Yes, Curator," one of the turbaned fellows said.

Then two of the brutes were upon Jonathan, grab-bing him by either arm. In a flash of blonde hair and pale flesh and glittery silver, the showgirl was hustled by one of the turbaned intruders over to a closet, where she was unceremoniously pitched inside, like a bag of dirty laundry. The door slammed over the sound of her yelping, "Hey!"

The small red-fezed character—clearly the leader of this sinister band, the "Curator"—walked over and spoke to the door: "Young lady, stay within, and be silent, and perhaps you will survive."

"I say," Jonathan remarked, "that's a trifle harsh, isn't it?"

The small dark man walked up to Jonathan and slapped him once, a hard, stinging blow.

Jonathan, blinking away a tear or two of pain, said

merely, "You wouldn't happen to be somebody's husband, would you, perchance? Sheila's? Cynthia's? Priscilla's . . . ?"

"I am unmarried," the Curator said.

"Imagine, a debonair fellow like you, still single. . . . If you work for Jimmy, please tell him I'll be able to pay him back on Tuesday."

"I know no one named Jimmy."

"Not your crowd, eh?" Jonathan stroked his chin. "Well, that about exhausts the possibilities on my end. I've been rather boringly well behaved of late."

The Curator nodded to his men, and Jonathan was dragged to an overstuffed chair and rudely deposited there, in a most undignified manner.

The Curator stood before Jonathan, hands folded on his belly. "Let us speak of the Bracelet of Anubis."

Jonathan shrugged. "Why not?"

"We are looking for it."

"Looking for what?"

"The Bracelet of Anubis."

"Ah. Jolly good! That would seem a smashing item for one's collection, the Bracelet of Anubis."

The dark glittering eyes hardened. "Where is it?"

"How should I know?" Jonathan shrugged again. "I've never heard of the thing before. If you're looking for it here, you're barking up the wrong tree. . . . I haven't the foggiest idea what you're talking about."

The Curator sighed. "Mr. O'Connell, you try my patience."

"O'Connell?" Jonathan sat forward. "Wait a minute, my friend—you have the wrong man!"

73

The Curator nodded to the turbaned devil at Jonathan's right, and suddenly the sharp point of a knife blade prodded the flesh just beside his Adam's apple.

"You are the white man who lives in this house, are you not?" the Curator asked, almost politely. "Or are you just an obstacle in our path, to be tossed aside?"

The point of the knife dimpling his skin, Jonathan beamed and said, "Oh, *that* Bracelet of Anubis! How silly of me . . . unfortunately, I lost it in a game of chance. You've played poker, perhaps?"

"For your sake," the Curator said, "I hope this is a lie, and the truth will shortly be forthcoming. . . ."

"I can give you the address of the fellow I lost it to, and you can . . . negotiate with him, in your own inimitable manner." The golden scepter still in one hand, Jonathan gestured with the priceless relic. "Who could say no to you?"

The Curator, getting his first good look at the scepter, responded with wide eyes and a hushed tone. "It cannot be!"

The dark little man snatched the object from Jonathan's hands and was examining it with an expert's eye when a tall, breathtakingly beautiful woman stepped into the bedroom, closing the door behind her.

Her hair was long and black, bluntly cut, Cleopatra-style; her slim yet curvaceous figure was poured into a black gown, her neck, her wrists, adorned with gold and diamonds that glittered across silky skin. She might have been going to a formal affair, not joining in on this abduction-cum-interrogation.

In one hand she carried a carved wooden box—perhaps not a relic, but in the Egyptian style—not much bigger than a cigar box. More jewelry, perhaps? Even with a knifepoint at his throat, Jonathan could not help but admire the fluid motion of this elegant, sensual creature as she crossed the bedroom to where he sat.

"Meela," the Curator said respectfully, even reverently, nodding to her—damn near bowing!—and stepped to one side, to allow her to stand before Jonathan. With a nearly imperceptible motion of her head, she commanded the turbaned devil to remove the threatening knife from Jonathan's neck.

"Hello," she said, her voice smooth and low.

The wooden box in her left hand, the woman with her free hand stroked Jonathan's cheek, caressingly, seductively. . . .

"Well, hello," Jonathan said, shifting in the overstuffed chair, much preferring this woman's style of interrogation and torture to the Curator's.

"Where is your wife?"

"My dear, I assure you I'm single."

She smiled mischievously. "Mr. O'Connell, if we're to have a relationship, we must be honest with each other. Do you think the fact you're married would dissuade me from getting to know a charming man like yourself?"

"Ah, you mean Evelyn. She went to Baden-Baden."

"I don't think so."

"You're right—I believe it was Tibet. The girl's always been a free spirit. Did I mention we have a modern arrangement, an open marriage?"

Still smiling, Meela shook her head, made a "tch-tch" sound, and placed the carved wooden box on a nearby table. The box, Jonathan noted, had a coiled snake carved on its lid—unpleasant image, that.

So perhaps he should not have been surprised when Meela opened the box and swiftly withdrew an asp—of a variety Jonathan believed, correctly, to be poisonous—by its neck.

Withering, Jonathan suddenly longed for the attentions of the Curator.

"Egyptian asps are the most poisonous in the world," she said melodically. "But also the most merciful."

"Really?"

"Yes. After only three or four minutes of extreme agony, death's blessing arrives."

She stepped closer to him, the asp in her grasp hissing—irritated, it would seem, at having been disturbed from its cozy resting place.

"Come to think of it," Jonathan said, beads of cold sweat forming along his brow, "it was something else I lost in that poker game. Suddenly I'm quite sure that bracelet is in this house."

"Where is it?" Meela hissed; so did the snake, minus the words.

"There's a safe in the library. The combination is three-twenty–fifty-eight–three-nine-three-four-five.

Would you like me to repeat it? Would you like to write it down?"

"The combination is three-twenty–fifty-eight–three-nine-three-four-five," Meela said. "You see, I have a photographic memory, Mr. O'Connell."

"That's a coincidence. I have a pornographic memory, myself. So. That would seem to conclude our business, then. . . ."

Meela nodded. "It would."

And she leaned in and raised the asp—specifically the hissing head of the asp—toward Jonathan's neck, just about where the knifepoint had earlier dimpled his skin.

Jonathan reared back as the hand of one of those turbaned bounders held him down in the chair. "Now, I simply must protest! I told you what you asked me! Wait . . . wait. . . ."

Meela, pausing, hissing snake in hand, looked at him curiously. "And what is your point?"

The asp coiled; Jonathan recoiled.

"My point? My bloody point is that I gave you that information so that you wouldn't kill me!"

"When did we make that arrangement?"

"Well, it hardly seems cricket to me—"

"Mr. O'Connell," she said, faintly scolding, "you might in future . . . which is to say, in your next life . . . consider the benefit of working out the terms of such an arrangement in advance."

Meela squeezed the asp's neck and its jaws popped open, displaying long, sharp, venom-dripping fangs.

Jonathan did what any self-respecting Englishman would do in such a situation.

He screamed bloody murder.

This took Meela aback, for a moment, which was fortunate indeed, because that moment was soon filled with the sound of the bedroom door bursting open, the woman whirling in that direction, blunt-cut hair swinging, the asp in her hand still fanging the air but not, thankfully, so close to Jonathan's neck.

"Jonathan," Rick O'Connell said, eyeing the intruders aligned about the bedroom, "didn't I tell you no parties while we were away?"

"I won't let it happen again," Jonathan said, grinning, grateful.

Evelyn's husband did something remarkable, then: he yawned. Jonathan knew that no one could outfight the former legionnaire; but his brother-in-law clearly did not seem really up for such a contest.

"Okay, folks," O'Connell said, patting the air with his palms in a gesture of reasonableness, "knowing Jonathan as I do, I'm quite sure he deserves whatever it is you're about to serve up to him."

"Well!" Jonathan said, indignantly, sitting up in his overstuffed chair. "I like that!"

With a sigh, O'Connell stepped forward slowly, saying, "But this is my home, and we enforce certain house rules here . . . first, no snakes. Second, dismemberments have to be cleared with the management."

Meela curled a lip in a sneer as ugly as she was beautiful and, in a sudden, vicious fling, sent the asp flying in O'Connell's direction.

O'Connell snatched the creature right out of the air, a perfect catch, even managing to clutch it by its dreadful neck.

"Good show!" Jonathan said to his brother-in-law.

O'Connell looked at the snake; the snake looked at O'Connell. "Nice asp," he said to the woman.

Lovely eyes flaring with rage, she cried, "Kill him!"

The turbaned character to Jonathan's left withdrew a pistol from his sash and aimed the weapon at O'Connell, who responded by flinging the asp at the man, whose neck became a new home for the snake to coil around. The warrior screamed and began flailing at the snake, which did not respond politely to this attention, sinking its fangs into the bloke's bearded cheek, causing him to scream yet again, and louder.

This distracted the other turbaned beast, the one who'd been at Jonathan's right, holding his knife on Jonathan, who took advantage of this diversion to seize the golden scepter from the grasp of the Curator, who was also caught up in watching the fun and games.

Then Jonathan, scepter in hand, flung himself backward, toppling the chair over and spilling himself onto the floor, and, to some degree at least, out of harm's way.

Meanwhile, the warrior with the knife drew it back and let it fly at O'Connell, who made another amazing catch, snatching the knife from the air, then sending it promptly back, as if this were a deadly game of catch.

The warrior preferred to play keep away, however, and ducked the oncoming blade, which wound up instead in the chest of a fellow warrior, who fell dead to the floor right in front of Jonathan.

Crawling over the dead body, like the inanimate object it was, Jonathan intended to aid O'Connell, using the scepter as a bludgeon; but before he got very far, Jonathan felt something, someone, grab him by the ankle.

Glancing back he saw the Curator, who leapt at him, clawing for the precious scepter, trying to wrest it from Jonathan's grasp.

Well, if the bloody fool wanted the scepter, Jonathan would give him the scepter.

Spinning around, Jonathan yanked the scepter out of reach from the Curator's greedy, grasping hands, and raised the relic high . . . and brought it down hard, bopping the bloke a good one.

As the Curator yelped, Jonathan—still crawling, keeping down—saw the cracked open door of the bedroom's private bathroom, and decided the better part of valor would be to retreat there. After all, the door could be locked from within, and a generous window would provide an escape route. . . .

Meela, however, saw Jonathan crawling toward safety—perhaps her asp was not the only snake in this room—and again screamed, "Kill him!"

Just as this command was given, reinforcements arrived, in the form of a single turbaned warrior, but one whose hands were filled with a submachine gun, right out of Al Capone's Chicago.

Near the bathroom doorway, Jonathan called, "This way, Richard!"

As the turbaned gangster blasted away with the tommy gun, O'Connell dove toward Jonathan, and the machine gun chattered and chopped up the bedroom, in particular riddling a radiator, which promptly emitted steam, quickly clouding the room. Shouts in an Arabic tongue added to the chaos, and—under the cover of steam and confusion—O'Connell rolled into the bathroom right behind Jonathan, getting to his feet slamming the door shut.

Immediately machine-gun fire chewed up the door, punching splintery holes in it, as Jonathan stepped to one side, and O'Connell to the other.

"What's that about?" O'Connell demanded of his brother-in-law between machine-gun blasts.

"Nothing to do with me! It was you they were after! I'm innocent!"

Another machine-gun barrage further chewed up the door, and the wall beyond.

"Innocent, Jonathan?"

"Well . . . anyway, not guilty."

As machine-gun fire further turned that door into toothpicks, O'Connell was taking in the large clawed bathtub, brimming with bubble-bath bubbles, a bottle of champagne cooling in a bucket nearby.

"I said no parties, Jonathan," O'Connell yelled, waiting for the machine-gunner to pause for reloading. He pointed to the windows that took up the better part of the wall on the far side of the large bathroom; Jonathan winced, shaking his head, but O'Connell overruled that with a curt nod.

Then, when the gunfire subsided momentarily, O'Connell yelled, "Come on!"

And O'Connell grabbed Jonathan by the sleeve of his tuxedo and, yelling, "Cover your face," they ran full-bore across the room and into that wall of glass, shattering it, sending them flying from a second-floor window, dropping down onto the grass in a shower of shards.

"Am I alive?" Jonathan asked, seeing his tux nicked and cut and slashed, but no blood.

"Technically!" O'Connell got up—shaking glass from himself like a dog ridding itself of water after an unwanted bath—and yanked his brother-in-law to his feet just as, above them, the window they'd so rudely "opened" provided, framed in jagged glass, a perch from which the Arab machine-gunner could—and did—rain lead down on them, chewing up grass, and the gravel of the drive.

Bullets were turning pebbles to powder just behind them, as O'Connell and Jonathan ran for their lives, ducking around a corner of the manor house.

"Let's get around front," O'Connell said, "and go in through the library—make sure Evy and Alex are okay!"

Jonathan had no argument with that sentiment, and followed as his brother-in-law raced around the manor, where they came upon the sight of a black limousine peeling out, throwing gravel.

In a side window of the limo, Evelyn was struggling, looking frantically out at them, her eyes huge, her mouth covered by a captor's dark hand.

"Evy!" O'Connell yelled desperately. "Evy!"

O'Connell ran after the limo, but it was no use, it had roared off into a night dark with storm clouds, taking Evelyn with it.

The last thing O'Connell and Jonathan saw was a red curtain being drawn back over that window, removing Evelyn from view, as if a final sign of sealing her within the dark speeding vehicle.

·❆ 6 ❆·

The Wrong Guy

As if the situation weren't already dire and melo-dramatic enough, the sky chose that moment to roar with thunder, and—as a wild-eyed Rick O'Connell, enraged, distraught—turned to his brother-in-law, a lightning bolt strobed the world white.

"Where's my damn car?" he demanded, grabbing Jonathan by both arms as if about to shake him like a naughty child.

"In back," he said, "by the garage!"

"All right." O'Connell pointed to the house. "Go check on Alex, and—"

Another roar filled their ears, not thunder this time, but an automobile engine, and they were again strobed, not by lightning, but the bright headlights of the limousine's twin rounding the corner from around back, bearing down on them, coming right at them.

O'Connell threw himself at Jonathan, tackling him, taking him down, rolling with him, narrowly escaping the prow of the vehicle, tumbling onto the grass.

For a moment they both sat there, helpless, watching as the limo accelerated down the gravel drive, throwing gravel as if mocking them. By the time O'Connell had gotten to his feet, the glowing red eyes of taillights had vanished around a distant corner.

"Damnit!" O'Connell said, fists clenched, pacing under the rumbling, charcoal-gray sky. His brother-in-law just stood there, arms hanging at his sides, impotent in his wilted tuxedo.

Blind with fury, adrenaline pumping, O'Connell didn't notice his son emerging from the front door of the manor, but when he heard the boy crying, "Dad! Dad!", he turned at once and ran to Alex, kneeling to take him in his arms, hugging him tight.

"Thank God," O'Connell whispered, clutching his son to his bosom. "Thank God. . . ."

"Dad . . . Dad . . . They took Mum!"

"I know, son." He held Alex out at arm's length so that he could look directly into the boy's moist eyes. "Your mother is very brave and very, very strong—she can take care of herself . . . until we rescue her."

The boy managed a smile, his chin wrinkling. "You will rescue her, won't you, Dad?"

"Yes, I will, son. *We* will."

That was when O'Connell saw an old friend walking toward him across the grass, having exited the manor house moments after Alex—an old friend . . . former adversary . . . with dark flowing robes and a trimly bearded face whose cheeks were decorated with bizarre ritualistic tattoos.

O'Connell stood, easing his son to one side, saying, "Ardeth Bay . . . Long time no see."

A serious smile flickered on the Med-jai's face. "That is what your wife predicted you would say."

O'Connell strolled up to his friend, said casually, "Did she?"

Then he clutched the front of the Arab's garment and practically lifted him from the grass, all but screaming into the man's face: "Who the hell kidnapped Evy? And what the hell do they want with her?"

Ardeth Bay's eyes were more woeful than alarmed. "My friend, please . . ."

O'Connell let go of the man, setting him down roughly. Hands on his hips, staring hard at the Med-jai chieftain, he said, tightly, "No. Scratch that—I don't give a damn who they are, or why they took her. All I want to know—all I *need* to know—is *where* they took her."

Ardeth Bay slipped a hand beneath his flowing cape and withdrew a photograph, handing it to O'Connell, who immediately recognized the Curator and several of the turbaned goons who'd invaded the guest room upstairs.

"They seem to be at a dig somewhere," O'Connell said. "Is this . . . are they . . . ?"

"Yes—that is Hamanaptra. The Med-jai are still

watching the City of the Dead . . . and this man was leading the expedition, the dig. . . ."

"A surveillance photograph," Jonathan said, having a peek at the candid shot. "You blokes have come a long way from just attacking like wild Indians with knives and rifles."

The sky growled.

"We would have done as much," Ardeth Bay said to Jonathan, "but we believe this man and the woman with whom he is allied are in possession of a dangerous artifact."

"So who is this guy?" O'Connell said, thumping the photo over the Curator's sharp-featured face.

"I do not know. But wherever this man is, my friend, so surely will be your wife."

Alex, on tiptoes, was getting his own peek at the photo. "Hey—I know who that creep is!"

"You do?" Ardeth Bay asked, surprised that the child had entered into this adult conversation.

"Who is it, son?" O'Connell asked.

"I don't know his name, but he's one of the curators over at the British Museum!"

Voice tight, Ardeth Bay put a hand on the boy's shoulder. "Are you positive, my son?"

"He's *my* son," O'Connell said, reaching a hand out to the boy with a proud smile, "and if he says he knows that guy, he damn well knows him."

It sometimes seemed to O'Connell that Alex spent more time at the museum than at home.

Jonathan, looking toward the manor, said, "Do you mind if I slip in and tell my date she can come out

87

of the closet now? Those brutes banished her there, you know."

"She'll keep," O'Connell said, already moving quickly around the side of the house. "Let's get the car!"

As they ran, Ardeth Bay fell in at O'Connell's side.

"You're here," O'Connell said, "and the bad guys are here, and they've kidnapped Evy . . . can I guess the rest?"

The Med-jai nodded gravely. "The 'bad guys' have liberated the creature from his grave."

"What, the Scorpion King?"

Unnerved, Ardeth Bay stopped, and said, "How do you know of him?"

O'Connell, barely breaking stride, grabbed the Arab's sleeve and got him moving again, saying, "You weren't talking about the Scorpion King, were you? You meant that those clowns have dug up Imhotep!"

Ardeth Bay nodded glumly.

They had arrived at O'Connell's prized possession, a brand-new powder-blue Beuford, which sat in front of the three-car garage, parked at the slovenly angle Jonathan had left it in when he and his showgirl had arrived from a night on the town and gone upstairs.

Jonathan dug in his tux pants pocket for the car keys, which he handed to a frowning O'Connell, who was saying to Ardeth Bay, "You just stood by while these guys hauled Imhotep outa the ground? Isn't it the Med-jai's job to prevent that sort of thing?"

"My friend, something terrible is afoot, something we cannot prevent until we grasp entirely what this cult intends."

"Cult?"

Ardeth Bay nodded. "The dark-haired woman who leads them, she knows things that no living person could possibly know."

"Like what?"

"It was she who directed them to the exact location where He Who Shall Not Be Named was entombed. . . . We were hoping she would lead us to the Bracelet of Anubis. We felt she either had it, or knew who did."

"*We* had it," O'Connell said, getting around on the driver's side of the car. "It was in that gold chest they snatched—that's why they grabbed Evy: leverage in case we came after them."

O'Connell opened the car door, but something was tugging at his sleeve—someone: Alex.

"Dad . . . you're wrong."

"What?"

"We have the 'leverage' . . . because they may have the chest, but they don't have the bracelet."

"No?"

"No, Dad. . . ." The boy pulled up the sleeve of his blue jacket and exposed the heavy golden bracelet locked onto him. A flash of lightning reflected off the bas-relief scorpion, making it almost seem to wriggle on his wrist.

Ardeth Bay went to the boy, gently taking his arm and examining the bracelet.

"Allah save us," Ardeth Bay said, dark face pale with shock. "It is indeed the Bracelet of Anubis!"

Excited, nervous, the boy burbled, "I was just looking at it and the stupid thing locked on me, like it had a mind of its own! Now I can't get the goddarn bracelet off, no matter how hard I try!"

The Med-jai clutched the boy by both shoulders. "Did you see anything, lad? This is important! Did you—"

"Yeah, I saw the pyramids at Giza, and, then—whoosh! I was floating across the desert to Karnac. It was better than a ViewMaster."

Ardeth Bay dropped the boy's arm as if it were on fire; backpedaling, the Arab's hands moved in ritual gestures, as he muttered, "Allah be merciful . . . Allah be merciful. . . ."

"Everybody," O'Connell said, disgusted. "Get in the car! That boy has a mother who needs saving."

"My friend," Ardeth Bay said, his tone grave, "you do not understand. By putting that bracelet on, your son has started a chain reaction that could bring the Apocalypse upon this world."

A flash of lightning punctuated this pronouncement, but O'Connell merely sighed and, pointing, sternly said to Ardeth Bay, "You—lighten up." Pointing to his son, he said, "You—you're in big trouble."

"What about me?" Jonathan asked, looking like a low-rent maitre d' in his droopy tux.

"Get in back with the other eight-year-old,"

O'Connell said, and he got behind the wheel, Ardeth Bay taking the passenger seat.

The grumbling charcoal sky promising more, the city had already seen a cloudburst come and go, the all-but-deserted, rain-slick streets like black patent leather as the Beuford rocketed toward its destination.

"I am sorry if I alarmed your son," Ardeth Bay said to the driver.

O'Connell, in no mood for further conversation, merely nodded, taking the next turn on two wheels.

Holding onto a door strap, the warrior leaned toward O'Connell and whispered, "But my friend, you must understand, now that the boy's wrist bears the Bracelet of Anubis, we have only seven days before the Scorpion King awakes."

"I tell you what, pal," O'Connell said tightly, "this time I'm gonna leave all the reawakened creatures to you and the rest of the Med-jai. All I want is to get my wife back."

Ardeth Bay was shaking his head. "If He Who Shall Not Be Named is not returned to his grave, he will raise the army of Anubis."

Jonathan leaned up from the backseat. "I take it that's a bad thing?"

Ignoring that, O'Connell said to Ardeth Bay, "Evy said the army of Anubis belongs to this Scorpion King character."

The Med-jai chieftain nodded. "But whoever can slay the Scorpion King can send his army back to the underworld . . . or take it as his own, to use it to destroy mankind, and rule the earth, having spared only his loyal followers."

Eyes narrowing, O'Connell asked, "This is Imhotep's cult, right? And they figure he's the only one tough enough to take out the Scorpion King?"

"This is madness!" Jonathan said, throwing up his hands. Alex, however, was listening to every word, intently.

Ardeth Bay was saying, "The Scorpion King must first be killed before He Who Shall Not Be Named can stand at the head of that demon army."

O'Connell took another corner and they all leaned to the right. "So these fools aim to wake up the Scorpion King, strictly so that Imhotep can kill him?"

Ardeth Bay nodded solemnly. "That, we believe, is their plan."

The sky underscored that, with a chorus of thunder.

"They must be lunatics!" Jonathan observed.

"Lunatics prepared to wipe out the world," O'Connell said grimly, "to serve their lord."

"Not the old wipe-out-the-world ploy again," Jonathan said, but his gallows humor rang hollow in the car.

On Great Russell Street, the Beuford skidded to a stop along a black wrought-iron fence in front of the immense classical graystone building that was the renowned British Museum. At this late hour, under threatening skies, not a soul was in sight; a stairway that hours before had swarmed with tourists stood empty. The nineteenth-century building, the intimidating columns of its Victorian Ionic facade looming in the night, housed the greatest and largest collection of art and antiquities in the world—but nothing as precious as the woman O'Connell loved, who was also likely somewhere within these massive walls.

O'Connell shut off the engine and craned around to look at his son. "I need you to watch this car, Alex—we may have to make a quick getaway."

Jonathan, raising his hand like a schoolboy requesting a trip to the washroom, said, "That sounds like a job I could handle."

"You're coming with us, Jonathan—we can use every man for this task, and that, strictly speaking, includes you."

Jonathan sighed and sat back as Alex leaned forward, his expression sarcastic. "You 'need' me to 'watch' the car? Come on, Dad, just because I'm a kid that doesn't mean I'm a dope."

"I would never mistake you for a dope, son." O'Connell ruffled his son's hair. "Stay here. Watch the car."

The boy squirmed away. "Stop doing that, Dad, please! Look, I know my way around in there better than—"

"You're staying with the car," he said, stern now.

Jonathan said to Alex, who was pouting, arms folded, "If you hear someone screaming and see a blur running out of there, open the back door—it's just me."

Reconsidering, O'Connell said, "Jonathan, you stay here and make sure Alex stays put."

93

"Yes, now you're thinking," Jonathan said. "The boy does have a reckless streak."

"You have a streak, too," Alex said to his uncle. "Guess what color?"

O'Connell was getting out of the car. "Behave—both of you."

"Dad!" Alex leaned forward, urgently. "At least let me tell you where to look!"

The father raised an eyebrow at his son. "How would you know that?"

"I told you, I know every inch of that place! On the main floor, off to the left of the entrance hall, are these huge sculptures of the pharoahs and Egyptian gods—you were with me that time, Dad, remember? I pointed out the Rosetta Stone?"

O'Connell, taking it all in, said, "I remember, son."

"They probably took her there . . . if not, maybe to the rear of the upper floor, the antiquities area . . . rooms sixty and sixty-one, that's where the mummies are. Also, there's this big storage area, in the basement, where they keep the extra Egyptian stuff—maybe they took Mum there. . . ."

Quickly, Alex gave his father instructions, O'Connell charting a mental map based on his precocious son's information.

"You might wanna try going in the skylight over the Egyptian display," Alex advised. "They've been repairing and restoring it—I bet you could slip in that way, and not set off any alarms."

Smiling, warmly proud of his son, O'Connell had

to restrain himself not to ruffle the boy's hair again.

Moments later, O'Connell was behind the Beuford, popping the trunk. More than just a spare tire was inside: a gunnysack, pregnant with weapons, lay within. Unzipping it, O'Connell displayed to Ardeth Bay the gunnysack's deadly contents—several revolvers and automatics, as well as a pump shotgun, a submachine gun and other assorted weaponry.

"You seem prepared for more than just a ride in the British countryside," the Med-jai observed.

"Yeah—after what we went through, last time around, I like to stay prepared. You want the twelve-gauge?"

"Thank you, no—I have become enamored of the repeating weapon."

"The Thompson? Take it." O'Connell was reaching for a pair of shoulder-holstered pistols, which he intended to sling on, when Ardeth Bay suddenly, dramatically, clutched him by the wrist, as if O'Connell were the one wearing the Bracelet of Anubis.

"What?" O'Connell said, crossly.

"You are marked!" Ardeth Bay was staring at the pyramid-shaped tattoo with the eye of Horus, which O'Connell had carried since childhood.

"Hey," O'Connell said, pulling his hand away, glaring at the Arab whose own cheeks, after all, bore bizarre puzzle-like tattoos, "who are you to talk?"

Respectfully, even reverently, and with a spooky intensity, the warrior said, "Were I to say to you, my friend, 'I am a stranger traveling from the east, seeking that which is lost. . . .' "

95

Without thinking, in a somewhat robotic fashion, O'Connell said—and heard himself saying, as if from a distance, "I would reply, 'I am a stranger traveling from the west. It is *I* whom you seek.' "

"How do you know this?"

O'Connell was slinging on the guns. "I don't know. It's some saying I've known since I was a kid. Long as I can remember."

Before he could remember. . . .

Ardeth Bay bowed his head. "Then it is true. . . . You are a Knight Templar."

O'Connell blinked. "*What* am I?"

"You bear the Masonic mark."

"This thing?" He held up his hand. "This got slapped on me back in the orphanage, in Hong Kong."

Ardeth Bay pointed at the tattoo. "That sacred mark means that you are a protector of man . . . a warrior of God."

Lightning flashed again, as if God agreed with this assessment.

But O'Connell didn't. He merely smirked, said, "Buddy, you got the wrong guy," and handed Ardeth Bay the tommy gun. He nodded toward the looming museum. "Ready to see if these bastards have my wife on exhibit in there?"

Ardeth Bay nodded. "I will follow you."

Somehow, O'Connell didn't like the sound of that.

·❨ 7 ❩·

Return of the Mummy

Those in the know said it would take a week to adequately explore the British Museum, with its Elgin marbles, Nineveh sculptures, antique vases and bronzes, and unrivaled Egyptian displays. Even so, there were places in the museum, secrets the vast building held, known only to the most knowledgeable staff members.

In one such area—a sprawling storage warehouse, deep in the recesses of the museum, cluttered with giant crates, ancient pillars and ornate statuary—an archaic and nefarious ceremony was under way. Though the museum's red-tinged electric worklights partially illuminated the bizarre doings, the ritualistic use of hand-held torches provided most of the light— flickery, orange and unreal—as the dark little man in the red fez, one of the museum's trusted curators, and the red-turbaned Lock-nah and half a dozen similarly red-turbaned minions—swayed in a circle, chanting incantations seldom heard since antiquity.

At the center, the idol they seemed to be worshiping, was the mighty slab of obsidian which shrouded the petrified, grotesquely disfigured remains of Imhotep—the man, the would-be god, the mummy who had in two separate centuries walked the earth. Like a black mirror, the obsidian reflected the flitter and flutter of the flames, as the frozen corpse of Imhotep seemed to scream for release from the stone. Off to one side, awaiting some ceremonial purpose as yet unclear, a large stone coffin, an ancient sarcophagus, was the home to a roaring, crackling fire.

Into this tableau, struggling wildly, having just emerged from a chloroform-induced sleep, came Evelyn O'Connell, not of her free will: two of the turbaned warriors were carrying her in on her own, smaller slab of black stone. It was as if she were being served up on a platter, her wrists lashed together, and her ankles. Her Egyptian print dress was torn here and there, and her entire form was bathed in the shimmering orange glow of torchlight.

Her struggling stopped, however, as she beheld the ritualistic swaying, the urgent chanting, of the Curator and his red-turbaned followers. Few scholars could rival Evelyn's grasp of the ancient Egyptian tongue, and—even in her distressed, slightly woozy state— Evelyn understood what these men were chanting, and worse, grasped *why* . . .

. . . as her eyes widened, beholding the horrific petrified corpse locked in obsidian.

"Imhotep," she whispered, as if afraid to speak the name out loud.

"Rise up!" someone was saying in ancient Egyptian.

The Curator—reading from *The Book of the Dead*!

Like a minister reading from the Bible to his congregation, the Curator held open in his hands the massive black volume whose obsidian covers were disturbingly similar to the stone imprisoning Imhotep.

"Rise up!" the dark little man said, his voice resounding through the room. *"Rise up!"*

A weaker woman—or for that matter, many a strong man—might have fainted at what Evelyn saw next . . .

. . . *the corpse of Imhotep was squirming within the stone!*

At the very moment Evelyn had been carted into the presence of the chanting cultists, Rick O'Connell and Ardeth Bay—the former with a shotgun in hand, the latter lugging his cherished Thompson submachine gun—were creeping through the museum's second-floor gallery. A crack of thunder made them both start, and they exchanged small nervous smiles. Moments later lightning flashed down through the skylight—the same one through which they'd entered, minutes ago, sliding down ropes—highlighting the sharp angles of the statuary looming around them.

Through the cavernous chambers of the museum

came the faintest echoing of men's voices . . . chanting.

"They're here," O'Connell said, tightly, pleased. "That means Evy is, too."

"It is as I feared," the Med-jai chieftain said, less than pleased. "They mean to waken He Who Shall Not Be Named."

Remembering the path his son had suggested, to that basement storage area, O'Connell motioned the Med-jai to follow him into, and through, rooms sixty and sixty-one, where the mummies were displayed. They were moving slowly past a sarcophagus—its lid removed and resting against the wall, to show off its bandaged contents—when thunder roared, lightning flashed, and the mummy within sat up.

"Damn!" O'Connell said, raising his shotgun, backing up against a glass case. Ardeth Bay, at his side, had done the same.

The mummy was merely sitting up, as if he'd woken from a long nap—reanimated, yes, coming after them, no.

O'Connell glanced at Ardeth Bay, giving the warrior a "what the hell" look, when just behind them, within the display case against which they were leaning, something slapped the glass, hard, jarring it, and them.

The two men turned and looked back at another wakened mummy, banging its bandaged body against the glass case.

O'Connell and Ardeth Bay stepped away, exchanging startled glances, just as lightning again strobed the room.

All around them, mummies were sitting up in their coffins, twitching, squirming, writhing in their glass cages, a dreadful dance recital lacking only music and a choreographer's touch.

Quickly, weapons poised to fire, they backed the hell out of there—the mummies not seeming to be in pursuit—and found the stairway Alex had told them about, the sound of chanting echoing up.

In the bowels of the building, in the sprawling storage area, the rite of revival had reached its crescendo, the turbaned men swaying, their torches flickering, the Curator reading from the massive obsidian book, the ancient words resounding.

The heat of the torches and the blazing fire in the nearby sarcophagus did not prevent the bound Evelyn from feeling a chill. On her slab—still hefted by the two warriors seemingly waiting for instructions she could not bear to imagine—Evelyn watched in horror as Imhotep's petrified corpse began to come fully alive, flesh reanimating, what had seemed stone turning to tattered tissue and rotted bone.

The Curator, looking up from the book, read from it no more. Evelyn caught a terrible glimpse of the exchange of demented, thrilled expressions between the Curator and Lock-nah.

As if it were a coat some invisible man were helping him out of, Imhotep stepped free of his obsidian cell—a gruesome figure washed orange-red in firelight, oozing gore, decaying muscle hanging off bone, fringed with shredded flesh, decomposing organs visible, wriggling as the creature breathed.

The red-turbaned followers stopped chanting and fell to their knees before Imhotep, lowering their gaze respectfully—or perhaps, Evelyn thought, they could not bear the ghastly sight of their "lord."

The monster cast its gaze around the room—even though its skeletal face had only two hideous empty eye sockets with which to do so.

"What is the year?" Imhotep demanded in his death-rattle rasp, speaking in his ancient tongue.

Exhilarated, the Curator—clasping the huge *Book of the Dead* to his breast, joyfully—stepped forward and said, also in the ancient language, "My Lord, we are in the Year of the Scorpion."

Looking at the little man, Imhotep's skull swiveled so quickly, Evelyn thought it might roll off.

"It is truly the Year of the Scorpion?" the mummy asked.

"Yes, my lord!"

Imhotep threw back his skull head and roared in triumphant laughter, and Evelyn shivered at the sight of half-decomposed organs, glimpsed through the tattered flesh and rotted bone, pulsing and shimmering and throbbing.

Then the mummy's laughter ceased, and a strangely reflective expression cast itself on the grisly mask of his face. Had he sensed something, or heard something . . . ?

Imhotep turned to look down a corridor between

stacked crates, and Evelyn cast her gaze there, as well.

The woman was slender and elegant in a clinging black gown accessorized with diamonds and gold jewelry, her black hair complete with blunt Egyptian bangs, her motion fluid . . .

. . . *and, without warning, another vision overtook Evelyn, and the elegant modern woman striding down the corridor of crates became an Egyptian beauty of ancient days, in palatial surroundings, gliding over the marble floor with a dancer's lithe grace, a living goddess wearing little more than golden body-paint.*

Evelyn blinked, and the black-haired woman again was in modern dress, in the here and now of the twentieth century—even if the woman did happen to be standing before the living corpse that was Imhotep, High Priest of Osiris.

The Curator looked at the woman and said, softly, "Do not be frightened, Meela."

This counsel was unnecessary: the young woman stared at Imhotep, unafraid—cool, even cold.

"I have no fear of my lord Imhotep," she said in the ancient tongue, head held high. "We have known each other before. . . . I am Anck-su-namun."

Evelyn recognized the name all too well—Anck-su-namun had been the chosen paramour of Pharaoh Seti. In 1290 B.C., Imhotep's forbidden love for Seti's lover—and hers for him—had set in motion tragedies that were playing out to this day.

"Anck-su-namun reincarnated," Meela was saying.

Imhotep stared back at her for several long moments. "Only in body . . ." His fetid lips and rotted cheeks formed something like a smile. "But soon . . . soon I shall return to you your soul. I will bring it back to you, from the depths of the underworld."

Lock-nah knelt and lifted something, resting it on a waist-high stack of crates. At first Evelyn could not see what the object was, but as Lock-nah turned, as he withdrew a vial of liquid from under his robe, she got a look at it—the chest, that small, golden ornate chest she and Rick had found at the temple at Thebes.

Lock-nah poured the liquid from the vial into the keyhole of the chest, and smoke sizzled out—acid, burning through the lock.

The Curator approached Lock-nah, and Evelyn could hear his whisper—in English. "Lord Imhotep will be greatly pleased."

Lock-nah smiled and nodded, then opened the chest—and his face fell. The vase he withdrew Evelyn recognized from the library of her own home—and at once she knew her son had substituted the heavy vase for the bracelet! *Did that mean Alex had the bracelet?*

"Where is it?" the Curator, face ashen, demanded of Lock-nah. "Where is the Bracelet of Anubis?"

The red-turbaned warrior stared at the vase, bewildered . . . then his features began to harden.

"The boy," he said. "The O'Connell boy."

The Curator glared over at a now trembling Evelyn, supine on her slab.

Meela leaned closer to Imhotep, unfazed by his

104

putrefying form. "I have acquired a gift for you, my love."

"A gift?" he rasped.

The woman stepped to one side and gestured, as if presenting an act in a show.

That was when Imhotep noticed Evelyn, those blackened empty sockets somehow seeing, and his grisly countenance distorted further, in fury.

"Her!" he cried, and crates rattled through the room.

"The O'Connell woman, yes," Meela said, with a matter-of-fact nod and a catlike grin. "I knew it would please you, watching her die."

With a snap of her fingers, Meela summoned several of the red-turbaned followers to attend to Evelyn, lifting her on her slab. Evelyn began to struggle with her bonds again, but it did no good, and then she realized where she was being taken: that large open stone sarcophagus, filled with flames that licked the air hungrily.

"Oh dear God," Evelyn said, her eyes burning with smoke, her ears filled with the dull, hoarse roar of a crematorium.

She was carted past the putrid reanimated corpse of Imhotep, who skull-grinned at her, saying in ancient Egyptian, "The underworld awaits you."

In the same tongue, Evelyn raised her head and cried at him, "I will put you in your grave, you monster—*again!"*

But her bearers had reached the crackling, fire-filled sarcophagus.

The Curator leaned in over her, gazing down with a smile almost as creepy as Imhotep's. "Not if we put you in *your* grave, first."

The stone coffin's flames reached out for her, greedily, its glow painting her orange, its heat like some monstrous oven door had been opened to receive her.

"Burn her!" Imhotep's voice, in the ancient tongue.

Meela looked on with unhidden delight as, beyond the walls of the great museum, thunder cracked like a whip of the gods.

The bearers tilted the slab, at the head of the sarcophagus, so that she would slide down into the flames; but Evelyn, wresting her body, managed to roll off the slab's side . . .

. . . and before she could hit the floor, she was in Rick's arms!

The briefest flash of relief and love and a hundred other emotions passed between husband and wife, as he scooped her up and carried her out to the relative safety of a nook between stacked crates.

Suddenly gunfire was echoing through the warehouse from above!

Evelyn glanced up and saw, on a catwalk, Ardeth Bay, raining down lead with a submachine gun, the modern implement of war a welcome anachronism against the robed figure of the Med-jai chieftain.

The Curator, Lock-nah, the red-turbaned rabble, all dove for cover as bullets chewed up wooden crates and shattered artifacts and zinged off the huge obsidian slab from which Imhotep had emerged, sending it crashing to the floor with a resounding *wham!* As more bullets flew, a pillar near Meela took repeated hits, powdering the air with ancient dust as the young woman screamed and hit the deck.

Rick was crouching over Evelyn, a shotgun in one hand, his other withdrawing a butterfly knife from a pocket; he snapped open the blade and began cutting the ropes at her wrists, even as he pumped shotgun blasts with his other hand, their roar deafening, her ears ringing, but she didn't mind, not when those blasts were knocking back into oblivion those red-turbaned bastards who had wanted to feed her to the fire in that sarcophagus, into which one of them fell, knocked back by a blast from the shotgun. The man within screamed as flames rocketed upward, and she shuddered—her hands free now—to think how narrowly she'd escaped that fate herself.

Throughout, Ardeth Bay had been racing along the catwalk, blasting down on the room, keeping their adversaries pinned down . . . with one exception.

The walking dead man was impervious even to machine-gun fire, and Imhotep was casting his black-socketed supernatural gaze around at this scene of carnage, as if bewildered by it all.

Then those empty eyes landed on Rick O'Connell.

And, as much in pain as rage, the mummy shrieked, *"You!"*

Consumed with fury, Imhotep stepped to a large black urn, which had seemed just another of the countless artifacts in this warehouse, and—though bullets from Ardeth Bay's machine gun were riddling him, to no apparent effect—he lifted the urn as if it were a giant goblet from which he intended to drink.

"Arise, my servants!" the mummy said.

Her ankles were free now, and Evelyn took her husband's hand, and they ran down the corridor of crates, toward a beckoning stairway. But Evelyn did not like the sound of the words she heard coming from behind her, words spoken by Imhotep, ancient words. . . .

"Collect your bones! Gather your limbs!"

She and Rick were at the stairway now, but Evelyn's blood ran cold as she heard Imhotep's impassioned chanting, behind her.

"Shake the earth from your flesh! Your master has returned!"

Evelyn, running up those stairs at her husband's side, did not look back, and perhaps that was just as well. Imhotep was ripping off the lid of the black urn, an action which caused—as if it had been held there under pressure—a mass of black sand to explode out. As the sand hit the floor, it mystically formed itself into four soldiers of death—materializing in shields and skirts and headdresses, with swords and spears at the ready—skeletal soldiers, mummy soldiers.

Pointing toward the fleeing O'Connells, Imhotep screamed to his soldiers, *"E-heeby-uut Setna!"*

The top of the staircase connected with the catwalk, and that was where the O'Connells met up with Ardeth Bay. Glad to see each other alive, they exchanged grins, fleeting ones, because—hearing an ee-

rie clanking accompanied by an unearthly screech—
they looked back to see the soldier mummies march-
ing down that corridor between crates, hunkered into
attack position, heading right toward them.

"I hate those guys," Rick said.

"You've always been a master of understatement,
dear," Evelyn said, as he pulled her through the door
and headed through an Oriental exhibit. Ardeth Bay,
machine gun in his hands, was taking the rear position, protecting them, moving backward.

"What's the quickest way out of this joint?" he
asked her.

Soon they were bursting through a side door of
the museum, and hightailing it down the alley.

"I think we've lost them," Rick said.

That was when, behind them halfway down the
alley, the side wall of the museum seem to explode,
spitting bricks, as the four soldier mummies jumped
through the new exit, in perfect, nimble unison, piv-
oting sharply and striding down after their prey.

Evelyn and Rick rounded the corner onto the deserted street, with Ardeth Bay bringing up the rear,
reloading, the mummies out of sight but the clanking
sound of them on the march said they were much too
near.

They ran, ran hard, knowing all they had to do
was make it to the car, and there it was, waiting, that
beautiful Beuford . . . only it was empty, as deserted
as the street.

Neither Jonathan nor Alex were anywhere to be
seen.

·❨ 8 ❩·

Double-decker Danger

While Rick O'Connell and the Med-jai chieftain were sneaking into the British Museum—and Evelyn O'Connell was witnessing a bizarre ritual of regeneration—Jonathan Carnahan and his nephew, Alex, were casually chatting under a growling charcoal sky. The rain-slick street all but deserted, they stood on the sidewalk, leaning against the powder-blue Beuford, a mature eight-year-old boy in short pants and an immature fortyish man in a slightly shopworn-looking tuxedo (it had been a long evening).

The boy had been regaling his uncle—who sipped from time to time from a silver hip flask—with the story of the adventures he and his parents had shared at the dig at the temple at Thebes. Right now, Alex was up to the part about the Bracelet of Anubis snapping itself on his wrist, and the resultant vision he'd experienced thereafter.

"And at the very top of the golden pyramid," the boy was saying, "sat an enormous diamond."

"Do tell?" his uncle said, mesmerized. "By 'enormous,' just what are we talking about, here—a millionaire's bride's engagement ring? A cabbage?"

"Uncle Jonathan," the boy said, whispering, as intense as if he were sharing a ghost story around a campfire, "that diamond was so big, it would reflect the sun and wink at distant travelers—beckoning them to their deaths."

Jonathan frowned, liking the sound of all of that, except for the beckoning-travelers-to-their-death part.

Thunder shook the world just then, as if God were suggesting the uncle take seriously what the nephew had said, and Jonathan was contemplating as much when more thunder caught the attention of them both.

Only it wasn't the sky making noise, this time, rather man-made thunder, emanating from within the museum—the muffled mechanical barking of gunfire, rapidly repeating gunfire!

Both Jonathan and Alex grabbed for the car door handle at the same time, momentarily fighting over it, panicking.

"Open it!" Alex cried. "Open it!"

"Let go and I will!"

Then Jonathan had the door open, and they threw themselves inside, gunfire popping within the nearby museum as if all the firecrackers in Chinatown were exploding.

O'Connell had left the keys with Jonathan, who dug them from his pocket, fumbling with them, even as his nephew impatiently prompted him, "Come on! Come on!"

Fear and adrenaline rushing through him in twin streams, Jonathan selected the correct key and jammed it into the ignition and turned it, hard.

The key snapped off.

"You broke it!" Alex said, wide-eyed, horrified, amazed by his uncle's incompetence. "You broke the key off in the dash! How could you do that?"

Jonathan shrugged elaborately, sputtering, "Can I help it if I have a forceful grasp?"

Gunfire continued to echo within the museum.

Alex was on top of his uncle, grabbing him by the tuxedo lapels. "Something terrible is happening in there—they're gonna come flying out of there, any second, and, Uncle Jonathan—*they're going to need a ride!*"

Jonathan sat there, a hand on his forehead, as if taking his own temperature. "There's a bus stop around the corner—we'll try there."

Alex looked at his uncle as if the man were insane. "We're going to catch a bus?"

"Do you have a better idea?"

They ran down the block, and around the corner. Just down a ways, idling at the curb, was a bright red omnibus, of the classic double-decker style so identified with London. Its heavy-set, uniformed, mustached driver was leaning against a lamppost, having a cigarette, apparently waiting to see if the storm was ever going to hit.

"I say, remember us?" Jonathan asked the man.

"Can't say I do, sir."

"My son and I took your delightful tour, earlier today. I neglected to tip you." Jonathan pressed a pound note into the man's hand.

"Well, thank you, guv'nor!"

"I wonder if you found a small book about Tom Mix anywhere on the bus? Do you have a lost and found?"

"Why, no, guv'nor . . . I didn't find any book, and we don't have no lost and found."

"Would you mind terribly if my son and I stepped aboard for a moment?" And Jonathan held out a second pound note. "Just to check our seats? It might have slipped back under, you know."

The driver grinned yellowly, snatching the pound note. "Go right ahead, guv'nor."

"Thank you so ever much," Jonathan said, smiling obsequiously, and he and Alex boarded the bus.

The driver was pocketing the pound notes when the double-decker groaned into gear. The driver's mouth dropped open as Jonathan, behind the wheel, waved a cheery good-bye and the little boy was waving too, as the bus roared off down the street and around the corner.

Exasperated, Rick O'Connell paced on the sidewalk, with Evelyn at his side and Ardeth Bay watching the rear, the clank of armor telling them that Imhotep's dead soldiers were on their inexorable way.

"Where the hell is Jonathan? What's he done with Alex?" O'Connell gestured to the Beuford. "Why didn't they stay with the damn car?"

As if in answer to O'Connell's question, the double-decker bus careened around the corner, with the tuxedoed, wild-eyed Jonathan behind its very big wheel, struggling nervously to keep the oversize vehicle under control, Alex jumping up and down at his side, having a wonderful time.

The bus whined to a stop, and Alex pulled open the door to welcome the passengers, saying, "Mom! I knew it! Dad *said* he would rescue you!"

"The rescue isn't quite finished yet, dear," his mother said, leaping aboard, O'Connell and his shotgun jumping on right behind her, and the machine gun–toting Ardeth Bay also climbing on, backward, the snout of the weapon aimed toward the mouth of the museum's alley.

Evy was hugging Alex as O'Connell flashed Jonathan a look-to-kill. "Is something wrong with my car? Tell me something isn't wrong with my car."

"We were forced to find alternative transportation," Jonathan said, hands gripping the wheel.

O'Connell's eyes were popping. "A double-decker bus?"

"It was your son's idea."

Alex, in his mother's arms, said, "Was not!"

"Was too!" Jonathan snapped petulantly back.

And the two children briefly exchanged *Was too*s

and *Was not*s until O'Connell—looking back toward that alley from whence those mummies could emerge any moment—yelled, "Just *go!*"

"*Go*, Jonathan!" Evy cried, clutching Alex to her.

"I'll just bloody well go, then," Jonathan sniffed, and hit the gas pedal, shifting up, the bus lurching forward.

O'Connell ran to the back of the moving vehicle and looked out the rear window—moments later, the four soldiers of death strode out of the alley, skeletal figures with swords and spears at the ready, in two-by-two assault formation. The creatures pivoted, with military precision, and marched right up and over the Beuford, severely crushing the trunk, roof and bonnet of O'Connell's gorgeous new car.

Devastated, O'Connell muttered, "Goddamn mummies, anyway."

Ardeth Bay was suddenly at his side, and a white smile flashed in the dark beard. "Now are you glad to see me?"

Out the back window of the bus, the two longtime allies in adventure could see the quartet of undead fanning out, four abreast, picking up speed, accelerating after the bus.

O'Connell gave the Med-jai chieftain a quick look, a mixture of apprehension and fondness. "Like old times, buddy. . . . Good luck to us both."

Then, as he was heading up the rear staircase, O'Connell heard the Med-jai—positioned at the back window with the machine gun poised—say, "Allah be with you, my friend."

On the upper deck, O'Connell saw out the window the mummy soldiers charging after the bus, at a speed that seemed unlikely on such spindly, skeletal limbs. He lowered the rear window and began pumping shotgun blasts down on the creatures, tearing holes in ancient shields and even blowing out several rib cages—and yet not stopping the bastards!

In fact, all he managed to accomplish, with his gunfire, was to incite the hellish soldiers to change their strategy, all four of the mummies fanning out and, logic be damned—a ghastly pair on either side of the street—running right up the face of buildings, like oversize spiders!

"Right," O'Connell said to himself. He had seen this tactic years before, in Imhotep's underground cavern; but somehow, in the context of modern London, the gravity-defying feat seemed even more surreal, and the extent of the mummy soldiers' supernatural powers might have sent him spiraling into despair, if he'd had the time.

Just then he saw one of the mummies, at left, leap from the building toward the bus, landing somewhere below O'Connell's field of vision.

On the lower deck, Ardeth Bay had been positioned at the back window—which he had not lowered—and seemed to be ready for anything. But when that mummy leapt onto the window with a *wham,* like a huge ugly bug landing, the fearless Med-jai warrior damn near soiled himself.

Ardeth Bay opened fire with the tommy gun, shattering the window into a thousand shards, and ripping

116

the undead soldier in half. The upper part of the mummy, still "alive," clung to the rear of the bus, while the lower torso dropped away, falling to the pavement like a bag of bones.

Breathing hard, Ardeth Bay—having emptied the machine gun into the creature—quickly reloaded, somewhat shaken, hands fumbling. He was not expecting—who could have?—the upper torso of the mummy he'd just blasted to swing its half-body, like a trapeze artist, through the window, shrieking with insane rage, hurling itself at the Med-jai warrior, whose weapon went tumbling from his grasp.

On the upper level, O'Connell continued firing out that open rear window, blasting at a mummy soldier whose leap from the nearest building seemed more like flying. But O'Connell's shots did not bring the creature down, and he heard it land above him, on the roof of the speeding vehicle, caving the metal in, somewhat.

O'Connell watched, in horrified amazement, as claws spiked through the ceiling and peeled it back, can opener–style. Firing up at the thing, its skeletal frame and skull-like visage visible through the torn ceiling, O'Connell tried to blast the monster off the bus; but it was no use: the thing leapt down and tackled him, knocking the shotgun from his hands, sending it skittering down the aisle.

Suddenly O'Connell was immersed in putrid death-smell and grasping skeletal limbs. Then an ancient sword was raised over him, as the undead executioner prepared to do Lord Imhotep's bidding.

117

Somehow O'Connell managed to thrust a fist into a decaying shoulder and the sword spilled from bony fingers.

But those same bony fingers thrust forward, seizing O'Connell by the throat, the skeletal form getting to its feet and lifting him toward the ceiling, as if the adventurer were feather-light. Apparently strangling O'Connell wasn't enough, as the mummy slammed the man's head into the metal ceiling, again, and again.

Dazed as hell, O'Connell nonetheless flailed and kicked, but it did no good, and his vision was blurring, going red and then black, the world turning obsidian, like *The Book of the Dead....*

Up in the front of the bus, near Jonathan, Evelyn—holding her son tight—watched in dismayed disbelief as Ardeth Bay fled backward down the aisle, pursued by the upper half of a mummy, scurrying over seats using only its hands, like a crazed, screeching monkey.

Evelyn yelled, "Jonathan—turn! Sharp turn! Now!"

Jonathan cranked the wheel, the double-decker slewing hard to the left, taking out a lamppost, sending Ardeth Bay and the fiendish half-mummy across the aisle, hurling them like rag dolls.

And on the upper deck, Jonathan's hard turn had a similar effect on O'Connell and the mummy strangling him, sending both tumbling across the aisle, the undead soldier losing its grip on the adventurer's throat.

Spotting his shotgun, down the aisle, O'Connell, on his hands and knees, scrambled after it. Soon his fingertips were touching the butt of the shotgun. . . .

But on the deck underneath them, Ardeth Bay—having leapt to his feet, unharmed—found himself again confronted by the half-mummy, who used its arms to rise over a seat, then lifted a deformed, skeletal hand.

Suddenly, supernaturally, the creature's fingernails began to grow, forming into razor-sharp, four-inch weapons. The clawed hand swiped at the Med-jai, ripping through the sleeve of his garment, tearing the flesh of his arm in four crimson slashes.

Screaming, the warrior clutched himself, falling back onto the floor. Evelyn and her son ran to Ardeth Bay, and pulled him back, and away, from the half-creature, which was just down the aisle from them, near the front.

Evelyn cried, "Jonathan, turn again—turn sharp, *turn!*"

And, once more, Jonathan cranked the wheel, this time slewing hard to the right, scraping past a parked car in a gnashing of metal against metal, throwing sparks.

On the level above, this tactic backfired for O'Connell, whose shotgun slid from his reach, and out an air vent. O'Connell was trying to get to his feet when the mummy soldier was on him again, picking up where it left off, lifting the adventurer up by his already scraped-raw neck.

Below, however, O'Connell's lost shotgun had

119

fallen onto the hood of the bus, landing there with a *klunk!* and staying there, shakily, but not falling off, not yet. Evelyn, noting this, extended her arm through the louvered window—but the shotgun was out of her reach! Then a bump in the road sent the weapon sliding into her grasp. . . .

Ardeth Bay—ripped across the chest by the half-mummy, four more scarlet streaks flaying the front of his garment—slammed against a seat, sliding to the floor, winded, barely conscious. The half-mummy slithered up and over and onto the warrior, one hand gripping the man's neck, the other drawn back, displaying its hideous, ready-to-strike claw fingers.

Evelyn blew the creature's head off with a shotgun blast.

Calmly pumping, she moved closer, undaunted, and blasted the thing again, point-blank, sending pieces of the half-mummy flying down the aisle, splatting here, splattering there.

Ardeth Bay looked at Evelyn and nodded his relieved thanks.

Alex had been watching this, astounded by what a keen mom he had.

"Uh-oh," somebody said.

Jonathan.

Alex and Evelyn and Ardeth Bay turned to look out the windshield and saw what had alarmed the bus's driver: a low-slung pedestrian bridge just ahead, with a sign announcing its height, warning buses and lorries to seek passage elsewhere.

Jonathan hit the brakes, and they squealed and

screamed, and the driver squealed and screamed, too: "We're not going to make it!"

Above, O'Connell—still trying his best to wrest himself from the vicious strangling grip of the mummy soldier—saw, over the monster's shoulder, the underpass coming. He threw several wild punches, giving it everything he had, and slipped from the mummy's stranglehold, throwing himself on the deck, covering his head.

The creature just stood there, looking down at a victim who seemed to be waiting for it to finish him off; then, sensing something, the mummy turned just in time to see the bridge coming, but not in time to do anything about it.

The bottom two-thirds of the double-decker roared under the bridge—the upper third, however, was sheered off, ripped away, taking the monster along with it.

O'Connell, on the floor of the now open-air bus, amid scraps of metal and shards of glass, felt the buffeting of wind on him. Cautiously, he opened his eyes and saw nothing around him but torn metal and the dark, stormy sky. He got gingerly to his feet, just as the bus raced out onto Tower Bridge.

Downstairs, Alex was embracing his uncle, saying, "Great driving, Uncle Jon! You're wonderful!"

Hugging the boy with one hand, steering with the other, an old pro at bus-driving now, Jonathan said, "You're not so bad yourself."

Evelyn, seeing this, for the first time realized just how close these two "children" were.

As a much-needed moment of calm settled over them, Alex heard a tiny rattle, and glanced to his right, seeing nothing but an open side window, and the gleam of the Thames beyond.

Then a mummy soldier popped its head up into the space of the open window—it had been clinging to the side of the bus, spiderlike—and Alex shrieked. So did his uncle Jonathan. So, for that matter, did the mummy.

"Cover your ears and duck, son," a familiar voice said.

O'Connell had come down the rear stairway to rejoin his family.

The boy covered his ears and ducked as his father leaned forward with the shotgun, inserting the barrel in the mummy's mouth. O'Connell squeezed the trigger and the skeletal head exploded into fragments, the mummy's headless body flying off the bus and out over the Tower Bridge, dropping into the water with a *ker-plunk*, like a stone.

Alex stood, yelled out after the creature. "Play rough, and somebody's gonna get hurt—right, Mum?"

"Right, Alex," Evelyn said, sitting down in the nearest seat, exhausted.

Jonathan shifted down, but the engine sounded sick, making strange noises, as if a pound of nails were loose inside and rattling around in there.

"I'm afraid this old darling is on its last legs," Jonathan said, steering.

O'Connell helped Ardeth Bay, his clothing soaked

with blood, to his feet. "Are you all right, buddy?"

"Yes," the Med-jai chieftain said, wincing in pain, "but I admit preferring travel by camel."

Finally O'Connell made his way to the woman he loved, the woman he had rescued.

"Well, that was easy," he said, with a hangdog grin.

"Com'ere, you," she said, curling her finger in come-hither fashion.

He came hither, and into her arms, and they began to kiss.

Alex grunted in disgust, preferring to skip the mushy stuff. Shaking his head, the boy wandered back down the aisle, to find a seat away from such nonsense.

The bus slowed down, though Jonathan had nothing to do with that; groaning, grunting, the vehicle clattered to a stop with an unmistakable finality.

Arm around his wife's waist, O'Connell said, "For a librarian, you lead a pretty lively life."

Evelyn said, "Without you, it would be ever so boring."

They were smiling at each other, relieved that this was over, when they heard their son's muffled yell.

Swiveling toward the sound, they saw the muscular red-turbaned Lock-nah, pulling the boy out the rear door, dark hand clamped over Alex's pale face, the squirming boy's eyes huge and terrified.

"Alex!" Evelyn cried.

O'Connell threw himself down the aisle, making it to the rear window in time to see Alex struggling with Lock-nah and two other red-turbaned men, stuffing the boy into the backseat of the waiting limo.

O'Connell tore out the back door of the bus, the limo's engine roaring to life as the long black vehicle charged out onto the bridge, past the dead double-decker.

Evy and Jonathan poured out the front of the bus, on O'Connell's heels. But the boy's father was faster, and raced out ahead of them, chasing the limo, just as the Tower's drawbridge began to rise.

Like a champion hurdler, O'Connell vaulted the traffic gate and ran after the limo, right up the ever-steepening, rising bridge. The limo made it over, easily, dropping down onto the other side. Fighting the incline, O'Connell made it to the top and, just as gravity threatened to send him back down, like a child on a slide, he gripped the lip of it, and pulled himself up.

But there was nowhere to go now but down, into the waiting water. He could see across to the limo careening off the far end of the bridge, vanishing down a dark street.

He let go, sliding down the rough surface of the bridge, winding up in a heap where Evy and Jonathan gathered around him, their faces distraught. He just sat there, like a man whose heart had been ripped from his breast, and said his son's name, over and over.

He did not cry, though—by the time his wife had helped him to his feet, O'Connell knew there would be no tears. To cry would be to admit defeat—worse,

124

to admit that their son was lost to them more than just temporarily.

Ardeth Bay, weakened from his wounds, had made his way to the stricken trio. "Do not fear, my friends—they cannot harm your boy."

Evelyn, holding onto her husband's arm tightly, said, "No?"

"No. They need him. The world needs him. He wears the Bracelet of Anubis."

This was the first Evelyn had heard of this, and her brow tightened. "Alex is wearing the bracelet?"

O'Connell quickly filled her in. Then he said to Ardeth Bay, "My son said he saw the pyramids at Giza, and then Karnac. Is that our path?"

The Med-jai chieftain nodded. "That is how our journey—how your son's journey—begins. At Karnac, the bracelet will reveal to him the next stop on his way."

Evelyn clutched her husband's arm desperately. "If we don't get there before Imhotep, and his crazed followers, we won't know where to go next!"

"Don't underestimate our son," O'Connell said to her gently. "Alex will know to leave a trail of bread-crumbs."

"We must go at once," Ardeth Bay said.

O'Connell was staring toward the Thames, which glittered like obsidian in the dreary night. The thunder and lightning seemed to have stopped; a gentle rain began to fall, like angel's tears.

Jonathan said, glumly, "We could use a magic carpet."

Nodding enigmatically, eyes tight, O'Connell said, "I may just know of one. . . . In the meantime, we'll charter a plane to Cairo."

"We're already packed," Evelyn reminded him.

"We'll take fifteen minutes at the manor," O'Connell told them. "That's all."

"Just time enough to get out of this tux," Jonathan said, "and let my date out of the closet."

And, abandoning the bus that had served them well, they went off to hail a taxi.

·❦ 9 ❦·

The Mummy's Kiss

On the uppermost parapet of the British Museum, surrounded by moldy copper gargoyles nearly as grotesque as himself, Lord Imhotep stood and looked out over the city. Though the sky remained threatening, the rain was faint, half-hearted. But Imhotep—his bearing noble despite the grim, semidecomposed nature of his form—would provide thunder, if the sky were no longer so inclined.

"Now," he roared in ancient Egyptian, "I shall go to Ahm Shere and slay the Scorpion King!"

Standing to his left was Meela, her black dress whipped gently by the wind, her blunt-cut bangs a reminder that she was the reincarnation of his lost love, Anck-su-namun.

"And together," she said to him, as he gazed at her, staring back with a look that promised every sensual pleasure, "we shall rule the world."

At his right hand was Faud Fachry, his high priest, the Curator. For all their triumphs this night, the man in the red fez seemed nervous, even troubled.

"My lord," the Curator said, stepping up to Imhotep, uneasily, "these people, the O'Connells, the Med-jai leader . . . They have the Scepter of Osiris."

Fury contorted the already grotesque features of Imhotep's rotting skull face. But he did not unleash his displeasure on this servant—he still needed the man.

Calming himself, Imhotep spoke ancient words: "To travel the road to Ahm Shere is to invite death. . . . They may have the scepter, but they will never live to have the opportunity to use it."

The undead Lord Imhotep turned to the beautiful living woman and leaned in to kiss her. For all of her devotion, Meela could not hide her fear, even her revulsion, for the corruption that was his corpse's face. He knew this.

"Trust in your love for me, Anck-su-namun," he said, and he stared at her from the empty sockets in his face, drawing deep from the recesses of who he had once been . . .

. . . and they were both in the pharaoh's palace again, face-to-face, the pharaoh's chosen olive-skinned beauty, the handsome high priest—head shaved, copper-skinned, features as well chiseled as any idol's—about to seal their forbidden love with a kiss. Anck-su-namun . . . for that was who Meela was in the vision . . . found her hesitation vanishing, and eagerly she leaned in to kiss this hypnotically hand-

some man, closing her eyes, offering her lips, her tongue. . . .

And it was fortunate for Meela, on the rooftop of the museum, that her eyes were closed, and that she was lost in a vision; otherwise she would have seen her lord's fetid, maggot-infested lips pressed against her luscious red mouth.

And she would have seen Imhotep's face rotting away even more from the simple touch of her, as physical contact with the living brought with it contamination to the undead.

Until his complete regeneration, such would be the price of the mummy's kiss.

PART TWO

The Mummy's Bride

·☾ 10 ☽·

Hell on Wheels

Steep towers and rounded domes ruled the rooftops of Cairo, a city stretching far to the north and south. To the east, rocky desert beckoned; to the west, an impossibly green valley bordered the wide Nile, a fresh north breeze swelling hundreds of sails. Just beyond the green land loomed the pyramids of the Giza Plateau.

By the bank of the Nile, cotton boats waited to be unloaded, their elongated masts forming a forest of dead timber against the modern iron backdrop of a railway bridge. While the style of the river craft and the costumes of the dock workers were unchanged since the pharaohs, the freight and passenger cars that rolled over that bridge carried people whose clothing was contemporary in manner, European in style, but for the occasional native fez.

An exception was a certain private train that had

carried—since pulling out of the Cairo train station—contingents of fifty armed guards in red turbans and flowing desert robes, sitting atop each car, watching, as silent as cathedral gargoyles.

Alex O'Connell, who loved riding on trains, was revising his opinion. Still in his short pants, the eight-year-old had for several days been in the less than tender care of the brawny Arab called Lock-nah. Right now the warrior had the boy by the arm and was pulling him along into a plush parlor car, where the red-fezed Curator and that beautiful dark-haired woman—Meela, she was called, wearing slinky black native attire and golden jewelry—stood facing each other, talking.

"When Lord Imhotep first encountered these O'Connell infidels," the small dark man was saying, "they condemned his immortal soul to the underworld. Because of this, our lord will be vulnerable, even when his powers are fully regenerated."

"Only when he stands at the head of the army of Anubis," she said, nodding, "will he again be invincible."

"Yes, my lady." From a seat by the windows of the richly paneled car, the Curator took a big black book, presenting it to the woman rather formally. "You must keep this with you always."

"Wow!" Alex said, pointing, the gesture unintentionally displaying the golden bracelet on his wrist. *The Book of the Dead!*"

Lock-nah slapped the boy's hand down, as the Curator and Meela turned to them, acknowledging their presence for the first time.

"Lock-nah!" she said, in a scolding tone. "Gentle, now—let go of his arm."

Meela gazed at Alex with what might have been fondness, moving toward him, fluidly—she was so pretty, and her expression was affectionate, yet she still scared him, for some reason. He resolved not to show his fear.

Looking down at him in a motherly fashion, she licked her fingertips and straightened his straw-colored hair. "My—what a bright little boy."

He shrugged. "I'm just interested in Egyptology. Because of my mother."

"I'm sure she's missing you terribly, right now." She touched his nose, lightly, cutely. "But if you wish to see her again, you must not only be bright, but very well behaved."

He smirked at her. "Lady, I don't behave for my parents. What makes you think I'll behave for you?"

She smiled ever so sweetly. "Perhaps because your parents would not slip a poisonous snake in your bed, after you fall asleep."

And for one wide-eyed moment, Alex couldn't hide his fear.

She stroked his cheek, then turned to the Curator, her eyes sending a silent order.

To Lock-nah, the Curator said, "Lord Imhotep will grant the boy an audience."

"Hey, that's okay," Alex said, backpedaling, "I don't really want one. . . ."

Nodding a bow to the Curator, Lock-nah latched onto Alex's arm again and hauled him across the luxury car and through the door into the next one.

And it was as if the boy had stepped into another dimension, or was having one of those crazy visions; but such was not the case: this was a common boxcar, made uncommon by an elaborate transformation into an ancient Egyptian temple. Lighted by torches, cluttered with artifacts and statuary, the air heavy with incense, smoke drifting like fog, the boxcar-temple's mood was somber and dark, an altar centered along the wall at left.

Presiding over all of this was a tall, eerie figure in a dark blue, hooded robe, standing with his back to Lock-nah and the in-tow Alex.

Lock-nah bowed down—not just a nod, Alex noted, but on his knees—and the hooded figure turned, robe swirling.

The hooded face looking down on the boy was a decayed, skeletal thing, with sick-looking flesh hanging off it, greenish, ghoulish.

Alex was the son of Rick O'Connell, and by nature no coward; he was also the son of Evelyn O'Connell, whose brains and spunk he had also inherited. Nonetheless, Alex was an eight-year-old boy, staring up into the desiccated face of a living mummy.

And, so, Alex screamed.

Lock-nah, still on his knees, raised a hand to slap the boy, but the creature—Alex had already figured out that this was Lord Imhotep—also raised a hand, for Lock-nah to refrain from the blow.

Another gesture from the gross, creepy creature told Lock-nah to rise, and the Arab took several steps back, as if granting some privacy to the boy and the mummy.

Imhotep spoke, and at first Alex couldn't understand his words. . . .

"Keetash issirian ibn . . ."

. . . and then it was as if the creature had begun to speak in English, though Alex knew that wasn't so, yet at the same time he could understand everything Imhotep was saying.

"It is you, young O'Connell, who are the chosen one. You who will take me to Ahm Shere."

Blinking, disconcerted by the supernatural translation taking place in his mind, the boy—less afraid now, sensing something strangely benign in the mummy's raspy tone—steeled himself.

The boy looked right up at the decomposing face, ignoring the maggots crawling in and out of the hole where a cheek should be, and said, "What if I don't lead you to this . . . Ahm Shere? What if I happen to get, you know, kind of . . . lost?"

Alex was unaware that he, like Imhotep, was speaking in an ancient Egyptian tongue.

"You have strength, little man," Imhotep said, his sinewy face forming a horrific semismile. "You are your father's son."

"That's right, and don't you ever forget that."

Empty eye sockets stared at Alex. "I will not—there is something you do not know ... but should ... and I promise you, this *you* will not forget."

"I don't know what you're talking about," Alex said, trying not to tremble. An awful stench came off the creature—that must have been why so much incense was burning.

Suddenly Imhotep grabbed the boy by the arm with a gloved hand, indicating the golden scorpion-relief bracelet. "The Bracelet of Anubis is both blessing and curse—the sands of time have already begun to pour out against you."

The hooded mummy let go of the boy's arm and went to a small ornate table where sat an hourglass—filled with black sand—which he turned over.

Swallowing, Alex stared at the sand trickling through the narrow hourglass neck, saying, "I already know about that—I put the bracelet on, seven days later, the Scorpion King wakes up. That's your problem."

"No, young O'Connell—that is my destiny ... but your *problem*. Here is what you don't 'already know': if you do not enter the golden pyramid before its apex is kissed by the sun, on that last morning ... the bracelet will suck the very life from you."

Alex felt as if he'd been struck a hard blow in the stomach. Gulping, he said, "That, uh, that part I hadn't heard before. . . . You mean, I'll die?"

"Death is a difficult concept for the young to grasp, but—yes."

Panic flowed through the boy. "Are you sayin' I only have five days left?"

Skull-grinning, Imhotep said, "Five days—and perhaps it would be best if you did not . . . 'get lost.' Do you agree?"

Breathing hard, Alex regained his composure. Gritting his teeth, staring the decomposing creature down, he said, "I think my dad is going to knock your block off—do you agree?"

Imhotep seemed to be considering that question when voices—male, adult voices—from just outside the boxcar-temple distracted him.

"Take him away," Imhotep said to Lock-nah.

And Alex—his arm in the tight, painful grip of his red-turbaned babysitter—was hustled out, into the next car down the line. But first the boy caught a glimpse of Lord Imhotep, spinning toward the altar, tucking himself into the smoky shadows, concealing himself from those who were about to be granted an audience.

Earlier, in the luxury of the plush parlor car—moments after the O'Connell boy had been hustled by Lock-nah into the adjoining boxcar, to meet Imhotep—a knock had announced the three mercenaries who Meela and the Curator were expecting.

The three men—Red Willits, the burly leader; Jacques Clemons, the strapping Frenchman; and spindly Jake Spivey—were an unshaven, dingy lot, with wide-brimmed cowboyish hats and hip-holstered sidearms to match. Jacques and Spivey were carrying a box of some kind, wrapped in a mangy blanket.

The Curator gestured toward the box. "You have acquired what we asked?"

"Oh, we 'acquired' it, all right," Red said. "We had to knock off a couple guards at that museum of yours, but we acquired it."

Like a magician performing a trick, Jacques yanked off the blanket and revealed an exquisitely ornate wooden chest, dancing with colorful hiero-glyphs in gold and black and blue and red. Meela smiled, warmth rushing through her as her eyes drank in the winged sun disks, griffins, squatting gods, falcon-headed Horus, and, of course, jackal-headed Anubis.

"You have returned the chest," Meela said. "Good."

"This is no ordinary chest, is it?" Jacques said, angrily. His blunt fingers glided over the hieroglyphs. "This is a cursed chest, yes?"

"You surprise me, Jacques," Meela said, folding her arms, resting them on the gentle shelf of her bosom. "Do you read hieratic?"

"No," Red said, stepping forward, "he reads mu-seum guidebook. Tell her what it says in there, Jacques. . . ."

" 'Death will come on swift wings to whoever de-files this chest,' " the Frenchman said, from memory. "There's this undead . . . thing . . . who will kill all those who open—"

"Who open this chest," the Curator interrupted dismissively. "Yes, yes, suck them dry and then he will become whole again. I wrote that guidebook entry, gentlemen. I know all about it."

Red stepped forward, his red-stubbled face twisted into a fierce grimace. "Then why in hell didn't you tell us about it? And why didn't you clue us in about the three Americans who found this box, ten years ago, and died horrible deaths?"

"Gentlemen," the Curator said. "Surely modern men like yourselves hold no stock in such primitive superstitions."

"We want more," Jacques said, flatly.

"More?" the Curator said.

"More," Spivey said.

Red stepped forward and thumped the dark little man on the chest. "Ten thousand."

The Curator's eyebrows shot up. "The agreement was for five!"

Bending down, Red patted the chest on its lid. "I got a feeling this little slice of history is worth more than even the ten we're asking. Pay our price, or we'll wrap 'er back up and look for a better buyer."

Meela approached the Curator, resting a hand on his shoulder, her eyes locking briefly with his, silencing any further argument.

Then, with her best catlike, most sensual smile, she purred to Red, "Ten thousand is reasonable. Ten thousand will be just fine."

Red grinned back at her, licked his lips, then looked at both of his comrades, with an expression of self-congratulation for displaying such savvy bargaining skills.

Palm outstretched, fingers curling in invitation, Meela said, "Follow me, gentlemen—and you shall receive all that you deserve. . . ."

Then they followed her through the door to the next car, the temporary temple Meela had had fashioned for Lord Imhotep. She stood just inside the smoky, gloomy boxcar, gesturing toward the altar, saying, "Your just rewards await, my friends."

Red, first one in, leaned close to Meela, near enough that he might have kissed her. "No tricks now, baby—we're not handing that chest over until we're satisfied."

She summoned a seductive look, bestowed it on him, and said, "There is much satisfaction to be shared."

Once Jacques and Spivey, lugging the chest, were within the dimly lit boxcar, Meela swept out, shutting the door from the outside.

Red heard the click, knew at once she had locked them in, and said, "What the hell?"

Then he turned, just as his partners were setting down the wooden chest. Surrounded by ancient artifacts, they stood squinting through the smoke, breathing hard, taking in the sickly sweetness of incense and a stench of decaying animal flesh. Shadows seemed to move in the steamlike air, one of them larger than the others, gliding toward them. . . .

"What the hell is that?" Spivey yelled.

142

His partners had no answer, other than to draw their pistols.

"What have we here?" Red asked, moving cautiously toward the shadow.

But this was not a shadow, rather a figure in a dark, hooded robe, and as Red was thinking, *It's just a man,* the figure stepped into a shaft of light and exposed a skeletal face draped in decaying flesh and maggot-ridden decomposing tissue.

"Christ almighty!" Red screamed, as he and his two hard-bitten companions all but jumped out of their skin.

Then the creature reared back its head and shrieked at them—half scream, half babble in some ancient language.

Spivey ran frantically to the door they'd come through, and clawed at the wood, screaming for help, staring at a metal plate covering a peephole, praying for an answer.

He got one.

The beautiful Meela's face appeared before him, advising Spivey, "He wants you to open the chest for him! Quick, open the chest! It will satisfy him!"

And the metal plate slammed shut, the peephole—and the beautiful face—disappearing.

Spivey, having no other option to speak of, took this one, scrambling back to the chest. The creature had retreated to the shadows again, and Jacques and Red were nervously fanning their pistols at the smoky nothingness of the boxcar.

Then Jacques noticed Spivey, kneeling over the

chest, obviously about to open it, and the Frenchman yelled, "No! Don't do it! The curse!"

But Spivey was following the counsel of the lovely Meela, grabbing onto the lid of the chest and forcefully pulling at it.

"Stop him!" Jacques said.

Then the lid popped off, a hissing emanating from within, accompanied by a discharge of white vapor.

"There," Spivey said, and he stood, and the creature was next to him, looming, staring with black eye sockets, unhinging its jaw, the skull face opening its mouth impossibly wide.

Spivey began to scream, a shrill scream that rattled that artifacts in the boxcar.

Red had retreated from this bizarre sight, and now the smoke concealed exactly what was happening to his partner. Jacques was nearby, and the two men looked at each other in horror, trying to make sense of the tornadolike sound, the sucking wind, that seemed to come forth from the hooded figure. They couldn't shoot without risking hitting Spivey!

And then that became a moot point: the shriveled corpse of Jake Spivey flew over their heads, slamming off the wall, dropping to the floor like the husk it was.

Red and Jacques, screaming in rage and fear, opened fire on the hooded figure, who merely turned to face them, grinning at them—an evil enough grin, but not as skeletal as before, the creature had changed, somehow, seemed . . . less a creature, more a man.

144

And yet the bullets were penetrating and doing nothing, impotent against the thing!

In the adjacent parlor car, Meela turned away from the closed peephole as the Curator—perched on a cushioned seat, reading a book of poetry—looked up with faint concern. Gunfire, after all, was echoing—two guns blasting next door.

Meela shook her head, sitting across from him. "Nothing to worry about."

Now only one gun was firing.

And in the temple car, Red kept firing, backing up as the creature advanced; as he witnessed its jaw unhinge and heard and saw a hellish wind emerging from the depths of that thing, coming for him, Red knew—much too late—that he should have settled for the damn five thousand.

Soon the creature was stepping around the shriveled shells of three once-dangerous men, a creature no longer—rather a handsome, muscular, tanned, perfect physical specimen, from his sandaled toes to his shaven head.

Lord Imhotep was as alive as the mercenaries were dead.

·❨ 11 ❩·

Izzy a Pilot?

Five miles beyond Fort Stack—itself on the outer-most outskirts of Cairo—lay the former headquar-ters of His Majesty's Air Corps. Ten years ago, it had been the province of the late Winston Havlock, and even then had been a ghost town of battered Quonset huts, with one sorry excuse for an airport hangar alongside a pothole-ridden asphalt runway, and no sign of a control tower, other than the looming dunes of the Sahara. In private hands since Havlock's heroic death, the airfield had deteriorated even further, mak-ing a joke of the shabby wooden sign whose crudely painted letters read: MAGIC CARPET AIRWAYS.

"*This* is your magic carpet?" Evy asked her hus-band.

O'Connell, his wife and brother-in-law had trun-dled here across the desert in the latter's Dusenberg. Jonathan had maintained the convertible over the years, storing it in the garage of the Carnahan family home in Cairo; even after acquiring the London manor, Evy had never sold the house because her work took her so frequently to Egypt.

"Izzy may not be a genie," O'Connell said, "but he's a pro. It'll be fine."

He got out from behind the wheel of the dusty car and the others followed suit, the eyes of his passengers widening at the sight of the rundown would-be airport. The trio looked like explorers in their desert khakis, Jonathan in a pith helmet, Evy in a wide-brimmed white hat, bare-headed O'Connell in full adventurer mode, a holstered revolver under either arm.

A door opened and out of the hangar stepped a small individual in grease-covered overalls, a wild-haired little man whose cheeks and hands were also dabbed with greasy black; under a scraggly mustache, a silver tooth winked in the midst of yellowish choppers. His eyes got as wild as his hair as he spotted O'Connell, and momentarily the grease monkey froze.

"Izzy!" O'Connell grinned at his old friend, holding out his arms, Jolson-style. "Is you is, or is you ain't my baby?"

"Ain't!" Izzy said, and ran back inside, slamming the door, clicking the lock.

Fanning herself from the dry desert heat, Evy wandered up to her husband's side and gave him an arched-eyebrow look. "And this is your 'old friend,' the pilot?"

O'Connell shrugged. "Izzy's always been a trifle shy. . . . Jonathan, unload the Dusie, get our bags."

"My hands are fairly full," Jonathan said.

O'Connell glanced at his brother-in-law and saw him smilingly lifting up the golden Scepter of Osiris. The precious artifact had in fact never left Jonathan's hands as he'd sat in the backseat of the Dusenberg while O'Connell drove.

O'Connell snatched the thing from Jonathan, and barked, "Now! Or do you think dawdling serves our purpose?"

Jonathan, head hanging, kicked at the sand and said, "All right, all right, I'll be your bloody native server."

"Good. And I'll deal with the flight details."

With a sigh, Jonathan scurried to the car, and O'Connell—Evy at his side—strolled up to the hangar office door, golden scepter in one hand, withdrawing a shoulder-holstered revolver with the other. As casually as a man tipping his hat, he shot the door handle off.

Evy jumped, then, quickly recovering, said, "Subtlety would not seem to be your strong suit, darling."

"No time for subtlety, dear," he replied, and kicked open the hangar door.

Stepping inside, O'Connell suddenly realized how unnecessary his action had been: the hangar had no far wall, revealing a view of a scenic handful of huts around a small oasis.

The little wild-haired man in the greasy coveralls was at a counter, quickly gathering up maps, looking

148

distressed, in the manner of one beating a hasty but necessary retreat.

Evy stepped inside and stood just behind her husband, saying, "Your genie doesn't seem terribly happy to see you—let alone grant your wishes."

"He's never turned me down yet," O'Connell said.

"Like any good genie," she said.

"Screw you, O'Connell!" Izzy blurted. "Begging pardon for my French, ma'am, but every time I hook up with this son of a bitch, I get bullets in me! Last time I got my ass shot off!"

He swiveled to show them, and, indeed, the part of his coveralls he pointed to was somewhat flat.

"You still seem to have a serviceable bottom to my eyes," Evy said, delicately.

"Not to mine, lady! Two years later, I'm still in mourning for my hindquarters!"

Evy looked at her husband. "Colorful. But is he really a pilot?"

"The best . . . Izzy, enough of this nostalgia. We can jaw over old times, later. No time for that now— we need a ride."

Izzy slammed the maps back down on the counter. "No way! I go with you, I get shot—that's the way it always goes. Cause and effect."

O'Connell folded his arms, as if he were the genie, golden scepter in hand. "Name once."

Izzy's eyes popped. "That bank job in Marakeesh? Huh? How's that for 'once'?"

Evy looked sideways at her husband. "Bank job?"

149

He gave her a pitiful smile. "It's not as bad it sounds."

"No," Izzy said, walking up to O'Connell, raving in his face, "it's worse!" Now the little grease monkey turned to Evy, as if she, perhaps, were capable of listening to reason. "I'm flyin' high, see, hidin' against the sun. So O'Connell, here, flags me down with a mirror, gives me the all-clear. So I fly in nice and low for the pickup, glide in nice and quiet, and that's when I see he's on horseback, with half the Marakeesh coppers on his tail, also on horseback. They start shooting at me, and I wind up in the middle of the road, my spleen hangin' out, and the big guy here goes galloping off with some belly dancer grabbing him around the waist!"

Evy cocked an eyebrow at her husband. "Belly dancer?"

"This was before I knew you," O'Connell said to her, lamely, "and, besides, he's putting a really negative spin on it."

"Tailspin, you mean," Izzy said, "which is what I went into when those Marakeesh coppers shot me!"

Evy found a nongreasy spot on one of Izzy's shoulders to pat. "Calm yourself . . . Izzy. You and I are going to be great good friends. . . ." She flashed her husband a look. ". . . It would seem we have much to talk about."

"Talk I'm up for," Izzy said. "Gettin' shot, that hobby I gave up."

O'Connell, prepared for this reaction, withdrew a fat bundle of cash from his back pocket. He slammed it on a nearby table.

"Quit whining," he said to the pilot. "You're getting paid this time."

Momentarily, Izzy seemed attracted to the cash; then he waved at it dismissively. "Well, that would be a helluva change of pace. . . . But I don't need your money. What do I need money for, in the middle of the desert? Anyway, I got an oasis in my backyard."

"Izzy, I'll get to the point," O'Connell said, gesturing with the golden scepter. "I have a son now— a little boy of eight. This is his mother. He's been kidnapped, and he's out there in the desert, with only a few days to live."

"That, uh . . . that's terrible. . . ." Izzy's eyes were focused on the golden scepter.

Noticing this, O'Connell slowly waved it before the grease monkey's close-set eyes, like a hypnotist's watch.

"I'm going to do whatever it takes to get my son back, Izzy," O'Connell said, softly. "And you're going to do whatever it takes to help me."

His grease-smeared hand trembling, Izzy pointed to the scepter. "You hand that gold thingamabob over to ol' Izzy, and I'll do anything you ask—hell, I'll do unspeakable things with a camel at the Cairo opera house!"

"Didn't you already do that New Year's Eve, 'twenty-three?" Grinning, O'Connell held the scepter out to the little guy. "Or was that in Tripoli?"

Izzy grabbed the Scepter of Osiris and scurried off, through the open wall of the hangar. Jonathan, making a trip with the luggage, had just staggered in, in time to see his big golden bauble disappearing in Izzy's greedy, greasy grasp.

In outraged disappointment, Jonathan dropped the bags heavily and said, "What's the idea of giving my golden stick to that blighter?"

"The idea is," O'Connell said, "rescuing Alex."

"Well, of course, but—"

Evy said, "If Rick thinks it was the right thing to do, Jonathan—it was the right thing to do."

But Jonathan didn't seem so sure, his expression that of a child asked to share his toys with a sibling.

O'Connell stepped back outside into the daunting desert sunshine, and both Evy and Jonathan followed him. From around the side of the hangar, Izzy appeared, without the scepter, wiping his grimy hands onto the blouse of his filthy coveralls.

Sidling up to the lovely Evy, the little pilot said, flirtatiously, "You know, droppin' in on me, like this . . . you're not exactly catchin' me at my best."

Sunlight reflected off the silver tooth in the yellow smile.

"Nonsense," Evy said, smiling politely even as she moved away from him, "you're positively charming, and we're very grateful to have you help us out like this."

"Damnit!" the pilot shouted.

Evy blinked, taken aback by this entirely inappropriate response to her pleasantries.

But Izzy hadn't been answering her. He was pointing a black-nailed finger at something.

Evy turned, but was not at all surprised—as this meeting had been arranged—to see Ardeth Bay, in the familiar dark turban and robes of the Med-jai warrior, on horseback, accompanied by twelve of his tribe's fellow warriors, also astride horses. All were heavily armed—rifles in saddle scabbards, scimitars and pistols at their waists. They were just sitting there, as if waiting to be noticed.

"I knew it!" Izzy said, shaking his head. "I'm going to get shot! I'm gonna get the rest of my ass blown to hell and gone!"

Ardeth Bay, dismounting, called out to O'Connell, "These are the commanders of the twelve tribes of the Med-jai."

The Arab strode forward, approaching the little group; then, planting his feet in the sand, he held out his arm, stiffly, crying out, "Horus!"

On the similarly outstretched arm of another of the Med-jai commanders sat a large, regal falcon, who at Ardeth Bay's command, took flight and flew to the Med-jai chieftain, landing nimbly on his waiting arm.

Jonathan said to the warrior, "A humanizing touch, that—you having a pet bird."

Lovingly, Ardeth Bay stroked the feathers of the falcon. "Horus is no pet. He is my best friend, my most clever friend. It is Horus who will let the commanders know of our progress, so that they may follow, at a distance."

O'Connell, nodding, said, "Good strategy."

Ardeth Bay turned toward the Med-jai commanders on horseback, touched his heart with one open palm, and then waved it, in ritualistic fashion, toward the burning sun.

"Harum bara shad!" the Med-jai chieftain called to them.

In unison, the commanders of the Med-jai made the same ceremonial sign, and, in unison, called back, *"Harum bara shad!"*

And the Med-jai warriors reared their steeds around and galloped off, horses' hooves raising clouds of sand and dust.

Ardeth Bay, watching them go, said to O'Connell, "If the army of Anubis arises from the dead, the Med-jai will do all they can to stop it."

Izzy laughed, and said to Evy, "I woulda sworn he said 'army' of the dead."

"Yes," she whispered to the pilot, awarding her new friend a small, prim smile, "such amusing notions these primitives have."

O'Connell said, "Izzy, cut the small talk—time is of the essence. Where's your plane?"

"Come and see," the pilot said, and he led them around the far side of the hangar, grinning like a proud new papa.

But Izzy's potential passengers stopped dead in their tracks, at the sight of the "plane."

"Shit," O'Connell said.

"Isn't she a pip?" Izzy asked, gesturing. "Isn't she the cat's meow?"

The pip, the cat's meow, was a gold-hued dirigible—small for a dirigible, but looming just the same. The blimp floated, held down by mooring lines, and slung to its underbelly was a decrepit fishing trawler that had seen two centuries—an airplane propeller extended itself rudely from the rear of the boat engine. No airship in the history of mankind had ever looked more jury-rigged, more handmade in the Rube Goldberg sense.

"It's a goddamn balloon," O'Connell said, walking up and down in the sand in front of the thing.

Izzy gestured like a ringmaster to his star attraction, saying, "It's a dirigible!"

"It's a goddamn balloon carrying an old fishing boat with an airplane propeller sticking out of its ass."

Izzy frowned, seeming hurt. "Rick, that's not fair. . . ."

"What happened to your airplane?"

"Airplanes are a thing of the past!"

"What happened to your airplane, Izzy?"

"I lost it."

"How can you misplace an airplane?"

"I didn't say I misplaced it—I said I lost it. In a poker game."

Shaking his head, fighting off despair, O'Connell said, "Izzy, you were right."

"I was?"

Nodding, O'Connell withdrew one of his revolvers

and trained it on the greasy little pilot. "You are gonna get shot."

Izzy held up his hands in surrender. "Whoa! Hold on, Rick! She's faster than she looks."

O'Connell pointed the revolver toward the big balloon. "Or maybe I'll just shoot that thing and put it out of its misery . . . and maybe you'll remember where you lost your plane and get us the ride we need, *now.*"

Patting the air, dancing in the sand, Izzy said, "Rick, she's perfect for this job. You got kidnappers to sneak up on, right? This baby is quiet as a shadow, perfect for sneakin' up on people."

O'Connell, considering that, holstered his revolver.

"Of course, if you stay true to form," Izzy said, sneering, gesturing toward the holstered weapon, "and go barging in, guns blazing, everybody will get their ass shot off! As usual."

O'Connell, face red not from the sun but a slow burn, said to the little pilot, "You're sure you don't have a plane?"

Izzy gestured elaborately. "Did you see one in the hangar?"

The adventurer sighed. "Then this will just have to do."

Ardeth Bay had been looking on at this conversation, aghast. A veteran of the airplane journey that had ended the life of the previous overseer of this airport, Winston Havlock, the Med-jai chieftain seemed to be speaking to the eagle on his arm when he said, "Can't these Westerners ever keep their feet on the ground?"

·❨ 12 ❩·

Desert Travelers

Over the eons, the wind and sand conspired to erase from the face of the Sahara any trace of men, covering the tracks of both pharaohs and British conquerors, consuming faithful and infidel alike, whether worshipers of the sun or the flocks of various prophets. Here a ceaseless procession of men had thirsted to their deaths, leaving their skeletons and those of their camels for bleaching by the unyielding sun under the cheerfully blue sky, the wind grinding those bones to dust to join the orange-yellow sand in the dry endless desert.

Only the night itself was more vast than the Sahara. The setting sun—the great god Ammon-Ra, in the form of a flaming crimson orb—boldly painted the barren landscape with streaks of red and purple, an impressionist masterpiece soon swallowed up by the haze of dusk. Before long, the desert floor turned a glistening black, and the sky came alive with count-less stars—Sirius, Cassiopeia's Chair, Vega and var-ious planets shining alarmingly near. A full moon dominated this glittering array, its glowing fingers touching dunes with ivory highlights.

Across that impossibly large moon glided the un-gainly motorized contraption that was Izzy's blimp, a lumbering fishing trawler somehow navigating the starry night sky.

On the deck of the boat, in the blimp's shadow, sat Jonathan Carnahan and his unlikely friend, Ardeth Bay, chieftain of the Med-jai. Jonathan—having as-certained that Captain Izzy was on the other side of this flying nightmare—was fishing . . . inside the open porthole of the captain's cabin. The golden Scepter of Osiris was on a table, inviting Jonathan's larceny.

"Your sister's husband," Ardeth Bay was saying, "is reluctant to embrace his destiny."

"Really," Jonathan said, not terribly interested, arm down the porthole, scrounging around inside.

Ardeth Bay—his falcon perched contentedly on his left forearm—nodded. "And yet O'Connell flies like Horus toward his destiny."

"How very fascinating." Jonathan, grunting, had his fingers on the scepter now—its smooth surface taunting him, denying him purchase. "But where does the golden pyramid come in?"

"It is written that no man since the time of the Scorpion King himself has ever laid eyes upon the golden pyramid, and returned to tell the tale."

"Well, if no one returned to tell the bloody tale, who told you?"

Ardeth Bay was lovingly petting the falcon, which all but purred at the attention. "It is written—"

"*Where* is it written? Who is doing all this writing? It's all bloody nonsense, if you ask me, and I'm sure you won't.... Ah! There! Got it!"

And Jonathan withdrew from the porthole the golden scepter, moonlight glancing off its shiny surface.

"Not bad, eh?" Jonathan said, displaying his prize catch to the Med-jai.

Ardeth Bay regarded the artifact with narrowed eyes. "If that curator fellow reacted to the sight of the scepter in the manner you reported . . ."

"He did."

". . . then this must be an important object, perhaps with significance beyond its monetary worth. I would, my friend, keep it close to your . . . what is the expression? Vest?"

Leaning back against the outer wall of the cabin, Jonathan hefted his prize, puffed out his chest, and said, "I'd like to see somebody take this away! The gods themselves couldn't—"

And that was when Izzy strolled by and snatched the scepter from Jonathan's grasp.

"Hey!" Jonathan got to his feet, calling out indignantly, "Come back here with that!"

Izzy turned, and held the scepter up like a club; his lip curled back over yellowed teeth, the single silver one catching a flash of moonlight. "This trinket is mine, Little Lord Fauntleroy—hands off, or you're goin' overboard!"

Izzy went along on his way, swinging the scepter like a beat cop with his nightstick. Jonathan, crest-fallen, dropped back down next to a chuckling Ardeth Bay, who sat stroking Horus.

"Well, I like that!" Jonathan said.

Ardeth Bay looked at the Britisher curiously. "You do?"

Up at the bow, Evy was staring out quietly at the sapphire sky, from time to time glancing down upon the fantastic, shifting landscapes below, the shadow of their ship chasing across the ivory-washed dunes. O'Connell—who'd been watching her from a re-spectful distance—stepped up to her side, and slipped an arm around her waist, drawing her gently near.

"How can it seem so lovely," she asked, "when it's so deadly?"

"The desert?"

She nodded, gesturing to the sands below. "When the great armies of the pharaohs moved through the hills of this desert, they perished in whirlwinds, vul-tures making carrion of them."

"Evy . . . I've never told you this, but when we first met . . . that day you and your brother came to my cell in the Cairo prison . . ."

She laughed a little, a bittersweet laugh. "I was so terrible to you."

"And I to you . . . and when we met, I had the strangest sensation . . . illogical, even crazy. I was facing death ... the hangman's noose ... and yet, meeting you, I knew I wouldn't die. I knew we were meant to be together, to share a life. So ... I wasn't afraid. I knew I couldn't die, not yet."

Now she was nodding; even smiling—still bittersweet, though.

He sighed, and said, "I felt that you and I ... well, that we had to be together. Kind of a screwball notion, huh? Maybe just a dying man's delusion."

"But you didn't die."

"No, I didn't ... thanks to you. Screwy as it all sounds ... the librarian and the legionnaire, meant for each other."

She beamed bravely up at him. "It doesn't sound crazy, Rick—it sounds ... it sounds just fine. We *are* meant to be together, darling, different as we are— we're like puzzle pieces, disparate shapes, fitting together, snugly, perfectly."

He turned her to him, and drew her close, kissing the tip of her nose. "I like your shape. . . . I like the way we fit together."

She clutched him, tight, her head against his chest, her face turned toward the sapphire sky and an infinity of stars and one moon.

"I'll get him back, Evy," O'Connell said softly, into her sweet hair. "I promise you."

Though there were tears prickling along her eyelashes, Evy said, in a quiet but confident voice, "I know you will. *We* will."

And they stood together, like that, for a very long time, as their ship sailed into the night.

162

• • •

The image of the flat Sahara was a misnomer, the desert a pathless wasteland whose perspectives were ever changing, landscape constantly milled into hills and valleys by the winds, only to be violently re-shaped by a sirocco or simoom. And yet men still invaded this shifting world, insisting on imposing permanence upon the transitory.

When, the next morning, the glorious smile of the great lord of the sun beamed from over the horizon at a train chugging on its track between giant golden sand dunes, Ammon-Ra might well have been amused by the doggedness of these creatures.

Within a tight little passenger compartment on that train—upon the top of every car of which rode armed guards—the red-turbaned warrior playing nursemaid to a certain eight-year-old boy was not amused.

Alex, seated across from Lock-nah, drummed his fingers on the windowsill and stared at the Arab, who stared right back. The boy had just asked the warrior, for the umpteenth time, that perennial question of traveling children, "Are we there yet?"

Lock-nah, unaware that his chain was being pulled, had responded, "No," on each occasion, as if the question were a legitimate, albeit irritating, one.

"Are we—" the boy began.

And Lock-nah leapt to his feet, a wicked knife appearing almost magically in his hand; the Arab hurled the gleaming weapon at the boy's drumming fingers and the blade slammed into the wood of the

163

windowsill and quivered there, between Alex's fore-finger and middle finger.

Alex sat quivering, himself. He did not complete his question—a question he would not again impose on this journey.

The boy also did not withdraw his hand from the sill, and did his best to stay calm and not betray any fear. He glared up at the cold, angular features of the Arab and casually said, "Nice aim."

"I missed."

Involuntarily, Alex's eyes widened.

Lock-nah fixed a meaningful stare upon the boy, yanked the blade from the sill, and sat back down across from him. He then began to use as the blade as a toothpick.

Alex knew the man was just trying to scare him—but what annoyed Alex was, it was working.

Glaring back at Lock-nah, the boy said, "I have to go to the bathroom."

"No."

"No? It isn't up to you, whether I have to go to the bathroom!"

The Arab's eyes were as cold as they were dark. "Having to go is your decision. Allowing you to go is mine."

"Then I'll do it in my pants. I'll just pee in my pants, and I'll tell your boss lady you wouldn't let me go to the bathroom, and they can just try to rustle up some more clothes that fit me, and—"

Loch-nah leapt to his feet again.

Alex swallowed.

But the Arab did not hurl his blade this time, rather he merely gestured toward the toilet at the rear of the car, and Alex got quickly to his feet and headed back there.

Alex opened the door and looked in at the most filthy windowless craphole this side of an Ozark outhouse.

"Maybe I *should* just go in my pants," the boy said.

"Get in there!" Lock-nah said, and shoved him within the foul cubicle, leaving the door open.

Alex, undoing the buttons of his short pants, glanced back at Lock-nah, who had stepped in behind him and was standing with his arms crossed, like an irritated harem eunuch.

Over his shoulder, Alex said, "What, are you just going to stand there looking at me?"

"Hurry up!"

Well, Alex thought, at least this bathroom had an attendant.

"Look," the boy said, "I just can't *go* when someone's watching. . . ."

"All right," Lock-nah snarled, and stepped out, slamming the door.

Alex looked around at his disgusting surroundings, then glanced into the pot itself, and almost gagged. Didn't anyone around there know how to flush a toilet?

Trying not to breathe the stench in, the boy reached out gingerly—not really wanting to touch anything in here—and yanked not Lock-nah's chain

165

this time, but the rusty one of the antiquated toilet. Turning away, he heard a flushing sound—a loud one—and looked down and saw that the way the thing functioned was for the bottom to open and spill the rinse water and waste right out onto the passing train tracks!

Alex urinated, buttoning up, flushing again, scheming all the while. He glanced back at the closed wooden door, beyond which Lock-nah waited. Then the boy grabbed onto the rusty toilet, banishing thoughts of germs from his mind, and pulled at it, finding it—as he'd suspected would be the case—to be loose.

Wrenching at the toilet, Alex pulled it off its slot enough to reveal a hole that would have been big enough for him to squeeze through. The thought of what else had gone through that hole was irrelevant: that craphole was Alex's escape hatch . . .

. . . if only those tracks down there weren't whizzing (so to speak) right by! He couldn't drop through that space without risking life and limb.

Lock-nah's muffled voice came through the door: "Hurry up!"

"I'm not finished!" the boy called, inserting a convincing grunt.

That might buy him some time. If only the train would stop, or even slow down . . .

. . . and, as if at his bidding, the brakes on the train suddenly locked up, metal screeching on metal. Alex was not aware of it, but the train had just drawn up to a stop near the temple at Karnac, its destination.

But Alex didn't have to know why they'd stopped. He didn't even think about the consequences of being a boy alone on the desert. All he knew was that escape beckoned, and via a craphole or not, he had to take it.

Shoving the rusty toilet aside even further, he dropped down through the hole, onto the tracks, kneeling down and crawling out from under the train, onto the sandy slope.

Then he saw the huge temple, with its staggering number of trunklike columns, recognizing this as the great Amon temple of Karnac. Even as he ran for his life under the relentless sun, over the hot sand, the boy knew that these were the very ruins first explored by his late grandfather, whose death had been attributed to the curse of King Tut.

Behind him, men were shouting in Arabic and broken English. He heard Lock-nah screaming, "The boy has escaped!" And—most terrifying of all—the sound of gunfire, rifle fire, raining down toward him from those guards atop the train.

Bullets ricocheting all around him, Alex dodged and scurried through the ruins, heading for the great temple. He heard something crashing behind him, but didn't know what it was.

The sound the boy could not discern was that of a boxcar door sliding forcefully open, revealing the regenerated Imhotep—his attention caught by the commotion—looking out, the lovely Meela at his side.

Hearing gunfire from the boxcar roof just above

167

him, Imhotep—in dark regal robes that displayed much of his hairless, muscular chest—leaned out, looking up at the red-turbaned guards who were shooting at the fleeing boy. Imhotep was infused with rage—his standing orders were that the O'Connell boy was not, under any circumstances, to be harmed.

Slowly, so slowly, the living mummy raised his arms. Meela watched, her eyes wide with wonder, as the golden-hued Imhotep seemed to be lifting some great invisible weight. Screams from above caused her, too, to lean forward and look up, where she saw the guards rising into the air, rifles dropping from their hands, harmlessly clunking onto the roof. Then, suddenly, the men were slammed together, in a sickening crunch of bone that silenced their screams; and flung from their perch like rag dolls into the sand and ruins.

Thrilled by this display of power, Meela embraced the arm of Lord Imhotep, who was slumping against the boxcar door, seemingly exhausted by this expenditure of psychic energy. She slipped an arm around him, lovingly, comforting him. But Imhotep—weary though he was—raised his eyes toward the limestone temple, into which the boy had disappeared.

And Alex indeed had raced into one of the great halls of the temple, looking for somewhere to hide, only to be possessed again by a vision sparked by the golden bracelet on his wrist . . .

. . . *the chamber around him as new as tomorrow, surrounded by the exquisite, delicately carved reliefs commemorating the triumphant campaigns of Phar-*

aoh Seti. Then the boy's vision raced, blurred across the desert, to another temple, the Temple Island of Philae, circa 2000 B.C. where a man . . . a muscular, large man of noble bearing . . . came striding toward Alex . . .

. . . who was suddenly back in the Karnac temple, a man still approaching, but that man was the golden-skinned, regenerated Imhotep, whose eyes froze Alex, preventing him from fleeing. Stopping before the boy, the stately mummy—unbandaged, regally robed— raised a hand to Alex.

Not to strike him—no.

Instead, Alex lifted from the ground like Peter Pan, levitating until he was at eye level with Imhotep, whose handsome face was ugly with contortion, with the effort of this remarkable act.

Then Imhotep exhaled, relaxed, and released Alex from his psychic grip—allowing the boy to drop roughly to the hard stone floor, in a human pile.

And Imhotep, grinning, almost as if proud of the boy, wagged a finger down at Alex.

"Naughty, naughty," he said, and held out his hand.

Swallowing, reluctant, Alex got to his feet, brushed off his short pants, and took the mummy's hand.

·❨ 13 ❩·

Pooled Visions

Against the brilliant orange of a sunset, Izzy's blimped boat floated high over the Nile, whose shimmering surface seemed on fire with the dying sun's reflection. For all the years, from childhood on, that Evelyn had spent in Egypt, the serene beauty of the desert, the knowing silence of the Nile, never failed to touch her deeply.

Now, as she helped her brother Jonathan pack gear in preparation for setting out on foot, she had a strange, tingling sense. Voices were calling to her—voices from the past, though not necessarily her past.

Nearby, the Med-jai chieftain and her husband were cleaning and loading weapons, making ready for the inevitable battle ahead.

"If a man does not embrace his past," Ardeth Bay was saying to Rick, "he is unprepared for his future."

"Okay," Rick said, with a sigh, "let's say I am

some reincarnated Masonic Templar. . . ."

"That is not precisely what—"

"Whatever the case. So I'm a Templar Knight— so what? What good does that do us right here and right now?"

"It is a spiritual thing. It is the missing part of you—of your heart, your soul. If you accept it, if you hold it near to your breast, you can do anything— including triumph against the approaching adversity."

"Swell," Rick said, shrugging. "Now, tell me— what kind of 'adversity' do you figure can we expect from our old friend, He Who Shall Not Be Named?"

Ardeth Bay smiled, faintly—he seemed to know he was being kidded. "Now that he is, no doubt, fully regenerated, there is no reason why we . . . I . . . should not call him by his name."

"Imhotep."

"Imhotep," the Med-jai said with a nod. "With his powers quickly returning, by the time he has reached the oasis of Ahm Shere, even the Scorpion King himself will be no match for him."

"And the Scorpion King is no pushover, right?"

Ardeth Bay frowned in confusion. " 'Pushover'?"

"A tough cookie—tougher than a whirling dervish."

"Ah—much tougher. No 'pushover,' no 'cookie.' "

Evelyn looked up from the rucksack she was packing, saying, "According to legend, after the Scorpion King gave up his soul to Anubis, he betrayed the great god, and was cursed for eternity."

"When ol' Imhotep was cursed," Jonathan said dryly, "it only increased his powers. Peculiar way to punish a person, making him stronger."

"The gods have their reasons," Ardeth Bay said, "and their ways."

"Jonathan's got a point," Rick said, as he filled an ammunition belt with cartridges. "Why do your gods indulge in these eternal curses? Why not just smite the blaspheming bastards, and let it go at that?"

Ardeth Bay had no answer, but Evelyn offered, "I can tell you this—the Scorpion King suffered a curse so vile, so horrible, the specifics were never written down, nor even handed down mouth to mouth."

Jonathan smirked at Ardeth Bay. "You mean, it wasn't 'written'?"

Ardeth Bay's expression was dark, despite being suffused by the orange glow of the sunset. "The lady is right—it has never been written . . . though it is whispered that the Scorpion King will take on some terrible, not wholly human form."

Evelyn smiled, just a little. "He's the boogeyman of Egypt—the parents and older siblings use him to tease and frighten their little ones."

That remark made Evelyn—made all of them—think of Alex, and a somber silence fell across the party. Brother and sister had finished their packing of gear, though the attention to weaponry of Ardeth Bay and Evelyn's husband continued.

She went to the bow, leaned there, looking out at the orange-tinged desert world, purple streaks mingling, now.

In the cockpit, Izzy sat, and—as Rick rose to join his wife—the wild-haired pilot caught the man's irritated expression and said, "I'm going as fast as I can! Dirty looks won't turn this thing into a rocket."

Rick nodded, moving toward Evelyn.

Behind him, Izzy called: "Rick, we'll be there before sunrise! You got my word. Cross my heart. Hope to—"

Rick looked back at Izzy.

"Well," the little man said, "cross my heart, anyway."

Joining her at the bow, Rick seemed to know that she didn't want to talk—words of assurance had done all they could. Nothing was left now but to find and rescue their boy.

But he did greet her worried look with a wink and slipped an arm around her waist, to give her a comforting squeeze. She smiled up at him, but it was a forced smile—they both knew it—and he nodded and left her alone, going back to his guns and the company of his fellow warrior, Ardeth Bay.

Evelyn did not see her husband pause, as he crouched beside the Arab, to look intently at the tattoo on the side of his hand—the pyramid formed by a mariner's compass and falcon's wings.

But the Med-jai chieftain did.

It would have interested Evelyn to know that her husband too felt some strange, prememory stirring; because right now she heard something, something that seemed to echo off the glimmering Nile . . . a chanting, in ancient Egyptian, in a too familiar, resonant, terrible voice . . . *Imhotep's voice.* . . .

When she turned toward Rick and the others, to say something, she knew at once that only she had heard the weird, rhythmic words.

Then she was leaning against the railing of the boat, in the shadow of the blimp, above the fiery surface of the Nile, weaving, almost as if drunk, or perhaps hypnotized, eyes glazing over, her body swaying, dangerously, at that rail.

At that very moment, in the temple at Karnac, in a chamber all but obscured by rolling fog, the Lord Imhotep—stately in robes that did not completely conceal his bronze musculature—stood beside a small pool, a sacred pool, over which the fog seemed to boil.

At his side was an obedient Meela, in a severely cut, gold-embroidered, deep-purple dress, with sheer sleeves and a plunging bodice that accommodated a golden bracelet—modern attire, yet redolent of ancient times.

As Imhotep raised his hands and uttered the ancient words, resonating in the chamber, Meela's eyes glazed—*just as in a craft hovering over the Nile, so did Evelyn O'Connell's*—and she began to gently weave, caught up in a trance.

Imhotep turned to her, his tone at once grave and kind, his words in ancient Egyptian. "It is time, Meela, for you to become who you were . . . and are."

Passing an outstretched hand over the foggy surface of the pool, Imhotep said, "It is time for you to remember who we were, together . . . who we *are*, together. . . ."

And, at Imhotep's gesture, at his bidding, the fog parted and on the glistening surface of the pool appeared an image from ancient Egypt, the vast limestone palace of the pharaoh.

This was the vision Meela—*and Evelyn*—saw.

"For our love," Imhotep's voice said, entering the consciousness of both women, "is a true love, an eternal love, our souls bound together, mated—forever."

In the high-ceilinged, many-pillared royal chamber of the palace, Pharaoh Seti—resplendent in his high, caplike serpent-embossed gold crown, his square goatee a black stain on his strong chin—sat upon his throne with his trusted high priest, the handsome, head-shaven Imhotep, standing beside him, the two men watching a remarkable entertainment.

A pair of apparent princesses—in headdress and golden regalia and clinging robes, their faces concealed by ornate golden masks—were engaged in a duel of sorts, hand-to-hand combat aided by tridents. Seti and his faithful high priest laughed and cheered and spurred on the sport, as the shapely young women in golden masks expertly traded blows, punching, kicking, elbowing, even backhanding each other, in a manner a skilled male warrior could easily envy. The metallic clang of the weapons, the slap of flesh on flesh, the grunts, the groans, were at once comic and erotic, and the audience of two living gods—a king and a priest—were reduced to mere men, enjoying the contest.

175

Even swept up by the vision, Evelyn knew: this was the duel, these were the contestants, depicted by the hieroglyphs on the sealed rock door in the temple at Thebes, where this adventure had begun!

One of the lovely combatants was hurled viciously to the floor, her golden mask knocked free, revealing the face of a lovely woman . . .

. . . a face identical to Evelyn's.

The comely, brutal foe who had forced to the ground this princess (with Evelyn's face) lunged forward, stopping her trident's sharp prongs an inch away from the fallen woman's pulsing throat.

The victor, the woman standing, snapped off the golden mask and revealed the beaming, beautiful, self-satisfied face of Anck-su-namun—the pharaoh's paramour, the woman for whom Imhotep would one day soon give up his life and soul to possess.

In the eyes of these women burned an unspoken rancor—the teacher, the woman Anck-su-namun (her official capacity one of instruction of self-defense), might have liked nothing better than to drive those triple spears into the neck of the princess who was her student. And the student might have liked to return the pleasure.

Yet Anck-su-namun smiled at her student and helped the slim, shapely young woman to her feet, saying, "You have improved greatly, Princess Nefertiri."

With a curt nod, the princess said, "I am honored by your praise, Anck-su-namun."

Applause rang in the marble chamber, as Seti, Im-

hotep and assorted courtiers cheered the two young female warriors.

The pharaoh stepped forward, saying, "Splendid! Splendid! You have taught my daughter well, Anck-su-namun." His loving gaze settled upon Princess Nefertiri. "Who better to protect the Bracelet of Anubis than the pharaoh's own daughter?"

The princess nodded a bow, and said, "I am your servant, father."

Then Seti turned to Anck-su-namun. "And what better protection could a pharaoh want than a queen who could guard his back from all betrayers?"

The openly sensual smile that Anck-su-namun bestowed upon the pharaoh was an insult to the princess—that her late mother would be replaced by a common concubine was an outrage! But there was nothing that could be done.

The princess hugged her father, and, with a warm laugh, Seti—a pharaoh, yes, but also a proud and adoring parent—hugged her back.

And in the embrace of her father, the princess saw, over his shoulder, the strangest look pass between the high priest and her future stepmother . . . a look that seemed knowing, personal, ripe with some private secret between them. . . .

The vision shared by Evelyn and Meela seemed to shimmer into darkness, and suddenly . . .

. . . it was night, the sky a curtain of sapphire flung with handfuls of diamonds, and as Princess Nefertiri stood upon her balcony, savoring the sweetness of the warm, Nile-touched breeze, her dreamy gaze

177

was broken by a flash of movement. The princess looked across the courtyard at Anck-su-namun's palacelike residence, where she glimpsed the familiar lithe form of Anck-su-namun slipping through a wall of drapes into her bedroom . . . and then another familiar form, the masculine, muscular, copper-hued form that was her father's high priest, Imhotep . . . and the two embraced, and kissed!

Horrified, furious, yet strangely relieved, Nefertiri drew back, not knowing what to do.

Hoofbeats announced the coming of a chariot, but the lovers in the window across the way did not hear the arrival of her father, or the echo of his footsteps striding across the courtyard, fury on his face. The princess smiled to herself, pleased that her father had found out his betrayers, sorry for the sorrow he would feel, but content that what was wrong would soon be made right, once again. . . .

The princess, turning away from this tableau, heard her father's voice, echoing across the courtyard, "What man has dared touch you?"

And, only human, she glanced back, to see how the traitorous Anck-su-namun and Imhotep would answer the accusation; but now only the concubine and the pharaoh could be seen, through the bedroom window—where had the high priest gone?

In the courtyard below, a phalanx of royal guards—who had been outrun by the pharaoh's chariot—were entering.

Panicking, Nefertiri yelled, "Quickly! My father needs you! He is in danger—hurry!"

Hands on the railing, she stared across and saw Imhotep on the balcony, something in his hand, the moonlight catching it, reflecting it—a knife blade!

Then they were stabbing him, both of them had daggers, and her father was screaming, in an agony that spoke not just of pain but treachery—and her father was on his knees now, dying, and Nefertiri was biting her fist, eyes brimming with tears and disbelief, and the cruelty continued, slashing, hacking, cleaving his flesh, as if they needed to kill him again and again and again, as the princess weaved in sickness and shock . . .

. . . and in the twentieth century, on Izzy's jury-rigged craft, against a blood-red sky, Evelyn O'Connell—experiencing these same sensations, living the memory of the long-dead princess—weaved in sickness, in shock, bobbing against the railing of the flying fishing trawler.

Rick O'Connell looked up from where he and the Med-jai chieftain were locking and loading weapons of war, and saw his lovely wife swaying, dangerously, at the rail of the ship.

"Evy!" he cried, scrambling to his feet.

But she did not hear him.

And he had not reached her when she went tumbling over the side, lost in her trace, afloat in the past, and the sky. He dove for her, grabbed for her hand, and at that moment, she snapped out of it—not in time to stop her fall, she was well over the side by then, but to latch onto her husband's hand . . .

. . . pulling him overboard with her!

179

O'Connell felt himself sliding over a rough surface, realized it was a fishing net, slung alongside the
decrepit trawler, and with his free hand grabbed hold
of a fistful of netting, catching himself and his wife,
breaking their fall, temporarily at least.

The hooks holding the netting to the old craft began to rip away from the railing, each one snapping
off—snap! Snap! Snap!

But then the snapping stopped, and the netting,
drooping, hanging down below the blimp-borne
boat, jerked to a halt, and held, as they dangled from
it, like a way too heavy earring on an overstretched
earlobe.

Evy was holding by both hands onto one of
O'Connell's outstretched arms, grasping for dear life,
her expression confused and shocked and appropriately terrified.

Straining under the weight, fighting gravity, holding on to the netting with a fist that screamed for
relief, O'Connell looked down at his wife's huge eyes
and casually asked, "Going somewhere?"

Soon, Ardeth Bay and Jonathan had hauled the
couple back up onto the deck, like two big fish, and
within minutes, they were all gathered around a barrel, glowing fire licking up from within, painting all
of their faces a warm orangish red, and Evy told them
what she had seen, and experienced.

The fright behind her, Evy seemed excited, almost
giddy. "Does this mean," she asked, posing her question to the Med-jai warrior, "that I am the reincarnated Princess Nefertiri?"

"Yes," Ardeth Bay said, not a tinge of doubt in his voice. "And the woman, Meela, is Imhotep's beloved, Anck-su-namun, reborn."

"Three thousand years ago?" O'Connell asked, both eyebrows up.

"Three thousand years ago," Ardeth Bay said, nodding solemnly.

"That makes me the brother of a princess," Jonathan noted. "I don't suppose an inheritance is involved . . . or that there are reparations to seek—"

No one bothered to respond to that, though O'Connell, gently, said to his wife, "Forgive me, dear, but . . . should you accept all of this so, wholeheartedly? So matter-of-fact?"

Her big eyes shrugged. "Why not?"

"Evy, you've been having those dreams, those visions, and—"

"Exactly! And those dreams and visions all make sense, now—they're memories of a previous life."

"You grew up the daughter of an Egyptologist— your entire life has been steeped in the facts and lore of this land. Couldn't that knowledge, and your interests, have fed these visions?"

Just the faintest bit cross, she asked, "You're saying, I'm deluded? Obsessed?"

"No . . . it's just—think of what we went through, ten years ago. The living nightmares we experienced. Why be surprised that your subconscious fed those experiences into your dreams?"

"Calling Dr. O'Connell," Jonathan said.

"Rick," Evelyn said patiently, taking his hands

into hers. "This explains everything—it all makes sense, now."

"You mean, this is why we found the Bracelet of Anubis?"

"Precisely! Princess Nefertiri was the guardian of the bracelet—which is exactly why I was led to find it."

Somberly, Ardeth Bay said, "Perhaps you were both led to find it. Surely now you believe, my friend!" He gestured with both hands to Evelyn. "Clearly your destiny is to love and protect this woman."

O'Connell shook his head, smirking. "Yeah, right—she's a reincarnated princess, and I'm a warrior for God."

"Such would be the response I would expect from you, if you were not, for the second time, seeking to do battle with a resurrected mummy."

O'Connell couldn't say much to that.

Ardeth Bay continued: "How else do you explain your wife's dreams and visions—not to mention her newly acquired combat skills? And how do you explain that you have worn, since your childhood, the mark of the Knight Templar?"

The red sky was darkening into night.

O'Connell shrugged. "Where I come from we call it coincidence."

"Where I come from," Ardeth Bay said, "we call it Kismet."

"Fate, you mean."

"Fate." Ardeth Bay put a hand on O'Connell's

shoulder. "You may say they are not the same, my friend—but in any language, in any culture, there is a fine line between coincidence, and fate."

In the temple of Karnac, at the fog-shrouded pool where she stood next to Lord Imhotep, Meela's trance had not ended at the same time as Evelyn O'Connell's.

The Egyptian woman's vision had continued on; she had stayed in the past, and witnessed—remembered—a further tragedy.

"You must go, my love," Anck-su-namun told Imhotep. "You must save yourself!"

She had seen Imhotep's priests pull him away to safety, leaving her standing alone, over the butchered body of Pharaoh Seti.

"Only you can resurrect me!" she had called to him, just before the doors splintered open and the pharaoh's royal guards, the Med-jai, had poured in, a sea of swords and spears.

She snarled a curse at the Med-jai, and plunged Seti's sword into her heart.

A shriek of agony both physical and emotional rang through the limestone temple of Karnac.

Meela's eyes snapped open, as blank as the eyes of the dead. She stood, frozen in the trace, as Imhotep—the huge obsidian-covered *Book of the Dead* in his hands—read from its forbidden pages.

Again fog parted from the surface of the small glimmering pool, and something strange, something black, something almost human, something dark gurgling from underneath the smooth surface, rose—a black sludge, an ooze that formed itself into a womanly, even comely shape, lifting itself from the pool and floating, like some strange black mirror image, until it was eye-to-eye with Meela.

Then the boglike spirit collided with the woman, covering her with its sludge, so that she was a glistening obsidian statue. Suddenly, somehow, the ooze was sucked within her body, disappearing, entering pores and orifices and becoming one with her.

Meela blinked, several times, and life came into her eyes.

She gazed at Imhotep and, slowly, lovingly, smiled.

The living mummy returned that loving gaze, and uttered, almost reverently, "Anck-su-namun."

"Imhotep," she said, with equal reverence.

"Our love has lasted longer than the temples of our gods," he told her, gesturing to the ruins around them.

"And it will last much longer," she said, "than the foolish men who would obstruct us."

They embraced, and they kissed—deeply, passionately, a kiss of humans, a kiss of gods. No longer did Imhotep's flesh rot away at a human touch; for he was now human, as was Anck-su-namun, Meela no more.

·☾ 14 ☽·

Sand Castles

Under the sapphire night sky, red-turbaned warriors led their camels through the encampment at Karnac, tents—some of them the circular, domed variety called yurts—pitched around the temple in a broken circle. Other than the stars and a Cheshire cat smile of a moon, the only illumination came from campfires and torches, shadows dancing on the hard, level limestone surfaces, flickering orange staining the stately ruins.

Alone within the temple, an eight-year-old prisoner paced in a circle, partly from anxiety, partly because—chained as he was to a thick iron stake driven deep into the sandy earth—that was all he could do.

Footsteps and the swish of robes announced someone approaching, and Alex glanced up to see a frowning Lock-nah round a limestone corner. In one hand was a tin cup in which water sloshed.

"Careful with that, partner!" Alex said. "You're spilling."

Lock-nah thrust the cup forward and the boy took it.

"It's your blood I will spill," the coldly angry Arab said, "when the time comes."

The boy looked into the cup. "What, no ice?"

Hands poised as if to strangle, Lock-nah took a step forward, his shadow falling ominously over the child, his voice a harsh whisper. "I will truly enjoy killing you. . . ."

Alex lifted up his left wrist with the ornate scorpion bracelet, jangled it, and the Arab took a step back as the boy said, "Maybe you'll get your chance, someday—but for now, Lock-jaw, you'd better be nice to me."

Lock-nah's eyes and nostrils flared; he was trembling with rage. Ever since Alex had made his escape from the train, the warrior-turned-babysitter had been suffering the ire of Imhotep.

"Or," Alex said innocently, "maybe you'd like me to tell your boss you've been smacking me around again?"

Lock-nah—emitting a sound that started as a growl, deep in his chest, and exited his lips a snarl—stormed out, cloak whirling.

Alex smiled to himself—how afraid could he be of the Arab, when the boy already had a five-day death sentence clamped to his wrist?—and turned in a circle, seeing if anyone was watching him. He had needled Lock-nah, after all, to gain some privacy.

He got down on his hands and knees and—after treating himself to a couple sips—tipped the cup, pouring water onto the sand. Sitting, legs crossed Indian-style, Alex might have been any eight-year-old boy on a beach, forming damp sand into a pliant pile, playing with it, fashioning a sand castle.

But Alex was not just any eight-year-old boy, nor was he on a beach . . . nor was he making just any sand castle.

The sun was a great gold disc grimacing midsky, blazing intensely, the desert heat fierce as an ancient curse, as Rick O'Connell—shotgun in his hands—and Ardeth Bay—Thompson at the ready—crept stealthily but quickly through the ruins at Karnac. The fine lines of delicately carved reliefs were highlighted starkly by the luminous sunlight and sharp-edged shadows of the desert climate, as the adventurer and the warrior made their careful way through these remains of grandeur. Camel dung and cold campfires and tent stake holes in the sand said that these ancient ruins recently had been an encampment of many men.

"Less than a hundred," Ardeth Bay whispered. "More than fifty."

But those men—whatever their exact number—had, apparently, moved on . . . unless they were aboard the train, which sat seemingly abandoned on the tracks, obstructing the railway Lord Kitchener had worked so hard to create before the turn of the century. And the small, well-armed rescue party who had traveled to Karnac by blimped boat were, it would seem, too late. . . .

O'Connell had to make sure. He dashed to a pillar, took cover, and with a nod signaled to the Med-jai chieftain, who returned the nod and raced across the sand, cloak and robes flapping, moving up to the silent train.

Then O'Connell followed, and as Ardeth Bay was bursting into the plush parlor car, O'Connell ran to the adjacent boxcar, its wide door slid open, both men ready for whatever they might meet . . .

. . . but meeting nothing.

The parlor car stood empty; the boxcar—elaborately, bizarrely outfitted as an Egyptian temple— brimmed with artifacts, but no people. And certainly no young boy.

Atop a small table edged with ornate hieroglyphs, the last few grains of black sand were slipping down into the lower half of an hourglass—time had run out.

O'Connell hopped glumly down from the deserted boxcar, meeting Ardeth Bay, who was shaking his head, indicating he too had found nothing, no one.

"Too late," O'Connell said, slamming a fist against the side of the boxcar, a wave of despair blotting out the desert heat. "Damnit, man . . . we're too late."

Resignedly, Ardeth Bay gazed out across the desolate Karnac complex, the grand temple, the pillars, the ruins. "We have indeed lost them. They are gone."

This was the race they had had to win—and they had lost. Now they had no idea where the Bracelet of Anubis—that supernatural map locked onto O'Connell's son's wrist—had led Imhotep and his followers next. No notion of where to look for Alex, much less how to rescue him. The shifting sands would make sure that no trail was left to follow.

Then a voice echoed across the ruins, Evy's voice: *"Riiick!"*

And hope leapt within O'Connell's breast, because that single word was not despairing, but excited, elated.

He raced across the sand, weaving through the ruins, with Ardeth Bay close behind. Evy called out again and they followed her voice into the temple, where she had gone out of desperation, grasping for any straw that might lead them to Alex . . . but the glimmer of hope on her face indicated she'd found more than just a straw.

She had found, in fact, a tie—Alex's little-boy tie, which had been draped over the arm of a statue of the temple's builder, Pharaoh Seti.

"Look," she said, smiling, pointing to the hanging tie, "at what Alex 'lost.' "

"It's a marker," O'Connell said, heart racing.

Now Evy pointed to the sandy earth that was the temple's floor—specifically, to an intricately, distinctly shaped sand castle, of sorts. But this was no kid's sand castle. . . .

"It's the Temple Island of Philae," she said.

O'Connell was grinning now, shaking a fist in the air, exhilarated, proud. "That's our next stop . . . way to go, son. Atta boy. . . . Let's go!"

189

Ardeth Bay nodded a bow, saying, "I must beg a few minutes' time before we depart."

O'Connell didn't question this; he knew the Medjai always had his reasons. He and Evy would join Izzy behind a nearby towering dune, and ready the blimp for departure.

And soon a scrap of paper with a message in Arabic was being rolled up by the Med-jai chieftain and inserted into a tiny metal tube. Standing next to his steed, with the falcon perched upon the saddle horn, Ardeth Bay held out his arm and Horus took his position between the Med-jai's wrist and elbow.

The tube was then attached by means of a magnetized tag on one of the falcon's rear legs. The bird put up with this indignity without a squawk or flap of wings.

Then Ardeth Bay, with a gesture of the arm on which the bird patiently sat, launched Horus into the sun-ruled sky. O'Connell watched as the regal falcon gracefully sailed over the temple, on its way to inform the Med-jai troops of their next stop.

That next stop—the island of Philae—on the following day proved as deserted as the temple ruins at Karnac. In fact, the only item of interest was Alex's jacket, which the boy had "carelessly" left behind . . .

. . . and beneath it was another intricately assembled temple of sand, a vista, including a conical mountain with four gigantic statues, which the absent boy's mother identified as the Great Temple of Abu Simbel.

The following day, when the blimp-borne boat

landed at Abu Simbel, again Imhotep's party had already departed; but a map in the sand—a river flowing through canyons—pointed them to a new destination: the valley of the Blue Nile.

And at each of these stops, over these three days of pursuit by air, a winged messenger—Horus—was dispatched to inform the Med-jai commanders, who were following on horseback, of the rescue party's next station. As small as the O'Connell team was, so was the Med-jai army large—ten thousand warriors strong.

But hearing a commander read the message the falcon had delivered—*"La Nile Azur!"*—sent a nervous murmuring through the warriors on horseback, for whom braving the Sahara's dangers was second nature.

The Blue Nile—the "second Nile"—was imprisoned in a canyon encircling the heart of great mountains, a ravine that could drop to a depth of five thousand feet, when it so desired. For five hundred inaccessible miles, the gorge of the Blue Nile was ruled by crocodiles, hippopotami, leopards and lions—a jungle paradise not yet ruined by man.

"Abyssinia," O'Connell said.

"You'll be seeing me?" Jonathan asked with a confused frown.

The blimp and its fishing trawler was now floating through deep canyons, following the river's twisting path.

"That's the Blue Nile down there," O'Connell said, looking over the side of the boat down into the glimmering river. Evy and Ardeth Bay were doing the same. "We're not in Egypt anymore."

"That is true," Evy said, "not in modern Egypt—but still in *ancient* Egypt."

From a rucksack, Jonathan withdrew the golden disc—the battle-banner masthead that had rested atop the Anubis chest when the O'Connells had discovered it at Thebes—and examined its elaborate bas-relief images. While the design was primarily of a scorpion, warriors with grotesque faces also stared out at him—men with the heads of dogs. And here and there were the grotesque, faintly comic, definitely horrific images of childlike figures with bared sharp teeth.

Jonathan stepped up beside his sister. "I say, Sis, quick question, before we do any sightseeing down there . . ." He pointed to the dog-headed warriors on the disc. "Who might these chaps be?"

"Anubis warriors," Evy said, matter-of-factly. "Minions of the Scorpion King."

"Ah. Mythical?"

"Mythical—or so it is thought."

"And these little fellows here, with the pointy teeth?"

"Cannibal pygmies," she said, touching one of the engraved figures with a fingertip. "The pharaohs used to catch the little blighters and bring them back to Thebes for show. Sort of ill-tempered jesters."

"Ill-tempered?"

"Very ill-tempered."

"Legendary creatures? Mythic?"

"No. Quite real—unheard-of in modern times, of course."

"Marvelous!" Jonathan said, his relief evident.

Evy was looking down at the craggy landscape below. "How ever are we going to find them in this maze of canyons?"

O'Connell slipped his arms around her. "Alex will leave us a sign, you'll see."

"But we don't have a temple to land at—we have an entire river!"

"Don't underestimate your son, darling," he said, keeping his tone upbeat, though he too had his worries. "He has a very brilliant mother."

Alex—who also had a very brave father—was closer to his parents than any of them might have guessed. Within a few miles of the blimp, the boy sat by the edge of the water, making a large design in the sand with his fingertips. He did this casually, as if he were just fooling around, goofing off . . . but he wanted to leave a sign for his parents, who he felt sure were coming for him.

In case they were tracking him over this gorge by air, Alex made the sign—a sun design ("son")—large and bold.

Finished, he leaned back to admire his handiwork, and a boot suddenly stomped on the design, erasing it angrily.

"How long have you been leaving such markers?" Lock-nah demanded.

"I don't know what you're talking about."

The warrior grabbed the boy's arm and yanked him to his feet. Lock-nah seemed about to slap Alex when a voice called out, in ancient Egyptian.

"You are very clever, my little man," Imhotep said to Alex.

Lock-nah and the child looked up and Imhotep was standing out in the Nile, water up to his knees.

The regenerated mummy continued to speak to Alex, in ancient Egyptian. "I hope your father and mother have enjoyed their journey—for it is about to come to an end. . . . They approach us, borne by a balloon—I saw them earlier, as they glided around a canyon corner. Your father is . . . your father *was* . . . a great adventurer. And your mother was a woman of remarkable beauty."

Alex trembled as Imhotep raised his arms—the mummy's strength largely regained, little effort was expended as a massive wall of water rose up out of the river.

The boy closed his eyes, opened them, and yet it was still there: a curtain of blue, hanging in the air, shimmering, waiting to do Imhotep's bidding.

Standing at the stern of the fishing trawler, O'Connell and his wife and Ardeth Bay were studying the riverbanks, looking for movement, scanning for any sign Alex might have left for them. A rumbling noise— faint at first, but swiftly building—made O'Connell think a waterfall might lie ahead.

As O'Connell turned toward the bow to look,

Izzy—in the cockpit—said, "For the luvva Pete—what the hell . . . ?"

A towering wall of water was crashing down the canyon, as if it had a mind of its own, rushing, roaring, charging right at them, reaching up toward them, pushing rocks and boulders out of its way as if they were pebbles.

"Izzy!" O'Connell yelled. "Starboard! Go right! Go starboard!"

Izzy cranked the wheel and the blimp began to corner.

O'Connell stared at the wall of water and he wasn't even surprised when a giant face formed itself within: the face of Imhotep.

Izzy had noticed this fantastic transformation, too, and was witnessing a huge watery mouth that was yawning open, and he said, "Shoot it! Shoot it! Somebody shoot the goddamn thing!"

But O'Connell—who had seen the giant face of Imhotep in a sandstorm, ten years before—knew how little good firepower would do.

"That won't work!" O'Connell told the wild-haired, wild-eyed pilot. "Try something else! Fly us out of here!"

Izzy jerked a lever and, with a *whoosh!*, flames shot out of home-made Buck Rogers–style booster rockets on either side of the trawler, gizmos that O'Connell had noticed but figured were functionless trappings courtesy of Izzy's eccentric mind.

But O'Connell was wrong: the boosters gave them

the speed, and the time, Izzy needed to make a turn and accelerate into a side canyon.

The massive watery face did not make the turn, screaming in anger as it passed, splashing into a canyon wall, the backwash drenching Izzy, mostly sparing the others.

"You just might want to take a gander at this, everyone," Jonathan said.

The others turned and had a look at the smaller ravine that Izzy had just flown them into, in time to see it empty out into an immense bowl-shaped canyon whose floor was an emerald landscape of fronds and foliage so rich and lush, this could only be . . .

"Ahm Shere," Ardeth Bay said, awestruck. "We have found the oasis of Ahm Shere!"

O'Connell snapped out his telescope and had a closer look, catching the sparkling tip of what seemed to be a pyramid . . . a golden pyramid.

"I think it found us," O'Connell said.

Behind them that waterfall rumble had begun again, and Izzy, looking back, said, "Son of a . . . *high tide!*"

Another wall of water was charging down the canyon at them, wearing the huge, crazed face of Imhotep, which seemed to laugh as its enormous mouth opened wide, ready to swallow the blimp and the trawler and all those aboard.

"Kick the throttle!" O'Connell yelled.

And Izzy did, igniting the booster rockets, flames again shooting out on either side of the boat, the blimp accelerating out over the jungle, out ahead of the hungry watery face.

That was when the booster rockets flamed out, sputtered and died.

"God's got it in for me," Izzy said, shaking his head.

And the huge watery mouth engulfed the blimp, taking it down into the jungle, where the jury-rigged vessel and all that water crash-landed.

At Imhotep's encampment—as a stunned, terrified Alex looked on—the regenerated mummy walked across the barely damp riverbed that, not long ago, had been filled with the Blue Nile.

Imhotep approached the boy, who backed up, swallowing.

But the mummy merely patted him on the head, as he passed.

·⟨ 15 ⟩·

Valley of the Dead

Ahm Shere may have been more jungle than oasis, but the sun beat down as relentlessly as if they were still trudging the sands of the Sahara. The thirsty earth had soon swallowed that massive wall of water that splashed down into the tropical tangle, having tossed the blimp and its boat and its passengers into a small clearing. Within an hour, the O'Connell rescue party was bone-dry, wilted but none the worse for wear.

The same could not be said for Izzy's cobbled-together flying machine, its blimp deflated, a limp husk on the earth, as if a dying animal had crawled out of its skin. The trawler was a torn-up mess, leaned up against an immense, towering tree, which Evy identified as a baobab.

Around them the emerald of the forest—fronds like the sharp blades of a surrounding army, festoons of wild vine draping every possible path—was shot through with other vivid colors, chiefly red and gold but also purple and shades of blue from pale to royal. The lushness of it suggested paradise; but you could be easily swallowed up here, strangled by vines, smothered in flowers.

Their supplies were in remarkably good shape, and none of them had been injured—ironically, Imhotep's watery ride had cushioned their fall, and the trawler had gotten the worst of it. Shaken, dazed, and at first drenched, the party had slowly gathered their wits and their gear. By now their rucksacks and other packs were loaded with equipment and weaponry, and the group was ready to set out.

O'Connell knew his son was all but within their grasp—they had seen the golden pyramid; and Imhotep's presence had manifested itself. The rescue was at hand.

But their eventual escape—fleeing this forest—remained at issue.

O'Connell approached Izzy, who was pacing, ranting, walking from the shriveled blimp to the busted-up boat and back again.

"Izzy," the adventurer said, "you're going to stay here and put Humpty-Dumpty back together."

"How in hell am I gonna do that?"

"I don't know. You're the pilot; you're the inventor. My job is to find my son, and get him back—and, when I've done that, I'm going to want to leave this place—quickly."

"No kidding!"

"So make it work, Izzy."

Izzy threw his hands up. "Don't you get it—this isn't a hot air balloon, it operates on gas! You got any helium on you? Any hydrogen in your back pocket?"

O'Connell shrugged. "Can't you . . . manufacture something? We're surrounded by natural resources."

"Oh, yeah, sure, we'll just refine and process some mangos and bananas. The only natural gas in this place comes from Tarzan's ass."

"Then convert the blimp to hot air."

"And how the hell am I supposed to . . ." But Izzy stopped; the wheels were turning.

Behind the pilot, Jonathan had sidled up and, over Izzy's shoulder, made eye contact with O'Connell, who gave his brother-in-law a barely perceptible nod. The two had a minor but necessary bit of larceny to perform.

"I suppose it's possible to jury-rig this thing to take hot air," Izzy was saying, eyes moving back and forth quickly, as he made assorted mental calculations.

Behind Izzy, Jonathan stepped up alongside the battered trawler. O'Connell slipped an arm around Izzy's shoulder and made sure the pilot's back stayed to Jonathan, who was in the process of plundering Izzy's damaged boat.

Izzy said, "But do you know how many cubic meters of hot air I'd need to come up with?"

Jonathan was lifting the Scepter of Osiris from the deck of the trawler.

Patting the pilot on the back, O'Connell said, "Iz, if anybody can fill this baby up with hot air, you're the guy."

"How long will you people be gone?" Izzy asked.

O'Connell's brother-in-law was stuffing the scepter into his backpack.

"I have absolutely no idea," O'Connell replied. "If we're not back by tomorrow this time, and you've got this contraption operating, come looking for us."

"Where do I look?"

"You might want to start in the vicinity of that solid gold pyramid."

Izzy's eyes lit up at the sound of the word "gold."

"All right, Rick—I'll see what I can do. But if I get the other half of my ass blown off, it's gonna cost you!"

Ardeth Bay stood in the clearing, attaching another missive magnetically to the rear leg of his beloved falcon. He stroked the bird fondly, then launched it. He watched the regal falcon fly up and out of sight over the canopy of the forest, then fell in behind Jonathan and Evy as O'Connell headed into the brush.

They had made only a little headway—O'Connell occasionally carving a better path with a machete— when a report of a rifle rang out over the jungle, followed by a shriek.

Not a human shriek: the cry of a bird.

Ardeth Bay could not know it, but Imhotep's man Lock-nah had spotted the falcon a day earlier, and had been keeping watch, waiting for its return, waiting for this moment, to shoot the winged messenger from the sky.

But Ardeth Bay did know that Horus had to be dead, or dying, and as he spun toward the sound of the shot, he called out the bird's name, his love for the creature apparent in the agony that colored his voice.

Staggering forward, the Med-jai chieftain stared into the empty blue sky, devastated.

O'Connell exchanged forlorn glances with Evy—they knew how much the falcon had meant to their comrade.

Ardeth Bay unslung the rucksack from his back and turned solemnly to O'Connell, saying, "I must go."

And with that, the Med-jai turned and began trudging in the opposite direction. Quickly, O'Connell stood in front of the warrior, blocking him, stopping him.

"I can't do this without you," O'Connell said.

"I must let my commanders know where we are," the Med-jai said. "If the army of Anubis arises—"

"First, we have to get my son back."

"My friend, I admire your son—he is a fine boy. But he is one boy. The army of Anubis threatens all mankind."

"Alex is one boy, yes—like Horus was just a bird."

Ardeth Bay stared into his friend's face; and O'Connell stared right back into the warrior's hard dark eyes.

202

With a nod and a sigh, Ardeth Bay picked up the rucksack and slung it back on. The warrior put a hand on the adventurer's shoulder.

"First," he said, "we must get your son back."

O'Connell grinned and put his hand on Ardeth Bay's shoulder. "Hey, you wouldn't want to let a Knight Templar down, would you?"

And the warrior grinned back. "I would not."

Moonlight and torches in the hands of red-turbaned, gun-bearing warriors lighted the path as Imhotep's caravan trooped through the jungle of Ahm Shere. No camels now—strictly on foot—the copper-skinned, regenerated mummy led the way; at his side strode the woman who had been Meela, but was now Anck-su-namun. Both wore dark, loose garments, and swaggered through the forest with heads high. It was almost as if the bladelike fronds made way for the princely pair.

Near the back, prodded along by Lock-nah, walked Alex, his hands tied in front of him. Brave though the boy was, he was afraid, and even showed it, a little. The eight-year-old was cowed by the jungle at night, and seized with a sense that his time was running out, the golden bracelet on his left wrist a constant reminder of that ticking clock.

Imhotep held up a hand, pausing the procession. From the branch of a tree just ahead, a large bag of netting hung, displaying its grotesque contents: human skeletons, armor-clad horrors, some still grasping shields.

The Curator, ever the guidebook author, leaned forward and said to Lord Imhotep, "Roman legionnaires . . . It should be remembered that the oasis of Ahm Shere has been called both Garden of Eden *and* Valley of the Dead."

Imhotep seemed unimpressed by this information.

And so, they proceeded, only to pause again when they passed another branch bearing a net containing skeletons in military uniforms, these European in design, perhaps dating to the nineteenth century.

"French," the Curator explained. "Napoleon's troops."

Alex took all of this in with wide-eyed, shivering wonder, properly terrified. Even the brutal babysitter seemed frightened.

"Who or what in the name of Anubis did this?" Lock-nah asked no one, and anyone.

The Arab referred specifically to several skeletons dangling from fire spits in the nearby underbrush—more recent corpses than the turn-of-the-century French ones. These poor souls had apparently been barbecued—alive?

Even the red-turbaned desert warriors wore their terror on their faces; the normally aloof Anck-su-namun gripped the arm of her lover in shuddering fear.

Of the entire caravan, only one of them showed, and felt, no fear.

Lord Imhotep.

• • •

Another small clearing presented itself, and—bathed in moonlight—the O'Connell party paused to drink from canteens, and to prepare for battle. From the rucksacks and other bags, the former legionnaire and the current chieftain of the Med-jai armed themselves to the teeth, slinging on revolvers and cartridge bandoleers.

O'Connell glanced up from loading a revolver. "Hear that?"

Ardeth Bay looked up from loading a rifle. "I hear nothing."

"That's right—nothing. Absolutely nothing. Any idea how many animals make their home in this little hothouse? And they're all dead silent."

Ardeth Bay nodded. "Never have I heard a jungle so quiet."

"This is how the desert sounds right before Tuareg warriors attack."

The two men exchanged anxious glances.

Jonathan—in the process of helping his sister load and stack rifles—spotted something in the brush nearby. Faces—he could have sworn faces were peeking out at him. He rose from his work and went cautiously over and brushed the foliage aside and looked right into the dead eyes of a dozen shrunken heads, dangling from a spiked pole.

He stepped back, frightened momentarily, then decided there was nothing to be scared of—these poor blighters weren't going to do him any arm—and pointed out his find to his companions.

"How do you suppose they do that?" Jonathan

asked idly. "Shrink those heads, I mean. Wouldn't you just love to know how they pull that off?"

O'Connell, Evy and Ardeth Bay simultaneously looked at him as if he were a blithering idiot.

Indignant, Jonathan released the leaves, covering his grisly find back up, and said, "What? Aren't we explorers? Shouldn't I be curious?"

Pouting, Jonathan returned to the weaponry and hefted a rifle, in he-man fashion.

Ardeth Bay arched an eyebrow at him. "Do you know how to handle that?"

"I should say," Jonathan sniffed. "Three times *Fox and Hound* champion."

Then, trying a fancy move with the weapon, Jonathan fumbled it, almost dropping the thing.

"Of course, I wasn't drinking, then," Jonathan admitted sheepishly.

Ardeth Bay's derisive laughter irritated Jonathan, who pointed to the scimitar the warrior was hefting. "Do you know how to handle *that*?"

"I hope I do," Ardeth Bay said, and he reached up with the scimitar and rested its blade against Jonathan's throbbing throat. "You see, the only way to kill an Anubis warrior is to cut off its head."

The Med-jai withdrew the blade, and Jonathan swallowed and touched his throat.

"Rather heavy-handed way to make a point," Jonathan said disdainfully, moving away from the warrior.

O'Connell knelt beside his wife, who was jacking a cartridge into her rifle.

Tentatively, he said, "Remember, darling, squeeze the trigger, don't pull . . . keep the barrel—"

"Don't worry, dear," she said, locking and loading. "I won't miss."

Then she leaned forward and kissed him softly, shutting him up.

Around them the jungle lay dark and still, so terribly still.

As his caravan crept through the jungle, Imhotep looked ahead, always ahead, seeking the landmark that would tell him their journey would soon draw to a close. Past further netting bags of bones they paraded, the sound of their movement the only disruption in a jungle that seemed strangely asleep, as if the presence of the living dead man, the regenerated mummy Imhotep, had sent every creature scurrying into its private, secret, silent hole.

Then Imhotep raised a hand, and the procession halted.

He could see, far off in the distance, the landmark he sought: the tip of the golden pyramid, spiking the star-flung sapphire sky. He began to smile—a wide smile, at first handsome (for Imhotep was nothing if not handsome)—but then something crazed came over that glazed grin.

Not that Anck-su-namun noticed, or the Curator, or Lock-nah, who had moved up closer to his lord, leaving Alex in the care of another warrior. These, the inner circle of his followers, merely smiled back at Imhotep, basking in the demented sunshine of a smile that lighted up the night.

Alex, at the rear of the caravan, the rough rope on his wrists burning his flesh, saw that pyramid's tip, too; and suddenly he knew he was in trouble. The bracelet on his wrist had led them to this place—but what use is a map, once you get where you're going?

In fact, toward the front, Lock-nah was whispering to the Curator—the warrior not daring to approach Imhotep directly. The dark little man in the red fez nodded to Lock-nah, then folded his hands on his belly and gazed up respectfully at his lord, who still stood staring at the pyramid point piercing the sky.

"My lord," the Curator said in ancient Egyptian, "now there is no need for the O'Connell boy."

This statement caught Imhotep's attention, and he turned to the Curator and said, also in the ancient tongue, "He is the son of a warrior—a brave boy, a smart boy."

"But he is of no further use, my lord."

"It would give me no satisfaction to see this fine spirit quelled . . . however, the pain his death would cause his father would provide me no end of pleasure." He looked at Lock-nah with a knowing grin. "Do with him as you please."

Lock-nah grinned back at his lord, and turned and moved down the caravan, even as it again began moving forward, the Arab heading for Alex.

The boy saw the warrior coming, and knew what that terrible smile meant: Alex was going to die, unless he could think of something, unless he could do *something*. . . .

He tried to bolt to one side, but the red-turbaned guard behind him latched onto the boy's shoulders, held him in place, as Lock-nah approached, hand on the handle of his scimitar.

Then the heat of the night—and the silence of the jungle—were cleaved by a gentle, whispering breeze, a wind strong enough to ruffle branches and leaves, to stir the bushes, wafting through the caravan as if a giant in the sky were blowing down on them.

The eerie breeze froze Lock-nah in his tracks.

An unearthly sound now accompanied the breeze as it swirled through the caravan, as if the wind were whistling through dry bones, a wind chime formed from a skeleton. . . .

Imhotep stopped, and he and Anck-su-namun cast their gaze around the jungle, as if trying to see this disruptive wind, bringing the procession to a halt.

The Curator—who had calmly witnessed man-eating scarabs fulfilling their purpose, who had sat reading poetry while a mummy sucked the life from three men—was finally afraid.

As the breeze mingled with the chilling bone music, the Curator swallowed and said, "Something . . . something is coming."

·❨ 16 ❩·

Jungle Fever

Rick O'Connell had the explorer's innate sense of direction, and distance, and—as the ghostly quiet of Ahm Shere was broken by the sounds of Imhotep's caravan, moving through the brush, up ahead—he knew his little group was closing in on the kidnappers of his son. And he knew his team was zeroing in on that pyramid, too, though the height of the overgrowth prevented confirmation.

Much as he hated to split up the rescue party, it had to be done. They had come upon a shelf of rock that would make a good vantage point both for surveying the landscape and for strategic placement of their limited troops. He knew both Evy and Jonathan had decent marksmanship skills, and keeping them out of hand-to-hand combat seemed desirable, as well.

So he sent his wife, his brother-in-law and their

rifles up the slope of rocks, on their way to that ledge-like perch.

Jonathan's eyes were uncharacteristically hard as he paused to look back at O'Connell, telling him, "I won't let you down, Rick."

"I know you won't," O'Connell said, and strangely enough, he wasn't lying.

Evy said nothing, not in words, anyway. Her expression, her eyes, spoke volumes.

Minutes later, O'Connell and Ardeth Bay were striding through the jungle, heading toward the rustle of brush that indicated the closeness of Imhotep's caravan, when a gentle breeze, a strange breeze, blew through, rustling foliage like wind through a window riffling the pages of an open book.

The two men froze, looking around; both instinctively knew this was something . . . otherworldly.

Then came the tuneless bone music, the clunking, chunking hellish wind chime that suggested something, someone, was approaching . . . a tribal sound. And O'Connell shuddered to think of the only tribe associated with Ahm Shere. . . .

Wind whistling around them, the hollow nonmelodic bone song in his ears, O'Connell slipped his shotgun into a scabbard over his shoulder and filled his hands with his revolvers; then he nodded at the Med-jai, who, nodding back, hefted the Thompson submachine in his grasp as that spooky wind fluttered his dark robes.

And the two men began to run.

They tore through the jungle full-bore, not worrying about who might hear them, knowing Evy and Jonathan were above them in the rocks, closing the distance between them and the caravan . . . and ready to face whatever that evil wind foretold.

Up ahead, the mummy's caravan was responding to the shouted orders, in Arabic, of Lock-nah, his slaying of Alex interrupted by the unearthly wind.

"Fan out!" the warrior was yelling to his red-turbaned underlings. "Eyes wide—guns up!"

Alex watched as Lock-nah's men spread out into the waist-high foliage, some with guns and torches in hand, others with scimitars at the ready—it was as if they were harvesting—but then one of them was jerked down into the undergrowth, disappearing as if the earth or the jungle itself had swallowed him up.

And then it was the red-turbaned men themselves who were harvested—the first to vanish down into the brush hadn't even had time to scream; the next man did have that luxury, his shriek a blood-curdling thing.

Now the warriors standing in that waist-high foliage knew they were in trouble, that they were standing in shark-infested waters, and one of them backed up, into a tree. He turned quickly, and saw something strange, something hideous, and yet childlike, lying against the trunk.

"Something here!" the warrior called out in Arabic, to Lock-nah.

But Lock-nah and the others were more concerned with the disappearance of the two warriors, and were circling around, robes twitching in the weird, bone-music breeze.

The warrior who had called out moved closer, slowly approaching what seemed now to be a withered carcass, almost molded to the trunk of the tree. Now he got a better look, and a worse one: this was the gnarled withered corpse of a pygmy, its bones bleached white, branches and vines grown through its exposed rib cage. The child body was topped by an adult-size head, with closed crusty almond eyes and a wide, impossibly toothy mouth, fangs razor sharp.

"It's . . . nothing," the warrior cried out in Arabic, even as he leaned closer in. "It's dead!"

That was when the pygmy corpse's withered eye-lids rolled back like window shades, exposing deep, empty sockets.

The warrior screamed, rearing back.

The pygmy hissed through its rotted razor teeth and a fleshless arm raised a small spear, a silly little toy spear that was nonetheless sharp—and deadly, when the tiny zombie jabbed it into the warrior's chest, piercing his heart.

His scream trailing off as he died, the warrior tumbled into the undergrowth, as the zombie pygmy yanked itself free from the vines and branches and scurried into the undergrowth, disappearing.

High in the rocks, positioned between boulders, were perched two unlikely snipers. Evelyn and Jonathan could see the strange goings-on below, watching the foliage shimmer under the bizarre breeze, seeing men pulled screaming into the under-growth. . . .

"What the hell is going on down there?" Jonathan asked, aiming his rifle at nothing.

Evelyn, settling in to take aim—thrilled to see her son alive, dismayed to have him down in the thick of it—said, "I haven't the slightest . . . but it's certainly *some* kind of hell. Remember, Jonathan, we have witnessed the impossible before—we must stay calm, and cool, and meet every challenge, no matter how uncanny, no matter how terrifying."

Jonathan, sweat beading his brow, poised at his rifle, said nothing.

"Jonathan?"

"Yes, Sis?"

"That's my son down there—and my husband. . . . You're my brother and I love you—but the time has come for you to make me proud."

Jonathan nodded, and his reply was earnest: "To-day, my darling sister, is that day."

And the ne'er-do-well brother of Evelyn Carna-han—who hadn't had a sip from his silver hip flask for hours—steadied himself at his rifle.

In the clearing below, Imhotep's caravan was in disarray, the red-turbaned warriors spooked, turning in helpless circles, their torches making orange smears in the darkness. One of them, entrusted with the precious obsidian-covered *Book of the Dead,* had not ventured out into the dangerous territory of the underbrush. But now, suddenly, he jerked forward, with a wail of pain that echoed through the night.

Spinning around, dying, he revealed the source of his pain to the others: his back was a sea of darts, deadly poisonous blow darts, sent his way from raiders lurking in the weeds.

His lifeless body had barely hit the ground when Anck-su-namun snatched the book from his limp fingers. Then Imhotep was at her side, latching onto her arm, grabbing her away, racing with his reincarnated love off into the jungle, abandoning his men, most of whom didn't even notice . . . though the Curator did.

As Imhotep fled, leaving the front of the caravan, at the rear O'Connell and Ardeth Bay came crashing through the jungle, onto the grisly scene.

At that moment, Lock-nah—obviously knowing a battle was about to ensue, with whoever was attacking from the cover of the underbrush—decided to take a moment to settle some unfinished business. The warrior withdrew his scimitar—the *shing* caught Alex's attention—and moved quickly toward the boy who had taunted him so.

Alex, eyes wide with terror, heart pounding, backed away; he was unattended now, the red-turbaned guards giving their attention to the danger in the weeds. Perhaps he could slip into the jungle, and run away—but he couldn't go into the undergrowth, the hazard of that was obvious.

As if to confirm Alex's opinion, the surrounding foliage came alive—the movement far more dramatic than mere wind could cause, even the supernatural variety—and a horrible hissing sound replaced the bone music, as spears, arrows and blowgun-driven poison darts flew out of the bushes, a rush of airborne death.

The red-turbaned Arabs—those not immediately struck by the barrage of primitive slaughter—panicked and wailed and aimlessly opened fire on their invisible foes, as if they were trying to kill the weeds.

Sprinting into this frenzy, O'Connell and the Medjai chieftain fired their weapons, O'Connell a two-gun kid with his revolvers, Ardeth Bay a jungle G-man with his Chicago chopper, cutting down Imhotep's red-turbaned minions like firewood.

"I'll get Alex," O'Connell said to his fellow human scythe, as they took time to reload; the Med-jai nodded, and the two men split off.

O'Connell could see his son, and he could see Lock-nah, scimitar in hand, making his way to the boy, who was backing up, weaving and dodging between dead and living red-turbaned warriors. It was obvious that, despite the confusion, and the raging battle, the Arab was taking the time to murder O'Connell's son. . . .

"Alex!" O'Connell cried. "I'm coming!"

Firing with both hands, he blew away one red-turbaned son of a bitch after another, carving his way closer to his boy. Pausing to reload, he did not see a burly red-turbaned bastard coming up behind him.

Alex did, crying, "Dad!"

But only at the last second did O'Connell turn and see the brute, scimitar raised to decapitate, just as the guy was blown off his feet and into the next life.

Glancing up, toward the rocks, O'Connell could

see the other half of his team, and he was damn glad he'd deployed them there. Evy and Jonathan were firing down on the clearing, steadily, unemotionally, doing their deadly job.

"Dad!"

As Evy and Jonathan took out two more of Imhotep's red-turbaned followers, O'Connell—knowing his back was covered—spun and ran toward his son.

Alex had backed up into a tree—dead-ended, Lock-nah moving in on him, less than ten feet away. The boy swallowed, looked toward the nearby underbrush, and saw a swarm of the pygmy creatures, all of them withered and white, cannibals that were no less hungry for being dead. . . .

As Evy and Jonathan continued to rain down death on the Arabs, firing round after round with emotionless precision, O'Connell charged through the chaos, a man possessed, red-turbaned warriors tumbling like bowling pins, getting out of his way.

Lock-nah's scimitar swung up—Alex covered his face with an arm, thinking, *It's all over but the funeral!*—and O'Connell was there, whisking the boy out of harm's way, even as the warrior swung down the blade, missing the child by inches. The blade thunked into the tree trunk, catching there, giving father and son precious seconds.

By the time Lock-nah had yanked the scimitar free, the Arab could see O'Connell throwing the boy up over his shoulder as he ran off. Fury raged through the warrior, and he drew back the scimitar, to throw it, taking aim at the fleeing O'Connell's back, but another blade clanged against his.

Whirling, Lock-nah was facing the chieftain of the Med-jai.

"Why not pick on someone your own size?" Ardeth Bay asked.

"A pleasure," Lock-nah said, and thrust his blade forward.

Parrying, thrusting, feinting, the two men pursued a private duel in the midst of the pandemonium, the steel of their blades singing and ringing.

Like a fullback carrying a ball, not a father his son, O'Connell charged through the foliage, running toward the jungle, intending to get his boy away from this field of carnage as quickly as possible.

Thrown over his father's shoulder like a sack of flour, Alex was getting a rear view, and he saw—emerging like ghosts from the underbrush behind them—a pair of grotesque skeletal pygmy zombies. Soon the death-white pygmies were hot on their tail, spears in hand, the massive misshapen heads on their tiny twisted bodies floating above the weeds, like bobbing apples.

"Dad!" Alex's eyes were popping. "Behind us!"

Without slowing, and in a casual manner that impressed Alex (to say the least), the boy's father spun, grabbing his shotgun from its scabbard, and blew their skeletal pursuers into flying fragments of bone and withered flesh.

At the carnage-cluttered clearing, the scimitars of the Med-jai chieftain and Lock-nah clanged and rang as the two skilled warriors battled away. The contest seemed even, until Ardeth Bay whirled and sliced, carving a deep wound in his opponent's chest.

Lock-nah, stunned, fell to his knees, a gash streaming blood across his chest like a scarlet sash.

"That," Ardeth Bay said, "was for Horus."

The warrior's eyes were filled with puzzlement and pain. ". . . Who?"

"Wrong answer," Ardeth Bay said, uppercutting him with the blade, across his stomach, finishing him.

The Med-jai did not see, coming up behind him with a revolver in hand, a hulking red-turbaned monster—the mountain of flesh that had stolen Evelyn O'Connell from her home, back in London. The man mountain might have executed the chieftain, then and there, simply and swiftly; but a shot rang out and the monster toppled.

Turning, Ardeth Bay saw his would-be executioner falling to the jungle floor, and looked up, seeing also his savior—Evelyn O'Connell, high in the rocks. They exchanged brief smiles and nods.

Ardeth Bay—knowing the boy was alive and in his father's hands, knowing too that Lock-nah was face-first in the mud, dead as Horus—fled quickly into the jungle, leaving the white zombie pygmies and red-turbaned warriors to their battle.

Up in the rocks, at her sniper's perch—seeing Ardeth Bay go, having seen Rick and Alex race off—Evelyn lowered her rifle.

"Reload," she told her brother. "Then it's time to go."

Jonathan lowered his rifle, too, and his emotionless mask dissolved into sheer frazzled exhaustion. "Thank God—killing people is simply ghastly work."

They reloaded and headed quickly down the rocky embankment.

Imhotep's minions were scurrying in various directions, meeting death wherever they turned. One group of a dozen red-turbaned warriors—their lord having disappeared from their midst—followed the only leader left to them, the small dark man called the Curator. They scrambled after him as he ran pell-mell into the jungle, their ears filled with the hissing war cry of the little zombies in pursuit. The tiny deformed creatures picked off their prey one by one, scurrying through the brush, sending arrows and blow darts and blades flying, reaping death.

A quartet of the red-turbaned warriors, running so fast they didn't see exactly where they were running, found the earth giving out under their feet—*quicksand!* As they flailed, sinking into the muck, getting sucked under, the Curator and the others skirted the area, taking more care with their steps than the unfortunate foursome had, and ignoring their pleas for help.

The pygmies in pursuit ran directly across the bed of quicksand, in an unusual, devilishly quick-witted manner: the warped creatures used the men as stepping stones across the bog, hopping deftly, nimbly from head to head, pushing the squirming, screaming victims down deeper into the sludge.

Now only a pair of red-turbaned warriors remained, with the Curator still in the lead. A swarm of the little zombies hurled themselves at the two men, tackling them, dragging them to the ground, and began to dine.

The Curator could hear the cries of the men, and the sound of the razor-sharp teeth feasting, gnawing, ripping the living flesh from the living bone of dying men.

And then he came to a thicket so dense, there was no possible passage—a dead end. Mind racing—he was a brilliant man, after all, a scholar of endless knowledge—he remembered that these creatures were, historically, the servants of the Scorpion King. He flipped through the file cards of his mind and—as the hissing of the scurrying skeletons drew closer—came upon a way, a possible way, to save himself.

The servants of the Scorpion King, the followers of that lord, indicated their loyalty, their deep faith, by performing on themselves an ancient Akkadian tribal ritual—removing the skin on their heads above the eyebrows, exposing their skullcaps.

As the pygmies approached, the Curator withdrew his dagger. His loyalty to Lord Imhotep was terminated—the regenerated mummy had, after all, abandoned him to die in the jungle. It was time for the Curator to serve a new lord, a new master—and to hope these tiny twisted minions of the Scorpion King would recognize the sacrifice he was about to make.

With one hand he grasped his scalp; with the other he placed the sharpness of his dagger's blade just above his eyebrows. And then he began to slice . . .

and to peel away flesh, to prove his fealty.

Minutes prior, in a small clearing, O'Connell paused and put down his boy. The hissing had stopped; the strange wind had ceased. Suddenly, from the jungle, came Evy, running with arms outstretched, and Alex ran to his mother, flinging himself into her arms. They stayed locked in an embrace as Jonathan, rifle in hand, also emerged from the brush.

O'Connell greeted his brother-in-law with a smile and a slap on the back. "Nice shootin', Tex!"

"Wretched work," Jonathan said, looking weary but managing a small, prideful smile. "Where's Ardeth Bay?"

"Now that Alex is rescued," O'Connell said, "he must have gone off to gather his Med-jai. Good luck to him."

A terrible scream echoed through the night—the O'Connell party didn't know it, but the scream had been caused not by the pygmy zombies, rather the painful process the Curator was putting himself through.

Dismissing the shriek as just one of many on this terrible night, O'Connell said, "Are you all right, son?"

These words seemed to snap Alex to attention; he left his mother's arms and ran to his father, grabbing him by the hand, tugging him forward. "I won't be, Dad, if we don't get going!"

"What . . . ?"

Alex lifted his left wrist, displaying the golden

scorpion bracelet. "I have to get to that pyramid—I have to get this bracelet off *now!*"

Jonathan—eyeing the valuable golden piece of jewelry—said, "Leave it on, Alex—looks good on you."

The boy gestured with both hands, turning in a circle, talking to all of them. "You don't understand! Imhotep said this thing will kill me if I don't get inside that pyramid before the sun hits it—that's tomorrow . . . *today!*"

"Oh, my God," Evy said. "That *is* the legend. . . ."

"It's close to sunup now," O'Connell said hollowly.

Faint but building, that horrific hissing sound was on them again—the little zombies were coming . . . in a hurry. Hungry again.

"Time to go," O'Connell said.

·❨ 17 ❩·

Curse of the Golden Pyramid

O'Connell held out his hand and Alex took it, and father and son tore off down a vine-draped pathway, in the direction of that golden pyramid, whose tip peeked tantalizingly above the emerald roof of the jungle against a night sky whose darkness threatened to fade into morning. Evelyn and Jonathan were right behind them, branches snapping, leaves underfoot crinkling, fronds pushed away, rustling.

Moving up behind them, in an appalling wave, came the pursuing pygmies, their hissing war cry mingling with the clatter and rattle of spears and tribal trappings and a crisp crunching that represented the bony limbs themselves of the skeletal creatures, living fossils whose very joints screaked, whose arms and legs and feet creaked like a thousand rusty gates.

Then the horrific horde of gnarled big-headed little men burst through the foliage, coming up fast, and

Jonathan and Evy at first tried to fire back at them, but the process only slowed their escape, and blasting a few of them would not prevent the insectlike swarm from overtaking the O'Connell party, and stripping the flesh from their bones in seconds.

Evelyn threw her rifle into the horrid horde, causing a couple of the creatures to stumble, and Jonathan followed suit—both were glad to be rid of the weight of the weapons, wanting to run ever faster—and O'Connell, too, hurled his shotgun back into them, taking off a pygmy head like a withered apple from a branch.

Either they had gotten off the pathway, in their haste, or the pathway simply gave out, because O'Connell and his crew now found themselves in ever thickening foliage, a denseness of brush that slowed them down—but would do the same, O'Connell hoped, for their tiny pursuers.

Jonathan soon got himself separated from the others—though he could hear them, smashing through the brush, just not *see* them—but he did see someone else, one of the red-turbaned warriors, in fact one of the fellows who had invaded his guest room back in London. The two men, running like hell, exchanged tiny frowns of recognition.

"Bloody little beggars!" Jonathan said to the warrior, who nodded in agreement. Not long ago these two would have been trying to kill each other; but now they were allies in fear and flight.

Suddenly they found themselves bolting into a clearing, a small one littered with white stones and

225

little earthen mounds, perhaps twenty feet across. As they dashed across it, Jonathan—who had picked up a certain amount of scholarship by osmosis, courtesy of his learned sister—brightened.

"I say," Jonathan said, "this is a sacred burial ground! We'll be safe on the other side—those buggers will never cross it!"

"Are you sure?"

"Quite sure!"

And the two men stopped on the other side of the burial ground, hands on their knees, breath heaving, grateful for at least a moment's rest.

A moment later, a single pygmy burst from the forest, and with no hesitation whatsoever sprinted across the burial stones with a spear lifted high. Jonathan took off running, but the red-turbaned warrior wasn't so lucky, the little white skeleton scampering up and thrusting the spear into his heart.

"Frightfully sorry, old boy!" Jonathan called over his shoulder to the stunned, dying man. "My mistake!"

He could hear voices—his sister's voice, O'Connell's as well—to his left, and, despite the denseness of overbrush, he pushed through, that hissing war cry and rattle-clatter of spears and bones coming up right behind him.

Shortly Jonathan found himself at the edge of a deep ravine, the bottom of which—assuming there was one—was not apparent, as a tangle of branches and vines obscured the view.

"Over here!" O'Connell's voice called.

And Jonathan saw, just down a ways, the rest of the O'Connell party on the other side, having used a huge log that served as a bridge over the bottomless drop. That hissing was building, as if all the pots on all the stoves in the world were boiling over. . . .

"Wait for me!" Jonathan cried.

Then the creatures were right behind him, waving spears, hissing their dire intentions, as he raced across the log, toward O'Connell, who was fishing something out of his shirt—a stick of dynamite! Half a dozen of the bony little bastards were in back of Jonathan, crossing the tree-trunk bridge, moving somewhat slower than usual, walking the tightrope that was the log.

As Jonathan threw himself from the log onto the ground, O'Connell—the fuse lit an inch from the dynamite—stepped out and, as if he were playing catch with a child, lobbed the lighted stick to the first little white walking skeleton.

Reflexively, the kid-size creature caught the fizzing red stick, looked at it curiously, as if trying to determine if it were food, and—the O'Connell party having already turned tail and fled—the ensuing explosion blew not only the lead zombie but the other five into pygmy powder.

They ran, and ran, and then they ran some more, until—once again—the hissing and clanking receded, and disappeared. When they emerged into another small clearing, they stopped, breath heaving, muscles aching. Because he'd stayed behind to toss that stick of dynamite, O'Connell was the last to enter the clearing; he, too, was breathing hard.

"All . . . all right," he said, "I think . . . think we lost 'em."

As if on cue, zombie pygmies moved through the foliage, all around them, at the edge of the clearing, encircling the hapless rescue party. Dozens of eyeless sockets stared them down, big heads bobbing on tiny twisted bodies, spears and shields and daggers and their very bones rattling and clanking, making discordant xylophone music.

And most of all—worst of all—the hissing . . . that snakelike sibilant sizzle emanating through fanged teeth from each skull head. What had been a war cry now somehow conveyed hunger . . . these nasty children were lining up for supper, or breakfast.

The O'Connell party formed its own circle, backs to each other; they were afraid, yes—but they had spent much of this long night doing battle, and were preparing for the worst, ready to go down fighting. Weapons in their hands, the small group of full-size human beings—faces clenched in determination— seemed to give the horde of tiny undead momentary pause.

Just momentary pause, however—one of pygmies, perhaps seeking someone his own size, lurched forward, brandishing a spear, hissing horribly, racing straight at Alex. O'Connell was moving to protect his boy, who held up his hands in front of him, like a boxer, ready to defend himself . . .

. . . when the skeletal white creature skidded to a stop.

The hissing it made turned fearful, and the little zombie cowered, backing away.

"The bracelet," O'Connell said, father and son exchanging glances.

"The Bracelet of Anubis!" Evelyn said, eyes bright. "They fear it—they fear the Scorpion King!"

"Like all good children in the land of the Nile," O'Connell said. "Hold it up, son—let all our little pals get a good look."

Grinning, Alex stepped forward and held his wrist high, moving in a circle, giving everybody in the audience a gander.

Now all of the monkeylike creatures hissed in fear. However loathsome the sound—and it made the O'Connell party's flesh crawl—the hissing signaled surrender, or at least retreat, as the little white zombies backed away in fear and reverence, disappearing into the jungle from whence they'd come, the hissing dissipating like a faucet shut slowly off.

The unlikely survivors allowed themselves a few moments of shock and relief.

"About time that bloody thing came in handy," Jonathan said to his nephew, nodding to the golden bracelet.

"The bracelet!" Evy said, and looked up.

From this clearing they could make out both the surrounding mountains, at their left, and—poking over the trees—the diamond tip of the golden pyramid, perhaps half a mile away, to their right.

"Oh, my God," Evy said.

The sun was about to crest the east face of the mountains.

Again, father held out his hand to his boy, yelling, "Come on, son!"

Their breath barely caught from the last chase, the two again ran like Olympic sprinters through the foliage, blasting through the jungle as if fired from cannons. Few athletes could compete with Rick O'Connell's physical prowess and, as for Alex, he was young and energetic and O'Connell's son. These two should have been able to win any race on earth . . .

. . . with one exception, perhaps. The sun was cresting the mountains, as O'Connell noted with a hurried look over his shoulder. He knew, all too well, that sunlight would momentarily begin its sweep across the canopy of the jungle in a great, inexorable tide, painting the emerald leaves as gold as the golden pyramid itself, soon to light that pyramid with God's torch, and send glittering rays of reflecting gold across the landscape—even as the pyramid's curse sucked the very life from an innocent boy.

And then they were in a clearing, the great golden pyramid just ahead, a ramp bordered with lions of solid gold, keeping silent guard, pointing the way. Behind them the sun, chasing them with deadly indifference, drew closer, closer. . . .

Alex, exhausted, his gut cramped with pain, stumbled, collapsing to the sand. His father, not missing a step, the night gone, morning all around, scooped up his boy with both hands, held him in his arms and ran for his son's life.

O'Connell, precious cargo in his arms, vaulted up the ramp, past the golden lions, and hurled himself and his son through one of many entryways.

Half a second later, the sun touched the tip of the golden pyramid and the entire golden structure flashed with blinding reflected sunlight.

On the temple floor, in a pile, lay father and son, panting, wrung out like rags. Finally O'Connell, still breathing heavily, sat up and leaned over and pulled his son close to him, hugging the boy. The hard-bitten explorer's eyes were closed, and moist, as he held his son and thanked his God.

Then he held Alex away from him, grinning at the boy—and he ruffled his son's hair.

"Oh," O'Connell said. "I'm not supposed to do that."

Alex, smiling back at his father, was shaking his head. "It's okay, Dad . . . really, it's okay."

"Not always easy, being a father."

"I know . . . but you're not so bad at it."

Father and son hugged again, an embrace unashamed of the emotion it displayed. In the midst of the clinch, the golden bracelet on the boy's wrist popped open, and fell with a metallic clunk to the limestone floor.

Alex picked up the precious artifact and flung it disgustedly away, across the entranceway.

As father and son were getting to their feet within the pyramid, they could be seen, in the open entranceway, by Jonathan and Evelyn, who had done their best to run after O'Connell and Alex, but could not keep up. Staggering into the clearing, brother and sister smiled at each other, warmly, thrilled to see that Rick and Alex had won their race against the sun and the pyramid.

And that pyramid—what a wonder! Jonathan, exhausted as he was, felt the familiar stirrings of greed within him as he craned his neck to take in the staggering sight of the huge, light-reflecting golden monolith, its diamond crest winking at him, daring him to come get it.

He was slow to react to the sound of movement from the foliage behind them, and when he turned— his sister had also turned toward the noise—a beautiful woman with blunt-cut Egyptian bangs and gold jewelry and dark robes stood before them, as if she had materialized.

In one hand, tucked under her arm, was the obsidian-covered volume of *The Book of the Dead.*

In her other hand was a dagger, raised to strike.

Which it did, swinging around, plunging into Evelyn's stomach!

As his sister doubled over from a pain as sharp as the blade Anck-su-namun was now withdrawing, Jonathan tried to catch his sister, but failed—she crumpled to the sandy earth, clutching her stomach, face tight with agony, blood oozing from between her fingertips.

The evil wench who had done this terrible thing was standing before him, laughing, in her hand the blade that dripped with his sister's blood. Enraged, Jonathan reached for his sidearm, but then another form, also as if materializing from the forest, slid between Jonathan and his sister's attacker: Imhotep!

The regal regenerated mummy reached out a hand, took Jonathan by the throat, and hurled him across the clearing, against the stone rampway. Jonathan, blinded by pain, dazed with sorrow, lay slumped there, the solid gold lions looking down on him in stately detachment.

Evy had made no sound, let out no cry, when the dagger struck so surprisingly; and it took the sound of Jonathan, flung against the ramp, to alert O'Connell. He saw his wife, on the ground, her stomach crimson, with Meela—Anck-su-namun—standing over her, her hand filled with the dagger, dripping rubies.

He screamed in protest as he flew from the pyramid, down the ramp, past the fallen Jonathan, Alex following. Imhotep and Anck-su-namun ran in a diagonal path that skirted the oncoming O'Connell, and took them to another rampway, up inside the pyramid—the beautiful attacker pausing to blow the bewildered Alex a cruelly ironic kiss before disappearing inside, *The Book of the Dead* snug under an arm.

O'Connell would deal with them later—now he knelt over his lovely wife, her face a mask of hurt as she lay curled fetally, hands trying to keep the blood in. Gently, he rolled her onto her back, ripped open her blouse, to see the wound . . .

. . . which was deep, gushing red, obviously mortal.

"God, no," O'Connell said softly. "No, no, this isn't happening . . . this *can't* happen. . . ."

But it was—and he knew, and Evy knew it. Her eyes knew it. Frantically, O'Connell covered the wound with the shredded blouse, holding on to it, applying some pressure.

Jonathan, coming up, said, "Is she . . . how bad . . . ?"

Alex, close by, said, "Dad—can you help her? Please help her!" .

"Son, you need to stay back—please stay back! Jonathan . . . keep him away from this."

Jonathan put his arm around the boy, affectionately, protectively, firm enough to hold him in place.

"She's all right, isn't she, Dad?" the boy asked, hope and despair battling in his voice. "Mum's going to be fine, right?"

O'Connell looked down into his wife's face, her lovely face, and her weak eyes.

"You're gonna make it, Evy," he said, keeping pressure on the wound. "You're strong. You hold on."

She shook her head—a small, terrible gesture.

His mind whirled with desperation; he'd left his rucksack behind, somewhere in the jungle, trying to lighten his load when those pygmies were after them. "Jonathan . . . see if we have any . . . she needs . . ."

Evy was trying to speak.

Touching her lips with two gentle fingers, he said,

"No . . . no, don't say anything. Save your strength. Listen . . . I have medical supplies in my rucksack. . . . I'll go find it . . . just stay here, don't speak, stay awake, stay alert, and—"

"Hold . . . hold me," she whispered.

Swallowing, he held her, held her close, so close even the Grim Reaper couldn't pry them apart. "Baby . . . baby . . . what can I do? How can I help you?"

Her lips were against his cheek. She whispered, "Take . . . take care of our . . . son."

The boy who had been through so much—who had kept a stiff British upper lip, who had met every challenge, greeted every danger, with all-American fortitude—began to weep, to sob. All of it finally poured out, as his mother lay dying a few feet from him, and his uncle held him close, very close.

Choking back tears, the hard-boiled adventurer held his wife away from him, just a little, so he could see her, so he could hold her eyes with his. He caressed her face with a blood-smeared hand and said, "Don't you dare leave me—we have so much left to do. I need you so much."

She summoned enough strength to bestow him a last smile, and uttered, "I love you."

He kissed her, gently, and in the middle of the kiss, she died.

He held her away from him, looking into those blue eyes one last time, the sparkle gone from them now. Gently, he closed them; she was still in his arms, and he held her tight, hugged her tight, but the Reaper had won just the same.

"Give me your jacket," O'Connell said numbly to Jonathan, reaching out a hand.

Swallowing, Jonathan complied.

Tenderly wiping his wife's blood from his hands on the jacket, O'Connell placed the garment over Evy, covering her with it, intending to cover her lovely face as well; but somehow he couldn't quite bring himself to do it. Instead, he snugged it under her chin, gently smoothed the khaki over her chest, like a parent tucking a child in for bed.

Then he stood and looked at his brother-in-law and his son—a hard steady gaze that demanded they obey, as he said, "Stay here—both of you. Stay with her."

Alex, clinging to his uncle, nodded; Jonathan nodded, too.

After one last bittersweet glance down at Evy, O'Connell—jaw muscles tensing—turned toward the pyramid, and strode forward.

Seeing O'Connell's stone-hard expression almost made Jonathan shudder—almost made him feel sorry for the bastards who would be on the receiving end.

Almost.

·❦ 18 ❧·

The Scorpion's Key

Within the temple, near the entranceway—when Rick O'Connell was still bending over his slain wife—a small dark figure bent to pick up the golden bracelet, which had been discarded by O'Connell's boy as if the object were not beyond price.

To the Curator—eyes aglow with near insanity and unbridled scheming, the skin above his eyebrows gone now, leaving exposed the red-stained white of his skull—the Bracelet of Anubis was the key to everything . . . a literal key.

He knew that to release the Scorpion King would set a course from which he could only benefit—whichever master won the clash, he would serve, and he would be of a new ruling class in a new world of ancient ways. He was, as the infidels would say, hedging his bet.

He snapped on the bracelet.

The man who had written the British Museum's Egyptian collection guidebook was nothing if not a scholar—even if now a half-demented one with the skin sheered from his forehead and eyes wilder than a rabid hyena's—and he knew his way around the interior of the golden pyramid as if he had been here often.

Glancing from time to time at the scorpion-embossed bracelet on his wrist, he passed through golden passages—the walls of gold shrouded in fungus and mold—using a torch to light the way. Soon he was in the keyroom itself, solemnly stepping up to a bas-relief formed out of human skulls and bones, exquisitely if hideously embedded into an elaborate design on the golden wall.

That design depicted a large, ominous scorpion—a bigger version of the one on the Curator's wrist—but in each of the bas-relief scorpion's claws was a hand-size golden close-quarter combat weapon—removable, functioning weapons. And the mouth of the scorpion gaped wide—a recession, a hole . . . a keyhole?

The Curator could only guess—scholarship did not cover this. He studied the bracelet on his wrist, then looked at the mouth-hole in the bas-relief scorpion, judging its shape and size.

Then he boldly thrust his arm into the hole, up to his elbow, and twisted his hand until the bracelet took hold in the passage, a human key in a golden lock. Looking at the bas-relief, it was as if the scorpion had swallowed his arm, which was disconcerting; but the Curator had come this far, and the bracelet seemed to have clicked into place. . . .

The dark little man shrugged, and turned his arm in the lock as if it were indeed a key.

The reaction was immediate: a vaporous charge spread out from the hole, around his arm, and a crackling electrical charge hummed and passed across the entire room in a flickering blue wave.

He felt only a mild throbbing—no pain—and looked around in wonder: the process had somehow cleaned the golden walls of their mold and fungus— the keyroom was a gleaming chamber of gold again! For the first time in countless centuries . . .

Unknown to the Curator, that vaporous blue lightning had travelled beyond the keyroom, throughout the rest of the pyramid.

Not far away, O'Connell—shirt shredded from the jungle chases, face smeared with dirt, hands stained red with Evy's blood, eyes hard and cold—crept through a tunnel, unarmed but for a torch, noting the fungus- and mold-cloaked walls. He reared back as the electrical storm clinging to the walls came rushing by him, wiping the golden walls clean in its wake.

The interior of the golden pyramid was soon new again, shining as it must have shortly upon completion, in the time of the Scorpion King.

His torchlight now bouncing blindingly off the glistening walls, O'Connell passed through an archway into the gleaming keyroom, where the Curator struggled, trying to withdraw his arm from the scorpion's mouth, the key caught in the lock.

Eyes widening at the bizarre sight of the skull-bared Curator, O'Connell said coldly, "That's a new look for you, isn't it?"

"You're too late, O'Connell!" The eyes under the red-stained bone were wild, crazed. "I have released the army of Anubis! Lord Imhotep shall soon take command!"

"He'll have to do it from Hell," O'Connell said, "because that's where I'm sending him."

O'Connell eyed the array of weapons that the bas-relief scorpion—in whose mouth the Curator's arm was still stuck—offered up, like a buffet of carnage. He selected an ancient battle-ax with a double-bladed head. The Curator was continuing his struggle to regain his hand, when O'Connell gave him a terrible smile, raising the ax above the man's arm.

"Maybe I can help," he said.

"No!" the Curator said.

But at that moment the Curator was thrust hard against the golden wall—not by O'Connell, but by someone or something on the other side, his arm yanked forward, bringing him flush to its bas-relief surface.

"Something's . . . grabbing at me!" the Curator said. "Little hands! Little hands!"

"Remember our cute friends in the jungle?" O'Connell said, grinning at the Curator, relishing the man's dilemma. "Ever consider this might be their house of worship? Maybe they take offense at intrusion."

"O'Connell, help me!" The Curator was using his

240

other hand to try to push himself away from the wall, but with no apparent success, his eyes wide with terror.

And then he began to scream, a scream so bone-chilling that even in his numbed state, O'Connell was taken aback.

An all too familiar hissing sound was accompanied by other hellish noises—teeth ripping, biting, chewing, bones crunching, as if greedy children were making a drumstick meal out of the man's arm.

Horrified, if not exactly unhappy with this bastard's fate, O'Connell backed away, just as the Curator ripped his arm free—or what was left of it, anyway. Under his torn robe there was only a gushing bloody stump. Weaving drunkenly, the Curator—who in hedging that bet hadn't factored in the hungry little cannibals—staggered off down a tunnel, screaming in agony.

O'Connell couldn't have helped the man if he'd wanted to: the poor son of a bitch would surely bleed to death, soon enough.

He backed out of the keyroom, battle-ax in hand, seeking Imhotep and the witch who served him, wondering just what exactly that fool Curator had unlocked.

Elsewhere in the golden pyramid, the man, the creature, sought by O'Connell—Lord Imhotep himself—strode regally down a stairway of sand, the beautiful Anck-su-namun (Meela was as dead as Evelyn) at his side, *The Book of the Dead* tucked under her arm, rulers seeking their next kingdom.

But the mummy did not see—and had he seen, might not have given it any particular consideration, anyway—a golden crest at the bottom of that stairway, embedded in the limestone floor. And so he stepped right on the crest, which was embossed with the image of the jackal-headed god, Anubis.

Energy surged through him, crackling electrically, and his copper-skinned, muscular body was seized by a spasm—he was held there, a prisoner of the pulsing power, helpless.

Anck-su-namun hopped to one side—she had not stepped on the crest—and watched in amazement and horror as Imhotep howled in rage, crackling blue bolts of energy veiling him.

Then, as if a switch had been shut off, the surge ceased, and Imhotep staggered forward, stunned, leaning against a pedestal.

"My lord!" Anck-su-namun cried, at his side now.

He was breathing hard, hunkered over. "I feel . . . I feel as if the very spirit has been drawn out of me."

"Oh no, my lord, my love . . . that is impossible. . . ."

Swallowing, trying to regain his dignity, and his balance, Imhotep straightened. He looked at the vase on the pedestal nearby and raised his arms, summoning his telekinetic powers.

But the vase did not rise, despite Imhotep's greatest efforts; it barely moved—simply shuddered. That was all.

The mummy leaned against a golden wall, exhausted, devastated.

"What has happened, my love?" Anck-su-namun asked.

He began to laugh—a raspy, almost maniacal cackle that echoed in the chamber. "It would seem the great god Anubis has diminished my powers."

"Why?"

"Perhaps so that the Scorpion King and I might fight as equals."

"Are you . . . just a man, my love?"

"No! Never. I am Imhotep. High Priest of Osiris. Grand Vizier of Zozer. I have died and lived again . . . and again. No, I will face the Scorpion King— and I will triumph."

She grasped his arm. "We will triumph, my love!"

Up ahead was an eerie, mist-shrouded gateway.

"I must go on from here by myself," Imhotep said.

Frightened, she clung to him. "No! Do not leave me here!"

"I must. I must face the Scorpion King alone."

"You must not, my lord! Without your powers, he might kill you!"

"And what of it?" He plucked the obsidian-covered book from her grasp and held it up, eyes glittering. "If he does kill me, my love . . . you will resurrect me!"

Terrified, Anck-su-namun shook her head. *"Niy!"*

Placing the book on a nearby pedestal, Imhotep took his lover in his arms, and kissed her passionately—she clutched him, returning the kiss, sealing it with desperation.

Then the handsome mummy pulled himself away from her and strode off through the gloomy gateway, over a small stone bridge, toward rock formations beyond—a cavern.

"Niiy!" she cried, lunging forward—but she did not follow.

Heart hammering, she went to the pedestal and the volume Imhotep had set there; she put both hands on its rugged obsidian surface, praying to her gods that she did not need to invoke *The Book of the Dead.*

Outside, in the clearing, not far from the ramp into the pyramid, Jonathan and Alex were kneeling over Evelyn's corpse. The boy had not stopped crying, and Jonathan could not blame him—though he had managed to hold in his tears, Jonathan felt ravaged, ruined, so desperately alone.

He took his nephew into his arms, held the boy tight. "Try to think of it this way, Alex—your mother is in a better place. Like the good book says—"

The boy's tears ceased. "What?"

"The good book. Like it—"

Alex jerked himself away from his uncle; his eyes were burning, moving side to side in thought. "That's not the book we need."

"What on earth are you talking about?"

"I've got an idea, Uncle Jon." The boy leapt to his feet. "Come on, help me get Mum—we're going inside that pyramid."

"What are you—what . . . ?

Alex was bending over his mother, lifting under her shoulders. "Help me pick her up! We have to get her inside that temple."

"But . . . your father said—"

"He's not here," the boy said, "and, trust me, Mum doesn't mind."

And the eight-year-old and his uncle—with a solemnity tinged with desperation and even a little hope—lifted his mother's corpse and carried it . . . carried *her* . . . up the ramp and inside the golden structure.

Beyond the lushly green Ahm Shere, the desolation of the desert waited, and at the crest of a golden dune, throwing shadows thanks to the low-hanging morning sun, so too waited ten thousand Med-jai warriors on horseback. They had heard the legend of the black sand, and Bedouins along the way had pointed the commanders of the Med-jai to this place, near la Nile Azur, the only signpost they'd been given.

Their twelve commanders were perched upon the highest dune, facing a dune nearly as high—consisting entirely of black sand.

As the Med-jai waited and wondered, a man on foot approached—a bearded warrior in the dark robes of their tribe, their chieftain, Ardeth Bay. They rode down to him, providing him a horse and, though his exhaustion was apparent, their leader soon took his place at their head.

Astride his steed, Ardeth Bay pointed across the

245

desert dunes at the reflective tip of the golden pyramid, the direction from whence he had come.

"We go there to seek the army of Anubis," the chieftain said to the twelve commanders of the Medjai tribes. "The Scorpion King will soon wake, and we will face the dog-headed monsters."

Next to him, Ardeth Bay's second in command asked, "But what of this mysterious black sand? What is its meaning?"

At that moment, the vaporous charge of energy—begun by the ill-fated Curator's insertion of his arm into the scorpion's mouth—reached beyond Ahm Shere, its blue energy waves rushing up and over the sand, stopping at the black dune, as if this were its destination, crackling, jumping, snapping, the shimmering landlocked lightning covering its surface like a blanket of electricity.

Then the energy seemed to have been sucked within the black dune, and the desert was silent again, the faintest whisper of wind flicking at the warriors' robes.

Ardeth Bay's eyes narrowed. He looked at his second in command, whose eyebrows were raised. What had they just witnessed?

"We must go to Ahm Shere," Ardeth Bay said, about to nudge his heel into his horse to begin the ride . . .

. . . when he sensed something strange in the air, something terrible, and his eyes traveled to the black dune just across from them, and he watched as the dark sands seemed to come to life, writhing forms

246

taking shape within the dune, terrible forms.

In seconds the black sand had formed itself into thousands of Anubis soldiers, alive again after thousands of years, fiends with canine heads and exo-skeletons overlaid with striated muscle, shields and spears and scimitars at the ready, eyes aflame with a centuries-old lust for blood.

"It would seem the Scorpion King," said Ardeth Bay, "has awakened . . . and so has his army."

Where the black dune had been was now an army two thousand warriors strong, waving their swords and spears, shrieking wildly, nothing human in those war cries, taunting the Med-jai, daring them to battle.

Ardeth Bay raised his scimitar and ten thousand Med-jai followed suit. Though they faced an other-worldly foe, these desert warriors were fiercely determined, unafraid to die for their cause.

An Anubis commander screeched a command, and the ghoulish army charged forward, racing across the sand; Ardeth Bay yelled a command, and his warriors on horseback galloped forward, down the dune. Soon the opposing forces collided at the base of the dune, crashing into each other, horses whinnying, metal whacking against metal, blades swinging, blood splashing, limbs, heads flying.

Any exhaustion from the long night prior evapo-rated in a flood of adrenaline as Ardeth Bay set the standard for courage, cutting down Anubis soldiers like kindling, decapitating them, always decapitating them, as there was no other way to kill the beasts.

All around him his Med-jai did him proud, battling the fearsome creatures to the death.

When one of the vicious demons dragged him down off his mount, Ardeth Bay stood toe to toe with the jackel-headed warriors, scimitar flashing, slashing.

Soon it became clear that the Med-jai were triumphing. Despite the almost insane, suicidal ferociousness of the beasts, Ardeth Bay's warriors vastly outnumbered them, perhaps five to one.

And before long, the last of the creatures went down, headless, defeated, dead.

The Med-jai had taken few casualties, considering the fierceness of these foes, and a resounding cheer went up across the desert battlefield as they stood victorious in the blood-soaked sand. But Ardeth Bay—surrounded by his commanders, who felt the same as he—knew this had been too easy. They were at war with the undead . . . surely this was not yet over. . . .

The chieftain heard something and was about to silence his men, when the sound built and the cheering stopped, without any prompting: their ears perked to a clanking of armor, of swords and shields, the distinctive sound of troop movement.

Holding up his hand for his men to maintain silence, Ardeth Bay dashed up the dune and took a look over the rise . . .

. . . and saw a contingent of perhaps fifty thousand Anubis warriors.

Now it was the Med-jai who were outnumbered five to one—at least.

"Allah save us," the chieftain whispered.

The massive horde of dog-headed soldiers, shrieking the wildest war cry imaginable, came careening around the dune, scimitars and spears high, heading for the Med-jai, already weary from doing battle with such creatures. It would be a slaughter—a quick one.

But Ardeth Bay—raising his sword high—screamed his own battle cry, a warrior to the bitter end.

This gave his fellow Med-jai courage to face such fiendish foes, to challenge certain death, and their swords too were raised high, and their battle whoops joined his, as they charged forward, even as the Anubis warriors raced at them, wolf-teeth bared, weapons at the ready, shrieking like the animals they were.

As the distance closed from one hundred yards to eighty to sixty to fifty to forty, Ardeth Bay thought of his friends, the O'Connells, and hoped they would fare better than he in the war against Imhotep and the Scorpion King, and—scimitar in hand—he prepared to die.

·❨ 19 ❩·

Eternal Warriors

Moving down a tunnel-like corridor of sheer breathtaking gold, Jonathan Carnahan—as dazed as a man in a dream—carried his late sister by her feet, his nephew Alex holding the dead woman under her shoulders. As man and boy conveyed the corpse through the recesses of the Ahm Shere pyramid, Evelyn looked almost peaceful, as in the funeral-home cliche ("She looks as if she's only sleeping!"), an effect aided by the khaki jacket draped over the fatal wound in her stomach. The eerie nature of this small procession was heightened by Jonathan's awareness of the mythic role of the pyramids of ancient Egypt, those mysterious man-made structures that at once honored death and hoped to cheat it.

"You do realize, of course," Jonathan said to the boy, as they bore the body down the tunnel, "that this particular ceremony can only be performed by some-one who can read ancient Egyptian."

"You're an Egyptologist, Uncle Jon."

"Well, of sorts. I'm more a plunderer of antiquities than anything else . . . though I did pick up a few tid-bits of knowledge from your mother. Still, I don't know about you, but I'm a trifle . . . rusty."

They had come to a fork in the tunnel. Evelyn wasn't terribly heavy, but they had already gone some distance in the pyramid's typically labyrinthian pas-sageways. It never occurred to them to set down this particular cargo, however, and take a rest. Somehow that would have been disrespectful; and there was an urgency, as well.

"We go left," Alex said.

"Are you guessing?"

"No."

"How can you know?"

The boy nodded toward hieroglyphs above the portal at left. *"Kasheesh Osirian Nye,"* he read. "More or less, that says, 'This Way to the Scorpion King.' "

"What a lovely prospect. . . . Seems you picked up a bit of this and that from your mother, as well."

With a sad little grin, Alex nodded, saying, "Mum taught me well. . . . I just wish I hadn't tossed away that God-darn bracelet."

Jonathan wished the boy hadn't done that, him-self—valuable damn trinket that it was. But he said, as they carted Evelyn's body through the archway, "Why is that?"

"When I wore it, I could understand ancient Egyptian. . . . I could even speak it!"

"No!"

"Yes."

"Do you think any of it stuck?"

"Maybe . . . between what I learned from Mum, and speaking the tongue like a native . . . we should do all right, Uncle Jon."

Rather stunned by the possibility, glancing down at the slumbering corpse of his sister, Jonathan uttered, "This just might jolly well work."

They continued on, and the trickiest passage was maneuvering the body down a stairway that seemed fashioned from sand. The sand-formed steps were a godsend, however, cushioning their footsteps and keeping them from alerting the dark-haired beauty whose back was to them, as she stood—as if on guard—staring through a strangely sinister, mist-shrouded gateway bordered by warlike statues, in whose golden hands resided various real weapons.

As they reached the bottom of the stairway of sand, Jonathan exchanged cautionary glances with his nephew, nodding toward the pedestal near the dark-robed woman—a pedestal on which rested the obsidian-covered volume they had come to get.

Speaking with their eyes, punctuated by nods, the man and the boy gently, soundlessly, set down the lifeless form of Alex's mother.

Heading toward the woman, but veering left, Jonathan motioned to Alex to hug the wall, at right, which the boy did, as they approached the woman, who seemed to be contemplating going through that gateway. It was as if she were arguing with herself about whether to stay or to go.

Jonathan positioned himself a few feet behind her, to the left—the pedestal, and the boy sneaking up on it, were at right—and cleared his throat.

She whirled, the blunt-cut dark hair swirling, her dark eyes narrow, her expression fierce.

Jonathan stood there before her, poised to fight, his dukes up in traditional English pugilistic style, having no idea how silly an ass he looked.

"Come and take your medicine, wench!" Jonathan said, bobbing and weaving.

She smirked, laughed softly, then approached him swiftly, moving in a straight line.

The reincarnated princess did not see, creeping up behind her, the boy grabbing *The Book of the Dead* off its pedestal. The boy, however, saw what the princess was doing: with the deadly precision of a trained expert in self-defense, Anck-su-namun pelted Jonathan with two front jabs to the face.

But Jonathan, licking blood from the corner of his mouth, may have looked the fool—and, to some degree, may indeed have been a fool—but he really was trained in pugilism, starting as far back as his boarding school days.

And he returned the blows, landing a sharp fist to her chin and doubling her over with a blow to the stomach—the same area where the witch had thrust her dagger into Evelyn.

Dancing on his toes, Jonathan said, "That was for my sister. . . . Hope you liked it."

Anck-su-namun straightened, sneered, and wheeled with a roundhouse kick, knocking Jonathan into one of the statues. Picking himself up, he plucked a spear from the statue's hands—playing fair didn't seem to be a priority at this point—and started toward her.

But the princess found her own weapon, snatching a trident from the hands of another statue.

The way she hefted the triple-headed spear made it clear the woman knew what she was doing. Fear traveled through him—he knew he was outclassed. As the princess moved in for the kill, Jonathan—trembling like the coward he desperately did not want to be—backed away.

"Hurry up, Alex!" he cried.

Anck-su-namun frowned, glancing behind her and seeing Alex, finally—down toward the stairway, next to his supine mother, the boy on his knees, hunkered over the big book as if it were the Sunday comics.

The Book of the Dead was open wide.

The princess snarled, a vicious animal sound, peculiar to emerge from so lovely if evil a creature, and was about to advance on Alex when Jonathan lunged at her with his spear, attacking.

Sitting next to his mother, leaning over her, as if he were praying—which, in a real sense, he was—Alex read from the book, his face tensed with concentration as the eight-year-old struggled to read words from a centuries-old language.

"Hootash naraba oos Veesloo," the boy read, tentatively. *"Ahm kum ra . . . Ahm kum Dei. . . ."*

Jonathan summoned all his strength, and every ounce of courage, trading blows with the skilled female warrior, slamming his spear against every swipe and swat of her trident . . . *almost* every one: a swift, skillful slash caught him across the chest, leaving a ribbon of scarlet.

Alex, wincing at the sound of his uncle crying out in pain, hovered over his dead mother, staring at the book, desperately trying to figure out the inscription.

Jonathan's wound was not deep, and he didn't have time to process the pain as he lunged forward, meeting every thrust in a manner that, while hardly deft, somehow did the trick.

But how could this woman be so strong, how could any woman be so strong? Even though he was blocking her blows, the power of her was rattling every tooth, every bone in his body, as if she might drive him down into the ground like a hammer would a nail.

Alex's voice echoed in the golden chamber: *"Efday Shokran. . . . Efday Shokran* something. . . . Uncle Jon! I don't know what this last symbol means!"

Holding up his spear sideways, desperately obstructing her blows, Jonathan yelled, "What does it look like?"

"It's a bird—a big bird . . . you know, a stork!"

At that moment, Anck-su-namun batted the spear

right out of Jonathan's grasp; then her hand was gripping his throat—in that same fashion that Imhotep seemed so enamored of, when it came to punishing Jonathan—and she slammed him against a statue, strangling him.

Jonathan—who knew very well what the stork symbol meant—did his best to squawk out a reply, hampered as he was by the princess's viselike grip on his neck.

"*Ah . . . ah . . .*" Jonathan began, and he might not have been saying anything at all, really, just crying out in pain. But then she eased up on him, to move him away from the statue and get him up against the wall, where she could assume an even better grip.

And, just before she slammed his back to the wall, Jonathan cried out, "*Ahmenophus!*"

Lighting up, the boy blurted, "That's it! *Efday Shokran Ahmenophus!*"

Jonathan could not share his nephew's enthusiasm, as he was currently being held against the wall, stunned, choking, his throat in the one-handed clamp of the powerful princess, who was leering at her victim, drawing back her trident for the killing blow.

And as Anck-su-namun's hand lunged forward, another hand gripped it by the wrist, stopping it, the triple-pointed blade inches from Jonathan's throat.

Jonathan turned to see who had saved him—and hope and happiness flooded through him in a rush as golden as the walls around him. Anck-su-namun's head turned, the black blunt-cut hair swinging like twin scythe blades—and the princess's expression was of dismay and disgust.

Evelyn Carnahan O'Connell—her blouse torn, the gaping wound in her stomach closed over, her hair tousled, her eyes hard, her jaw firm—gave Anck-su-namun a sneer the princess could only envy.

"Leave my brother alone," Evelyn said, and shoved the princess halfway across the chamber.

Alex was suddenly at Evelyn's side. "You and your uncle," his mother said, "go help your father."

"Yes, Mum—you'll be all right, Mum?"

"I'm a new woman."

Anck-su-namun was getting to her feet. She started toward them, lithe as a cat.

Alex clutched his mother's sleeve. "But—"

"No 'buts,' dear. I'll be just fine. Leave this bitch to me."

The boy grinned, involuntarily. "Mum—language!"

She smiled, touched her son's shoulder, lightly. "Go. Jonathan, take him away!"

And Jonathan took the boy by the arm, hustling him away, as Alex said, "We can't leave Mum!"

The princess seemed to be prowling after Evelyn now, approaching in a battle-ready crouch, wielding the trident.

"She said she'd be fine," Jonathan said, all but dragging the wide-eyed boy across the small stone bridge through the gloomy gateway into the cavern beyond. "She wants us to find your father. Anyway,

257

when was the last time your mother was wrong about anything?"

Then her son and brother were gone, leaving Evelyn in the golden chamber, to face the reincarnation of the combat-savvy Anck-su-namun.

"Do you know who I am?" Evelyn asked, circling, waiting for the woman to attack.

"Nefertiri," the princess said.

"As my husband would say . . . long time no see, Anck-su-namun."

The princess smiled, and stopped moving—stood to her full height. "It is good that we both know who we are."

The two women faced each other—a strange respect mingling now with their mutual hatred.

"Isn't it?" From a nearby statue, Evelyn plucked a trident for herself, hefting the weapon, getting the feel, judging the weight. "Now we can pick up where we left off, not so long ago . . . in my father's palace. But we won't have to . . . as they say nowadays . . . 'pull any punches.' "

Anck-su-namun nodded her agreement—but the gesture was more than that: it was a bow, the sort of signal one gladiator might send to another.

The two women raised their weapons.

Simultaneously, they lunged toward each other, and a battle begun three thousand years ago was continued, no golden masks this time, just vicious, expert blows traded one for one, clangs of metal against metal, smacks of flesh against flesh, punches, kicks, elbows, backhands, no prowess lost over the passage of mere centuries.

In and around the golden statues they fought, a pair of twentieth-century women possessed by, and possessing, ancient warrior skills, thrusting, parrying, feinting, the staffs of the deadly tridents pressed against each other, as first one, then other, of these powerful women would toss the other aside, only to return to take, and deliver, more punishment. Relentlessly they fought, brilliantly, hating each other, admiring each other, each astounded by the proficiency of the other.

Finally, Anck-su-namun saw an opening, and took it, diving toward Evelyn, the trident points headed right for that healed-over wound—nothing would have pleased the princess more than to open that gaping gash and spill this woman's blood once again, one last time.

But Evelyn stepped aside, and slammed a vicious elbow into the back of Anck-su-namun's neck, sending the princess to the floor in a tumbling sprawl, trident flung from her grasp, skittering across the floor. And when Anck-su-namun flipped over, to get back to her feet, she never made it, because Evelyn lurched toward her, the deadly trio of knife-points freezing her.

This was how their previous confrontation had ended, only now Evelyn—Nefertiri—had traded places with the princess. This time the wicked prongs of a trident were an inch from the pulsing throat of Anck-su-namun . . .

... who looked up into the face of Evelyn O'Connell, though the eyes gazing down on Anck-su-namun—eyes that were on fire—belonged to Nefertiri. Yet the trio of razor-sharp points did not plunge forward, remained poised to kill but did not kill. . . . Was the twentieth-century woman Nefertiri had become struggling with civilized notions that would not have impaired the former Meela?

And the princess smiled up at Evelyn. "You have improved, Princess Nefertiri. It would seem the instructor has taken a lesson from her student. . . ."

Evelyn tensed herself, to ram the blow home, when a bellow of rage, an otherworldly roar as if from some unimaginable beast, echoed out of the cavern through the misty gateway.

This momentary distraction allowed Anck-su-namun to bat the trident away from her throat, and out of Evelyn's grasp, and the princess—in a most undignified manner—scrambled from harm's way, taking off running, fleeing through the gateway over the stony bridge and into the mysteries of the cavern.

Evelyn, furious, took off after her—neither combatant taking time to rearm herself—racing through that gateway into the unknown.

Having chanced his own way in, O'Connell—torch in one hand, double-headed battle-ax in the other—found himself in a weird, shadow-flung, smoke-drifting netherworld quite unlike the gleaming interior of the golden-walled pyramid. The catacomblike passageway gradually opened into a vast chamber where cavelike walls and massive gray stalactites mingled with Egyptian temple–style limestone pillars, as if God or the devil had collaborated with man to fashion an ominous underground cathedral. As he walked on into this strange landscape, his torch added orange highlights to Stygian depths punctuated by dripping water, underscored by the howl of distant wind.

And then, across the cavernous chamber, O'Connell saw the man—the creature that walked as a man—he sought: that dark-robed, copper-skinned, bald-headed bastard who some misguided sons of bitches considered their lord, the living mummy— *Imhotep*.

A curious emotion surged through O'Connell— rage fused with delight. This man who had never been sadder had never been happier to see vengeance so near his reach. . . .

The woman who had murdered Evy was nowhere in sight. But Imhotep—his back to the approaching O'Connell, unaware he was being stalked by the adventurer—stood before an immense golden gong, in his hands the great padded hammer with which that gong could be struck.

The gong was mounted near two mammoth wooden doors, an enormous gate built right into the stone walls of the cavern; this would appear to be an altar of sorts, a monument to the Scorpion King, as several life-size golden scorpion statues—similar to the bas-relief on the Bracelet of Anubis, and to that wall-size bas-relief in the keyroom that had cost the

Curator so dearly—stood silent guard on either side of those looming wooden gates. Like the bas-relief, these statues displayed in their claws various weapons of combat, as if the repository of the arms once used by guards—living and breathing ones, not just icons—who had long ago stood watch here.

Separating O'Connell and his quarry was a crevice, perhaps five feet wide—nothing the adventurer couldn't easily leap, though doing so would announce his presence to the mummy. As O'Connell jogged quietly forward, Imhotep—his back still to the avenger—raised and drew back the hammer-headed pole. Just as O'Connell jumped the crevice, the mummy forcefully banged that giant golden gong.

The resultant vibrations were of a supernatural force, causing the entire chamber to tremble, every stalactite, each temple-like pillar shuddering, a shimmering *whoooom* resonating through the cavern.

O'Connell, who had just landed on the other side of the crevice, damn near lost his balance, losing his torch down the hole, glancing over his shoulder at a rocky drop that seemed to end nowhere, giving over to a blackness that swallowed his torch's flame and fell to eternity.

But the banging and echo of the gong covered the sound of O'Connell's jump, as well as any sound he made as he ran toward Imhotep, who was in the process of setting down the hammer-headed pole.

O'Connell was swinging the battle-ax down on the inviting target of the mummy's robed back, when Imhotep—finally hearing or perhaps sensing something—spun and swung the pole quickly up, blocking the blow. O'Connell's ax blade cleaved into the rod, its big steel tooth sinking into the wood, catching there, holding.

Both men gritted their teeth, jaw muscles clenched, as they struggled with their interlocked weapons. Inadvertently, they simultaneously put their muscle into a sideways motion that sent the ax-and-pole sailing out of both their grasps, sliding across the smooth rock floor and slipping down into the hungry crevice.

Instinctively, both men backed away—and now they were facing each other.

Imhotep said, in his ancient language, "And so the eternal warriors meet again."

O'Connell, of course, did not understand this—nor did he understand the mummy's smile. Personally, O'Connell was in no mood for smiling. . . .

"Now," Imhotep said, still speaking the ancient tongue, "we shall see what the gods have in mind for us."

They advanced on each other, O'Connell with fists raised, Imhotep with hands poised as if to strangle; but the mummy's hands closed into fists as the two men did hand-to-hand battle across the cavern floor, ever skirting the crevice that might claim either or both. Viciously, relentlessly, they exchanged punches, kicks, elbows and backhands, drawing blood, and though the eyes of both glittered with fury, burned with hatred, they seemed to share a peculiar respect, of a sort known only between worthy foes.

263

Suddenly an earthquakelike tremor interrupted them, freezing them both in midpunch. The tremor continued, the cavern trembling around them. Exchanging winces of confusion, the two men seemed to know, their expressions seemed to say, *Something's coming!*

O'Connell recovered first, slamming a right hook into Imhotep's jaw, sending him reeling into one of the scorpion statues. Wiping blood from the corner of his mouth with one hand, Imhotep with the other grabbed two weapons from the golden claws: a trident and a scythe.

The mummy did not move forward, not yet; his expression . . . again, that peculiar respect was at play . . . told his opponent that the time had come to up the ante of their deadly game.

O'Connell nodded, and stepped over to the other golden statue and selected the same two weapons.

Then the two men began to circle, like gladiators in the Coliseum, looking for the right moment, seeking an opening. When they went at each other, each blow, every clang of steel against steel, was lightning quick, expertly placed, two warriors perfectly matched, while around them the cavern shook, rumbled, with the approach of . . . something.

Something getting closer. . . .

O'Connell, frustrated by how even this match was, stoked the fires of his fury, remembering that this was the creature responsible for his wife's death, picturing in his mind the mummy's smiling mistress standing over Evelyn with a blood-dripping dagger in her hand, and he screamed and leapt forward and hammered at Imhotep, startling him, staggering him, the mummy meeting the adventurer's blows but getting battered back, even as around them the cavernous walls shook with their own fury.

Imhotep forced himself forward, and trident was pressed against trident, scythe kissing scythe, as the two warriors stood locked in a warriors' embrace, locking steel. Nothing but hatred burned in the eyes of both men, each staring into the other's—respect forgotten now.

The wooden doors flung themselves open, bursting, exploding open, the sound of it echoing through the cavern making that banged gong seem a whisper!

The two men, blades locked together, turned their eyes from each other toward the vast, empty, yawning doorway, a portal draped in fog, offering nothing but smoky darkness.

Then something, something large, began to lower itself into view, from the ceiling within that other chamber, and the vaporous haze and shadowy darkness still obscured the creature . . . no, it was a *man* . . . from view. Only the upper half of him was visible, at first . . .

. . . a muscular, handsome, dark-hued warrior, of fierce mien, a big man, but just a man.

Only his arms, there was something strange about them, and as the fog lifted, the arms revealed themselves as ending not in hands, but claws. . . .

O'Connell, instinctively, backed away from Imhotep; and Imhotep did the same from O'Connell.

Both men were petrified by the presence, the appearance, of this third warrior, about to join the fray.

Imhotep said something in ancient Egyptian, but O'Connell required no translation. None was necessary to know that this was the Scorpion King.

Because now O'Connell and the mummy could see—as the man, the creature, scuttled out through the doorway from the mist into their midst—that the king of the scorpions was a scorpion himself, a sort of Egyptian minotaur.

Handsome as he might be from the waist up, from the waist down, the Scorpion King *was* a scorpion—a very large scorpion at that, with multiple claws and a tail, and an enraged expression that said he wasn't at all happy about being awakened from his slumber.

·❆ **20** ❆·

A Knight in the Scorpion's Lair

Of all the surprising, terrible things O'Connell had encountered in his Egyptian explorations, this half-man, half-scorpion—this towering collection of claws and curling tail—was in an appalling class of its own. At once repulsive and regal, the creature held its head high even as its insectlike movement dragged massive claws scuttering scratchily like fingernails on the blackboard of the cavern floor.

Both of them staring in awestruck horror at the monster, O'Connell and Imhotep instinctively separated, the former to the left, the latter to the right, to divide their forces strategically against what seemed potentially a shared foe.

The creature stood between them, looking down at them, first O'Connell, then Imhotep, perhaps deciding which one to take out first. Then the Scorpion King's gaze returned to Imhotep and settled there—

something seemed to pass across the handsome face of the hideous beast, whether recognition or some instinctive, even supernatural cognizance, O'Connell could not say.

Whatever the case, that awareness on the creature's human face darkened into anger, and the thing was moving toward the mummy, scudding toward him like a crab on beach sand, scribbling on the hard cave floor with its claws.

As the Scorpion King advanced, Imhotep backed away, but even from across the cavern, O'Connell could see the regenerated mummy's eyes flashing with thought, mental wheels turning. O'Connell watched in bewildered amazement as the mummy raised a hand to his forehead, just above his eyebrows, and ripped away the scalp!

Shaking his head as if to clear cobwebs, O'Connell at first thought the mummy had gone mad; then questioned his own sanity as he saw Imhotep's exposed skull, a hideous dry skullcap—no blood, Imhotep spared that scarlet indignity . . . the mummy was himself part creature, part man.

O'Connell realized at once that this self-mutilation mirrored that of the Curator, and—seeing Imhotep kneel down, slapping his exposed skull, genuflecting before the approaching creature—O'Connell gathered correctly that this must have been some ritual, perhaps some primitive Akkadian display of fealty.

Eyes lowered respectfully, raising his arms like a revival-tent preacher praising Jesus, the mummy knelt before the half-man, half-scorpion as it dragged itself menacingly toward him, and cried in ancient Egyptian, *"Mi Phat Ahs! Mi Phat Ahs! . . .* I am your disciple!"

The creature stopped, stared down at the mummy, then slowly began to nod, recognizing a true believer.

"Oh, hell," O'Connell said to himself.

The Scorpion King swung itself around, its lobsterlike extremities scraping on the rock floor, turning its attentions toward the other intruder. The beast did not see the self-satisfied, wicked grin of its "disciple," who now rose to his feet, eyes no longer lowered in reverence, retreating into the shadows to allow his two foes to battle it out—hoping the worst for them both.

O'Connell had backed himself into a pillar, the creature closing in on him, and he wished he could trade this clawed monstrosity for something easier to deal with, like a couple thousand Tuaregs maybe, and rather desperately he slapped his own (flesh-covered) forehead, mimicking Imhotep's ritualistic gesture.

And he did his best to say what Imhotep had said, coming as close as he could: "My fat ass! My fat ass!"

This declaration of loyalty failed to impress the Scorpion King, who lashed down at O'Connell with a massive skeletal pincer.

The adventurer dove out of the way, and the claw swung through the ancient limestone pillar, shearing it, turning it to dust-stirred rubble. Running like hell, O'Connell damn near stumbled into a figure that staggered out of one of the catacomb tunnels, a familiar

figure, whom O'Connell was surprised to see alive
. . . the Curator!

The dark little man staggered into the cavern,
clutching the bloody stump the scorpion keyhole had
bestowed, his eyes looking up at nothing, a ghastly
sleepwalker.

As the Scorpion King scraped its deadly way toward them, O'Connell—noting the whimpering Curator's red-stained exposed skull—thought quickly.
This bastard was already a dead man, walking or
not—and what Scorpion King didn't appreciate a human sacrifice . . . ?

From a nearby weapons-laden statue, O'Connell
snatched a golden helmet and jammed it down over
the head of the already lurching Curator.

"*Your* fat ass," O'Connell said ruthlessly, grabbing
onto the man's arms, turning him around and kicking
him in it, pitching him forward.

"What?" the Curator said, stumbling, blinking stu-
pidly . . . and then his eyes widened as the monster
that was the Scorpion King loomed in front of him,
regarding him with narrow eyes, pincers poised.

The Curator decided immediately which master to
serve: he dropped to his knees, raised his hands high,
eyes lowered, as he cried, *"Mi Phat Ahs! Mi Phat
Ahs!"*

And yet the Scorpion King scuttled slowly forward, this pincer raised, then that pincer raised, as if
the creature were trying to decide which one to
use. . . .

The Curator, snapping out of his funk, suddenly

realized what O'Connell had done to him—the little man patted his head, felt the smooth metallic surface, and knew that the ritual he'd so painfully performed upon himself was doing him no good: the bone he'd bared for the Scorpion King was concealed by the helmet!

And the helmet was stuck tight to his head . . . he tried to get it off, tried desperately . . .

. . . but the Scorpion King made his decision, and grabbed the Curator around the waist by a massive pincer, raising him high, looking at him curiously— a bug inspecting another bug—and then, with a horrendous bellow that echoed like thunder, closed his claw, squeezing, squeezing, squeezing . . . cutting the man in half, flinging the pieces to the cavern floor in two bloody piles.

O'Connell used the time the Curator's destruction had bought him to select a weapon from another of the statues, a trident seeming the best bet, and as he turned to hurl it, a huge claw swung around and sent him flying in one direction, and the trident in another.

He slammed up against a cave wall that, fortunately, was smooth and didn't impale him on any sharp rocks, merely jolted every bone and muscle in his body. Getting painfully to his feet, he found himself next to a life-size cartouche depicting not an Egyptian figure, but a medieval knight. In the process of catching his wind, and pulling himself together, O'Connell noticed the image depicted the knight holding not a sword or a lance but a scepter . . . the golden Scepter of Osiris!

271

And the knight's hand, holding the scepter in the image, bore that same tattoo—the pyramid formed of mariner's compass and falcon's wings, centered with the eye of Horus—that O'Connell had worn since childhood!

The mighty tail of the Scorpion King swung around and pulverized the cartouche, missing O'Connell's head by inches, inspiring him to leap out of the way in a dive that became a roll, and when he popped to his feet he was standing before the wall he'd been slammed into moments before.

No wonder he hadn't been spiked by rocks: the wall was smooth, carved, bearing a hieroglyph-style pictograph of the same knightly figure whose cartouche had just been shattered by the scorpion's tail. The cartouche wall was a damn how-to-do-it display, depicting the knight in a series of images preparing the Scepter of Osiris for battle, revealing that the golden object telescoped out into a spear . . .

. . . and the final image portrayed the knight hurling the spear at a likeness of the Scorpion King!

For many long centuries, the Med-jai had stood watch at Hamanaptra, guarding against Imhotep's return; had Knights Templar during the Holy Crusades learned of the Scorpion King, and kept guard here?

And was O'Connell one of them?

Right now, he was ready to believe—and it wouldn't take ripping the flesh from his forehead, either.

As that enormous tail, with its deadly stinger,

whipped around again, O'Connell dove out of the way, the tail powdering the cartouche wall and its helpful pictograph; but O'Connell already had the knowledge he needed.

And as he ran from the scuttling creature, O'Connell saw Jonathan—with Alex at his side—come dashing into the cavern on the other side of the yawning crevice. While he hardly relished having his son present, the adventurer had never been gladder to see his brother-in-law.

The pair skidded to a stop, their eyes widening in wonder and shock at the sight of the Scorpion King.

"Jonathan!" O'Connell shouted. "The scepter! That gold stick of yours! It's a spear—it opens up into a goddamn spear!"

"Really," Jonathan said, confused to be getting such information at this juncture, backing away from the sight of the horrific beast who ruled here. "How fascinating . . ."

"It can kill this son of a bitch!"

"Ah! Splendid!"

Jonathan fished the scepter out of his rucksack, and began clumsily fiddling with it.

Alex said, "Give me that!" and snatched the scepter away from his uncle.

Across the cavern, watching from the shadows, Imhotep—already possessed of the knowledge O'Connell had just gained regarding the golden artifact—whispered to himself, in his ancient tongue, "The Scepter of Osiris . . ."

The weapon was what the mummy required to

smite the Scorpion King—but if that reborn Knight Templar or any of his covey hurled the scepter's spear into the beast, O'Connell would rule over the army of Anubis, and the Scorpion King would have to do the adventurer's bidding.

The foolish Britisher and the boy had the scepter, on the other side of the sprawling cavern, across the narrow though bottomless crevice. Imhotep emerged from the darkness and charged toward them.

And just as Imhotep ran toward the boy and his uncle, Anck-su-namun rushed into the cavern, with Evelyn on her heels; but the two women lurched to a mutual stop, standing nearly side by side, their duel forgotten, as they took in the terrifying tableau: the monstrous Scorpion King, claws snapping at the air, tail raising, then swinging, pincers and stinger slashing and tearing through pillars, plowing holes into walls, as it closed in on O'Connell, who was scrambling out of its path. The halves of the corpse of the Curator littered the cavern floor, splashing it with blood, a dire display of the beast's capabilities.

Anck-su-namun—or was she Meela now?—backed away in abject fear, a hand covering her face but her eyes peeking out at the fearsome creature, which swatted O'Connell, as if he were the bug, sending him spiraling through the air, smashing into a cavern wall, not a smooth one, this time. He slid down, landing on his ass, a spread-eagled sprawl.

Evelyn cried out to him: *"Riiick!"*

And he looked up, and saw that his wife was alive,

274

and for all his pain, however dreadful the circumstances, he had never been happier.

Half-smiling, half-crying, he yelled, "Evy! Get out of here! Take Alex!"

And the scorpion's great stinger whammed down, slamming between O'Connell's outstretched legs, carving a hole in the rock floor.

Leaping to his feet, he saw his trident, snatched it up, and backed away, looking up at the looming monster, not as afraid now, reinvigorated—*Evy was alive!*

And O'Connell had to keep her that way.

"Jonathan," he yelled, "will you hurry the hell up and figure that damn thing out?"

He threw the trident, aiming for the human flesh of the creature's chest, but it reared back, and the three-headed spear bounced off claw shell.

Imhotep was leaping the crevice, and would soon close in on Jonathan and Alex, who were trying to decipher the hieratic on the scepter, working with various indentations around the head of the thing.

The mummy was perhaps twenty feet away from them when Jonathan twisted the bottom of the scepter, which suddenly slid open, revealing a sharp tip. Alex grabbed onto the artifact and yanked it, telescoping the scepter out a good four feet, into a deadly looking, sharply pointed spear.

Imhotep was coming.

Jonathan snatched the spear away from his nephew, saying, "Out of the way, lad—this is man's work."

Taking careful aim, Imhotep almost on top of him,

Jonathan flung the scepter's spear at the Scorpion King, past the mummy, directly at the creature.

Thwarted, the furious Imhotep swatted Jonathan aside and screamed, *"Niiiiy!"*

But the Scorpion King turned an ungainly pirouette and its stinger whacked the spear away, sending it spinning, churning through the cave like a propeller.

O'Connell leapt for it, nabbing it nimbly from the air, hitting the ground running and, like a javelin champ, hurled the spear back at the Scorpion King, aiming away from crustacean exoskeleton and seeking human flesh.

The spear sank deep into the monster's chest, through the man-half's heart, sending the creature skittering back, screaming in surprise and pain and fury, a bellow at once animal and, eerily, human.

Forgetting Jonathan and Alex, the mummy cried, *"Niiiiy!"*, running toward the Scorpion King, howling in rage, vaulting the crevice, but too late to do anything. . . .

The Scorpion King, weaving drunkenly, gazed down at O'Connell in anger and agony, bellowing what would have been a battle cry if the thing had not been dying.

And the adventurer—ignoring his own pain, gritting his teeth, stared back at the monster.

"You have to do my will, now," O'Connell said to it—to him. "So . . . go to hell."

The Scorpion King's eyes widened as the final stage of the curse of Anubis took effect, the creature exploding into black vapor—O'Connell covered his face with an arm, but no hurtful fragments of the thing went flying, no careening claws, no sailing chunks of flesh, because the king of the scorpions had disintegrated into black nothingness.

And on the desert beyond Ahm Shere, where the valiant Med-jai, hopelessly outnumbered, battled the hound-headed warriors of Anubis on sand dunes soaked with Med-jai blood, a bizarre—and yet wonderful—event transpired, which would become the stuff of desert legend before the end of that day.

Ardeth Bay and his commanders—minutes from death—witnessed the vast army of Anubis erupt harmlessly into the black sand from which they'd emerged, dissipating across the Med-jai, who found themselves brushing what remained of their foes from their battle-torn, blood-dampened robes.

"Allah be praised," Ardeth Bay said, astonished to be alive.

He would have been astonished, as well, to witness what was occurring at the oasis of Ahm Shere. Thick black vapor was bursting from the archways of the golden pyramid, mushrooming into the sky, forming into a giant cloud in which the human face of the Scorpion King could have been seen—had any man been present—giving one last enraged and ultimately impotent bellow before the cloud imploded and the black vapor sucked itself back into the pyramid, whose golden structure shuddered with the impact.

Those in the cavern below had not seen this unearthly incident transpire, but the aftermath was unavoidable: the Scorpion King's lair shook with earthquake-level vibrations, just as O'Connell and Imhotep—the eternal warriors, as the mummy had said—stood facing each other across the crevice, ready to continue their clash.

But the tremors rocking the cave overruled any such intention, tossing both men into the suddenly widening crevice.

The world coming down around her, Evelyn cried, "No!" and ran forward, but found her path immediately blocked by falling stalactites—razor sharp, dropping like deadly missile-size icicles in a sudden thaw.

Within the crevice, the eternal warriors were side by side, sharing a crevice wall, holding on for their lives, dangling like ripe fruit about to drop from the vine. Below them awaited that seemingly infinite drop, a fall to the nowhere of eternity.

Both man and mummy had endured much, in this struggle—and neither had much strength left. Joined in a sudden shared predicament, the two exchanged glances that admitted neither could hold on much longer. Hero and villain alike needed help to survive.

They could, from the ledge to which they barely clung, see up the slope of the cavern floor—O'Connell and Imhotep were both aware of the lethal rain of stalactites frustrating any rescue effort, as the cavern around them quaked. And they could see the women they loved, torn with agony, wanting to help.

Gulping for air, the tremors trying to throw him off his precarious perch, O'Connell called to Evy,

"Stay back! Stay there! Stay with Alex!"

Desperately clawing at the ledge, Imhotep called to his resurrected, reincarnated love in their ancient tongue, *"Anck-su-namun! Help me! Please help!"*

The two women stared toward those they loved, who seemed about to die, spears of rock falling like bombs all around them, between them and their men.

But Evelyn wasn't afraid to die—she'd done it before.

And she ran across the minefield of fatal falling stalactites, running like mad for the father of her child, for the safety, the life, of the man she loved.

"Stay back!" O'Connell demanded, but she didn't listen, and he was furious with her, thrilled with her.

Anck-su-namun—who had also died more than once—stood frozen, just another statue on the cavern's periphery.

And then Meela turned and ran, ran down the tunnel back toward the gateway—getting the hell out, leaving her ancient lover to the precipice.

Imhotep, hanging by his fingers, screamed in disbelief: *"Anck-su-namun!"*

But she had vanished down the tunnel.

O'Connell glanced over at his foe, and could see in the mummy's face that his world had just collapsed much as this cavern was coming down around them.

"Anck-su-namun?" the mummy whispered.

At that moment, Evelyn reached the edge of the crevice, leaned over its edge, and grabbed onto her husband's arm. Quickly she yanked him up and over the crevice, to relative safety.

279

O'Connell, Evy at his side, looked down at the helpless Imhotep, and—strangely, unbelievably—he found himself wanting to reach down a hand to help this worthiest of foes.

But Imhotep, devastated, stared up at them and something like a smile etched itself faintly on his lips. He spoke a few words in ancient Egyptian, and then he let go of the crevice wall, falling into eternity.

The Disappearing Oasis

The O'Connell party went out the same way Anck-su-namun had—back through the gateway, over the stone bridge, up the sandy staircase and into the golden tunnels of the pyramid itself.

Once in the tunnels, however, Anck-su-namun—well out ahead of them—took a different pathway, and found herself in the keyroom, where the late Curator had first unleashed the secrets and terrors of the golden pyramid. But as she moved through, past the bas-relief scorpion with its keyhole mouth, a wall collapsed and barred the archway exit with blocks of solid gold.

Turning to see if the fallen wall had opened up a new avenue of escape, she found herself instead teetering at the edge of a wide moat filled not with water but deadly wriggling scorpions, who themselves seemed to be panicking as the world quaked around them, climbing over each other in a disgusting black teeming mass.

Eyes wide with horror, she touched her chest, gasping for breath, relieved she'd caught herself in time. Blunt-cut hair swinging, Anck-su-namun turned to flee back the way she had come—no pathway here—when the keyroom shook violently, tossing her off balance.

Flailing wildly at the edge of the scorpion-filled trench, mind racing with the ramifications should she fall in, she regained her equilibrium, sighed in relief, and a quake promptly tossed her in.

The Scorpion King was dead, but his subjects remained loyal—and they dealt with the intruder.

The lovely young woman—Anck-su-namun or Meela, what did a name matter now?—was swimming in a black sea of stingers and tiny pincers, arms windmilling, her screams stifled, choked off, as the creatures filled her mouth, swarming over her, enveloping her, pulling her down beneath the moat's wriggling black surface.

In the entranceway of the pyramid, the O'Connell crew was finding its way up through a hole in the floor, only to discover themselves in a virtual hurricane—black vapor and massive foliage was being drawn through every archway and down into a huge sucking hole in the middle of the chamber, a whirlpool of wind.

Plastering themselves behind a golden archway, which blocked them from getting pelted by flying debris, they had to scream to be heard over the howling wind.

Evelyn, holding onto her husband—her hair, her clothing whipping in the wind—yelled, "There's no way out of here!"

"Always a way!" her husband yelled back, looking around desperately, spotting something. "Come on!"

And he led them up through a stairway inside the arch.

Though the wailing wind echoed up the stairwell, no flying rubble or black vapor followed them. About midway to the top, a narrow fissure in the golden wall seemed oblivious to the siphoning effect, and allowed O'Connell to peer out at what his destruction of the Scorpion King had wrought.

The others joined him at the crack, peeking out at an amazing, terrifying vista: the entire oasis was being swallowed up into the pyramid—palm trees, brush, bushes, the earth itself, red-turbaned corpses, shrunken heads, even squirming, protesting, hissing zombie pygmies, swimming through the flying dirt and debris.

"This goddamn place is a vacuum cleaner," O'Connell said, "sucking everything in!"

"Why don't we leave, then?" a wild-eyed Jonathan suggested.

The pyramid, already alive with tremors, began to shake violently. Remembering that hungry whirlpool-like hole in the entranceway, O'Connell realized that the pyramid itself was going to be drawn down into the earth.

"This ship is sinking!" O'Connell said, and ran up the stairs, yelling, "Let's go, let's go, let's go!"

The stairway opened into a small, open landing near the tip of the pyramid, but a press of jungle foliage, sucked up against the side of the pyramid, blocking their way, kept them from knowing how high up they might still be, preventing them leaping, even so.

The fronds slapped at them, insultingly, as the wind drew the jungle itself into the ravenous waterless whirlpool.

"Are we trapped, Rick?" Evy asked, eyes huge.

O'Connell had one arm around his wife, the other around his son, facing smothering green. He saw no way out. None. After all of this . . . after braving so much . . . enduring so much . . . triumphing over so much. . . .

"There's always a way," he said.

But he didn't have to think of one, because a voice yelled out from above: "Hey! Need a lift?"

And they whirled to see the blimp rising over the diamond tip of the golden pyramid, just behind them.

"Izzy!" O'Connell yelled.

"Hurry up—this sucker's gonna suck me down, too! We ain't got all day!"

Then O'Connell was hoisting first Alex and then Evy up and over the side of the battered trawler, and jumped aboard himself. Jonathan, lingering a moment for a look at the diamond just out of his reach, turned to jump, but did so just as Izzy yanked a lever that caused flame to shoot from the bellows and rise into a hole in the now hot air–driven blimp.

The quick rise of the blimp caused Jonathan to miss the lip of the trawler, and he slipped down its side, and a collective gasp went up from the rest of them.

But Jonathan's feet caught in the fish netting strung alongside the boat, and got tangled there; so he'd caught his ride, after all—though in a slightly undignified manner, as he was now hanging upside down.

To Jonathan this inconvenience was well worth it, because just below him glinted that diamond, that huge wonderful diamond, cracked off its perch by all that quaking. Deftly, he snatched it off the pyramid just as the structure was sucked down into the earth.

Then that wave of foliage crashed down past the rising blimp, narrowly missing them, as the whirlpool of wind sucked this last big bite down, drawing it into the earth with a roar, followed by a concluding *whump*.

"What, no burp?" Jonathan asked dryly, as he climbed up the netting into the helpful hands of his sister and brother-in-law.

And as the proud new owner of the largest diamond in the world tumbled onto the deck of the trawler, the others looked down over the side at what had been the jungle . . . or oasis, if you will . . . of Ahm Shere, now just a valley of dust and desert, with not a whisper of wind remaining.

Soon Izzy was receiving hugs and profound thanks

from Evy and Alex, attention that seemed to both please and embarrass the wild-haired little pilot. Jonathan was busy, sitting on the deck cherishing the big chunk of polished diamond, grinning like the fool he sometimes was, perhaps even deserving this reward for the hero he'd become.

Rick O'Connell leaned against the trawler's cabin wall, exhausted, wincing at pains he only now realized he was suffering, clothing torn, face smeared with dirt and blood.

Izzy wandered up to his old friend. "My cat pukes up hair balls that look better than you. What the hell have you people been up to?"

"Nothing much," O'Connell said. "Raising the dead, killing zombie pygmies, skewering giant scorpions, sending mummies back to hell . . . you know— the usual."

Izzy grinned. "No belly dancers?"

O'Connell nodded toward his wife, who was standing with Alex at the bow of the trawler. "With a woman like that, who needs 'em?"

Thinking that over, nodding, trying to grasp his pal's point, Izzy went back to the wheel.

"Rick!" Evy called. "You should see this!"

O'Connell joined Evy and Alex at the bow. Even Jonathan pried time away from contemplating his diamond to join the rest of the family as they looked down on the sandy terrain.

Thousands of Med-jai on horseback were riding away—alive, triumphant—from their desert battlefield. One rider—at their head, pausing atop a high dune—stood out, even at this distance.

Ardeth Bay, smiling up at his skyborne friends, touched his heart with an open palm, and then waved at the blimp-carried boat silhouetted against the sun.

"Harum bara shad," the Med-jai chieftain said. "My eternal thanks, my courageous friends."

On the trawler in the sky, they could not hear these words; but they knew—and shared—the sentiment. O'Connell saluted his compatriot, relieved to see him alive, hoping they would meet again, whether adventure called or not.

Evy was waving, too.

O'Connell said, "Thought I lost you, there."

"You did—for a little while."

"A little while is way too long. Don't do that again. . . . What did he say, anyway?"

"Who?"

"Imhotep—before he fell. He said something in ancient Egyptian."

She nodded. "He said . . . 'Love that lasts longer than the temples of the gods.' "

"No kidding. Talking about himself and that dame . . . ?"

"Talking about us, I think—I think at the end . . . he envied us." Shaking off the somber moment, she gave him a mischievous grin. "Care to know what heaven looks like?"

"Naw." He just gazed into his wife's lovely face, into her beautiful blue eyes. "Hell, I already know."

And the adventurer took the librarian into his

strong, tired arms, and they shared a long, hard, passionate kiss worthy of a Knight Templar and an Egyptian princess.

"Oh, brother," Alex said, making the face that all self-respecting kids make when confronted with the mushy stuff.

"Leave me out of this," Jonathan said, returning to his diamond.

Izzy, however, was nodding, enjoying the romantic view, understanding how O'Connell could leave belly dancers and any other women behind, for this remarkable female. He throttled up, and the blimp sailed off into the sunset.

They were heroes, after all, and had the right.

A TIP OF THE PITH HELMET

I must first acknowledge Stephen Sommers for his fun, lively, action-packed screenplay, one of the rare sequel scripts that compares favorably to its predecessor. I am grateful to him and to Cindy Chang of Universal Studios for allowing me to write this sequel to my novel version of the script for Mr. Sommers's entertaining movie *The Mummy*.

Cindy, as usual, provided excellent, ever timely support.

I refer interested readers to the rather lengthy list of reference works cited at the end of my previous *Mummy* novel, and would like to add the following: *Birdseye Views of Far Lands, Vols. IV and V* (1926 and 1927), James T. Nichols; *The Nile* (1943), Emil Ludwig; *Temples, Tombs and Hieroglyphs* (1964), Barbara Mertz; and *A Woman Tenderfoot in Egypt* (1923), Grace Thompson Seton.

Thanks, too, to my friend and agent, Dominick Abel; and to my wife, Barbara Collins, who frequently interrupted her own writing to guide me on this expedition.

MAX ALLAN COLLINS has earned an unprecedented nine Private Eye Writers of America "Shamus" nominations for his Nathan Heller historical thrillers, winning twice (*True Detective*, 1983, and *Stolen Away*, 1991).

A Mystery Writers of America "Edgar" nominee in both fiction and nonfiction categories, Collins has been hailed as "the Renaissance man of mystery fiction." His credits include five suspense-novel series, film criticism, songwriting, trading-card sets and movie tie-in novels, including such international bestsellers as *In the Line of Fire, Air Force One, Saving Private Ryan, U-571,* and *The Mummy*.

He scripted the internationally syndicated comic strip *Dick Tracy* from 1977 to 1993, is cocreator of the comic-book features *Ms. Tree, Wild Dog* and *Mike Danger,* and has written the *Batman* comic book and newspaper strip.

Working as an independent filmmaker in his native Iowa, he wrote and directed the cult-favorite suspense film *Mommy* (1995) starring Patty McCormack; its sequel, *Mommy's Day* (1997); and the innovative *Real Time: Siege at Lucas Street Market* (2000). He also wrote the HBO World Premiere film *The Expert* (1994) and wrote and directed the award-winning documentary *Mike Hammer's Mickey Spillane* (1999).

Collins lives in Muscatine, Iowa, with his wife, writer Barbara Collins, and their teenage son, Nathan.